RELEASE THE DOGS OF WAR

The Kurtherian Gambit 10

MICHAEL ANDERLE

COPYRIGHT

DEDICATION

To Stephen Russell
May you recuperate
quickly and
not lose
your mind as you
get better!

RELEASE THE DOGS OF WAR
The Kurtherian Gambit 10 Team

Beta Editor / Readers
Bree Buras (Aussie Awesomeness)
Tom Dickerson (The man)
Heath Felps (Vacation - Bah!)
Dorene Johnson (DD)
Lisa Mitchell (Damn Woman! Amazeballs)
T S (Scott) Paul (Author)
Diane Velasquez (DD)

JIT Beta Readers
Andrew Haynes
Kelli Orr
Leo Roars
Hari Rothsteni

Editor
Ellen Campbell

Thank you to the following Special Consultants
for RELEASE THE DOGS OF WAR

Jeff Morris - Asst Professor Cyber-Warfare, Nuclear Munitions (Thank God!)
Stephen Russell - Ideas & Suggestions
Heath Felps - USN
Dorene Johnson - USN (Retired)

CHAPTER ONE

FORT LAUDERDALE, FLORIDA, USA

What I'm saying," Eric said, as he and John moved among the exotic supercars on the floor of the dealership. "Is we need two of these bad boys to properly support following Bethany Anne whenever she's driving hers."

Bethany Anne had come out of her temporary suite in the Australian Outback at close to eight thirty PM and told Eric that he and John were going shopping with her. Then she promptly turned around and ducked back into her room saying she was going to change. John showed up with Eric's cup of coffee three minutes later, and Eric informed him they were going shopping.

"Any idea where?" John had asked as they sipped their drinks.

"Not a clue," Eric said. "Popped out, we're going shopping, popped back into her room."

RELEASE THE DOGS OF WAR

John stepped up to the door and knocked twice, sharply. He heard her answer 'come in, John' so he poked his head in and asked where they were headed.

Thirty minutes later they were at Ferrari of Fort Lauderdale looking at the new F12berlinetta. The salesperson was shocked as hell when Bethany Anne walked in with John and Eric right as the store opened, then shocked again when he realized who she was.

John and Eric had a moment of peace as she was sitting in the car going through the sales review. There weren't any other people looking at the cars on this Tuesday morning, as they had walked in just five seconds after nine AM. Their salesperson, Sheldon, hadn't even finished his Starbucks yet.

John looked around to make sure nothing seemed amiss. "I've talked with Jeffrey. If she buys anything, the guys will be here right as she takes possession, if not earlier, and upgrade it."

Eric grinned. "They'll have to make that three!"

John laughed. "Yes, I agree, it will have to be—"

John turned from Eric when Bethany Anne slid out of the drop dead sexy car. "I want three, all Rosso Fiorano and I want them fast," she told her salesperson. "I'm completely open on negotiations, and I don't care where they are in the world. Find them, buy them and let me know how fast I can get them. Also," she added, "There's a twenty thousand sales bonus if you get three found and ordered before close of business today."

Sheldon was just able to get his voice back. "Ma'am, we don't have three in stock..." Her look caused him to pause a moment as he realized how his customer could help him over the hump. "If you needed to provide transportation? Would that be acceptable?"

Bethany Anne's smile lit up the store. "Perfectly! You send any information to the email I give you and I'll have them picked up from their location and back here within a couple of hours." Her face lost its smile. "If it becomes a circus because people find out," this time, she shook her head. "You lose the sales, understood?"

Sheldon considered his answer before saying, "Ma'am, you know that pictures of you are going for more than fifty thousand, correct?" He put up his hand. "I'm not telling you this to bump up the bonus, I'm just making sure you're aware there will be some people that will give up a job to get a picture and that sort of payout. But it won't be me. I love these cars, and I'm building my career on being discreet. So, I feel it necessary to let you know what could happen." He shrugged. "If I'm going to prove how discreet I am, I can't do better than being discreet for you."

Bethany Anne nodded and leaned toward Sheldon, who looked around and then got closer. "I'll tell you what, Sheldon. You tell everyone that you have a photo opportunity for your handpicked support people. If not a single word about this comes out before me and the two men with me are ready to drive off, I'll do five minutes of photos with those who helped you keep this secret. Who you pick is up to you, but don't make it too many. Then I'll make sure to give you a fifteen-second video support message on how you handled my purchases. Deal?"

Sheldon straightened up and held out his hand. "I'll have your car information within two hours. We have one here, so I just need two more. I'm pretty sure where to find them. If I have to sweeten the deal?"

Bethany Anne shook Sheldon's proffered hand. "Money, within reason, is not a problem. Secrecy is. So, when it comes time to pick up the two cars no one on that side can breathe a word."

Sheldon said, "I understand, and let me thank you. You've just made my career... if I don't screw this up."

"No opportunity for you if you hadn't been here early on a Tuesday morning. So, consider what it took for you to be in the right place before you throw all the credit my way, okay?"

Sheldon nodded. John came over and handed him a business card. "Our contact information for this deal is on the card. It will expire in thirty-six hours, or as soon as we drive off the lot. I need you to let me know as soon as the cars are here, as we need to go over them ourselves." John's visage turned slightly harder. "Security."

Sheldon looked down at the card and back at John. "I'll sleep here tonight."

John clapped him on the shoulder and pulled a second card out. "This is my card. You ever want to talk about a different job, call me. People with your work ethic are hard to find."

Sheldon held the second card with serious respect. The first card was a business deal that would make his career.

The second was an honor.

Sheldon had worked on the deal for an hour before he got his first dealership to give up their F12berlinetta. The deal was at a twenty percent premium, but the salesperson didn't ask any questions, so he was going to call it a win.

The second, however, wanted to know who it was for, so Sheldon hung up after a polite good-bye. The third choice, over in Las Vegas, didn't care who it was for either. It was all about the money to her.

The dealership had just received their car, and it wasn't prepped yet. Sheldon promised that not prepping it was going to be perfect, and if they just got it ready for pickup, he would give them an additional two grand on top of the deal.

The final agreement arrived via email and Sheldon whooped, hands pumping in the air.

With eighteen minutes to go, he sent the information to the temporary contact email address and had an immediate reply. Who to talk to regarding money transfers and any other legal information about the cars was delivered to his email immediately. There would be two trucks with twenty-foot long shipping containers to pick up the cars at the dealerships within two hours.

Sheldon was about to reply that there was no way to drive the vehicles to Miami quickly enough and then remembered who his client was.

He snorted to himself and started his follow up. He told his boss that they had two hours to finish any paperwork because trucks would be arriving to pick them up, he was damned sure.

Not surprising, the financials went through immediately. Sure enough, Sheldon called both dealerships at the end of two hours. Both had trucks with big, black shipping containers on the trailers ready to load the vehicles.

One even remarked that ever since the TQB company put black shipping containers on the moon, everyone now painted their shipping containers black. As if, he said, they could all fly.

Sheldon kept his mouth shut. His contact would just have to find out about it some other time.

He got an email that said the cars would arrive at ten PM so most of the crew would be gone. Would that be a problem?

Sheldon had already pulled three of the absolute best people from the back and told them he would pay them each three grand to help him prep his three sales that night, or they could trust him, and if everything stayed quiet, they would get something worth far more than three grand.

All three guys agreed that their lips were sealed, and it became a small spy scenario for the four men. Their manager shrugged and handed over the keys. He knew what was going on and after being in the business for twenty-two years, he had worked with very big names. So, not being involved in the lady CEO's purchase wasn't a big deal.

Sheldon was pretty sure his boss didn't pay too much attention to celebrity news and apparently hadn't put two and two together. Too much time on the golf course with the elite around town was his best guess.

Oh well, it wasn't Sheldon's job to make sure his boss understood who they would be delivering over a million dollars worth of automobiles to in the morning.

He considered the massive opportunity to take pictures and picked up the phone. He had a family friend back in Orange County, California that had done pictures for many Los Angeles and Orange County luminaries such as Gene Simmons of KISS and President Reagan, as well as having International Photograph Hall of Fame & Museum recognition. Whatever it took to get Mark to arrive by seven the next morning, Sheldon was going to spend it.

After a few minutes talking with Mark, he finally was able to convince him that it would absolutely be worth his time, but no, he really couldn't tell him who it would be. Just that he would have exclusive shots that would be on the bylines of most of the world's news sites within forty-eight hours.

Sheldon hung up, and then looked to see if he could book a ticket for Mark from John Wayne International in OC to Fort Lauderdale, but they had no non-stops. He was able to go LAX to Fort Lauderdale and back, so he grabbed those tickets and sent the information to Mark immediately.

The 'spy posse,' as they had named themselves, were working to get the first car ready and laying out the plans to make sure they could bring the other two F12s online as fast as possible when they arrived. Everyone was going to take naps and make sure there were no screw ups.

Now, it was going to be a waiting game until ten PM.

———

WASHINGTON D.C. USA

Johann from the subassembly for the Advancement of the Human Race stepped into the outer office of Congressman McKinney and nodded to his secretary who picked up her phone and put up a hand showing two fingers.

Johann cooled his heels for just under two minutes when the door opened and Congressman McKinney stepped out still speaking to a gray-haired gentleman. "Tom, I'm sure my voting record for retroactive immunity for telecoms' warrantless surveillance speaks towards my high regard and understanding of how we need to support technology while supporting local and national authorities. Don't worry, I'm sure that the communication technologies these people must be using will come to light, and then we will stomp on the use and ban it for not having proper licensing."

"Just so that all of the jobs are protected, George," the older man said. "If they have something that's revolutionary, your constituency will be affected if we have to compete in the future. I've got fifty-seven senators and two hundred and twenty-seven congressmen ready to back up a moratorium on the introduction of new technology."

Johann watched the two men shake hands as Congressman McKinney put his second hand into the handclasp. "Tom, that's two-hundred and twenty-eight."

"Thank you, George." They separated and Tom knocked on the secretary's desk as he walked by and stepped out.

McKinney turned. "Johann, good to see you. Come on in."

Johann nodded to the secretary and stepped into the office ahead of McKinney, who closed the door behind him. "Please, let's sit over in the easy chairs. That damned desk chair hurts my ass."

Johann turned to the left, where lounge chairs and a bookcase made up a conversation arrangement. Johann sat down and settled comfortably. "Thanks for seeing me, Congressman."

"George, please," he said with a smile. "I know, it's all official until I say otherwise every time with you. But after six conversations and six amicable separations, we've never done any business. Why do I sense that this time is going to be different?"

Johann smirked. "Because a birdie told you something?" He continued, "Because you have an important person in your district that we are concerned with, and finally because the fifty-thousand dollar check from one of the companies I represent was cashed."

George said, "Yes, an interesting situation there. It seems I have become a leading congressman recently, since I represent Miami and the surrounding areas. Those districts contain some very, very rich people and for that reason I have always had a certain amount of influence, but it's night and day now."

Johann agreed. "I imagine it has. Not too many people have access to quite so many important contacts as you, nor do they know them that well. The Colorado representatives haven't had much luck since the site was previously an Army base, and so they didn't focus as much on that remote spot."

"So, what is it that you're asking of me?" Congressman McKinney interrupted. "Because I've had a conversation with a former congressman who was kind enough to go out of his way to 'accidentally' run into me and warn me not to mess with a certain individual. Would you know why that is?"

Johann's eyebrows drew together. He wasn't sure which congressman McKinney could be talking about.

"No guesses?" McKinney asked. When Johann finally shook his head in the negative, McKinney said, "I'm going to give you a hint, 'salt.'"

"Pepper?" Johann said. "Didn't he leave for health reasons? I mean, not the typical health reasons, but real ones?"

"Well, if you allow mental problems to be considered as health issues, then certainly." George McKinney continued, "But no one here knew why he quit. Oh, a lot of people knew he had something fishy going down in South America and would fly down from time to time. Since Miami's an important hub for flights and business, that isn't strange. But he came back from one trip and within ninety days he was gone. His own secretary said that he seemed to be off after the trip."

"Okay, but what does that have to do with the CEO of TQB Enterprises?" Johann asked. "I can only imagine that everyone, including Tom Carpenter, who just left, is focused on what TQB was going to do to interfere with their businesses."

"Yes, everyone is, and no one can explain to me exactly

what's going on to frighten them so much." George said. "As far as I can tell, TQB hasn't upset anyone here on Earth. Oh, I know she's giving NASA fits, but when I ask anyone on that committee, everyone says they don't get involved with anything. Regardless of how much money is thrown at them, everything is ignored. You cannot buy them," he finished.

"We know that." Johann leaned forward in his chair. "What do you know about Sean Truitt?" he asked in a tight and quiet voice.

George asked, "The CEO?" Johann nodded. "I was led to understand his was a missing persons case? That happened what, a few months ago?"

"Three," Johann said. "They found him. He was at the very bottom of Cle Elum Lake. He was in his car in over three hundred feet of water."

"Okay," George replied. "So, am I to take it from what we're talking about that you believe there's something fishy here?"

"George, that part of the lake is a few hundred yards from anyplace that could be reached by car. He didn't drive his vehicle off the road across three hundred yards of water and then sink. We believe he was dropped."

George sat back in his chair. "You guys think that TQB retaliated for the attacks on their base? Why?"

Johann was annoyed. George had never taken any of their carefully worded requests seriously and certainly never accepted any of their donation checks, and he was just as big a pain-in-the-ass as Johann had expected. Too many questions and too few offers to help.

Dammit, he was going to have to be blunt with this idiot.

"George, we only know of one technology that can float anything metal, and that would be TQB's containers to the moon. So, the working theory is one of them was put on the car and when Sean got close, it took him out to the lake and dropped him right where he was found. Well," Johann corrected himself. "Three hundred feet above where he was found."

"Okay, but why?" George asked. "Let's suppose you're correct and TQB is behind the killing. Why did they do it?"

Johann shrugged. "Who knows? Maybe Sean asked their CEO for a date and she took offense."

"Sean Truitt was married. I've seen the sobbing wife on TV," George replied dryly.

"Yes, I merely make a point of saying we don't know why Sean Truitt would have been a target. But if they're going around killing high-level CEOs, do you think they'll stop there? What's to prevent them from coming after congressmen and senators?"

"Why, have some of them done something to piss them off, too?" George asked.

"Of course not," Johann replied while thinking, *Hell yeah they have, and they're doing more.*

"Don't lie to the Congressman, he doesn't believe you." George retorted. "Of course there are people on Capitol Hill who are looking to either get in TQB's good graces or get something out of them so they can be in someone else's good graces."

"Like yourself?" Johann asked. "Not to put too fine a point on it, but you did accept our donation and Tom left pretty happy."

"Tom is easy." George replied. "I don't believe anything TQB has is going to come out into the commercial telecommunication sphere anytime soon, so what does it hurt to support something that won't come to pass?"

"Ah, that makes sense," Johann agreed, even if it did annoy him to think that his one major leverage point wasn't going to do him any good.

"So, let me ask you again, Johann. What is it you want me to do?" George was polite.

Well, Johann thought, *I'd like you to tell your buddies to arrest the bitch by knocking down her front door, but since that doesn't look to be in the cards...* "How about sharing the rumor with a few important ears that there's some backchannel talk about TQB possibly being responsible for Sean Truitt's disappearance?"

"This is what you want for your donation?" George asked, surprised.

"How about that and one additional conversation, when we have something a little more concrete to talk about?"

George considered his request for the necessary amount of time before nodding. "I can agree to that and I've got three people I can share this information with by this afternoon. Two are local down in Miami, the other one is down there, but is Fed."

Johann rose. Now that negotiations were done, the congressman would need to move on to his next appointment. He stuck out his hand. "Congressman McKinney." He smiled at the joke.

George stood up. "You ass!" But he didn't keep the smile off of his face.

Johann left that office and worked his way to the other side of town.

He had another meeting to attend, and this one was going to be a little more candid.

CHAPTER TWO

FORT LAUDERDALE, FLORIDA, USA

When they arrived, Sheldon felt a bit intimidated. At first, it wasn't a big deal as they had just knocked on the door. It wasn't until Darryl checked out the cars and confirmed they were clean that it became apparent just how they had gotten there.

By air.

Darryl had Sheldon open the door into the warehouse. When it was fully open, a black… something… came down from above and glided in. Tim was quick enough to start the door closing as William opened the pod and started pulling out white boxes about a foot square and six inches in height. There was a total of eighteen of those, and then three larger boxes. Sheldon found out that six were to be installed underneath the car and then one large device put into the trunk.

It took William twenty-three minutes for each car. When he finished with one, Marcus would start talking to himself and typing furiously on a laptop. They had pulled up a rolling table for the laptop so he could type then take a few measurements and then type some more.

"Sheldon?" Marcus called over to him.

Sheldon was watching William working on one of the cars, high on a lift, and had to jog back over to where Marcus was working. "Yes?"

"Can I get something destructive?" Marcus asked.

Sheldon was confused and slightly alarmed. "Destructive? These are very, very expensive cars, and I'd prefer they didn't get damaged while they're still in our garage."

Marcus looked at the sales guy for a second. "Oh, nothing like that! I just need something like a long metal rod or something like a bat."

Sheldon's eyes opened a little wider. "Still not liking where this is going…"

Marcus dipped his head down to look over his glasses. "Young man, these cars will not be scratched." Sheldon looked at Marcus for a moment before turning to search. "I think," Marcus finished quietly.

A minute later, Sheldon came over with a lever used for full-size car jacks. Marcus touched a couple of buttons on the laptop and then typed in a sentence and waited for a reply before holding his hand out to grab the bar. It dropped when Marcus caught it, he didn't expect it to be so heavy.

"This will do nicely," Marcus said. "Here goes nothing!" To Sheldon's horror, the man grabbed it in both hands and swung it over his head to land on the hood of the beautiful F12.

"What the HELL!" Sheldon asked as he jumped to pull the lever out of Marcus' hand. He rubbed the spot where the bar had slammed down.

Marcus looked up at the surprised salesperson. "See, nothing." He waved a hand for Sheldon to take a look. Sheldon touched the hood, but it was spotless, and more importantly, dentless.

He continued rubbing the spot while turning his head to look up at Marcus. "How?"

Marcus smiled. "It's a feature of the engines we installed. Since we aren't changing the glass like we would on her SUVs, we're making damn sure it has a protective field. Mind you, I'd prefer you didn't tell anyone," Marcus said.

"I won't," Sheldon agreed. "This whole thing except the pictures and whatever she decides to video for me won't be talked about by me."

"Good, good," Marcus said. "Now for the second part." He turned back to the rolling table. "Ah, you might want to come over here with me."

Sheldon stepped closer to Marcus.

He typed again and Sheldon watched as the F12berlinetta lifted off the ground six inches. "What the hell," Sheldon murmured. He stepped closer to the car and went down on his knees to confirm all four wheels were off the ground.

"See any problems?" Marcus asked, concern in his voice.

"Problems?" Sheldon asked, looking back up at the scientist. "If by problems you mean a wheel is touching the ground, then no. They all seem to be at the same height. The problem," he continued as he turned back around to look under the car. "Is that we shouldn't be watching a Ferrari floating."

"You get used to it," Marcus said.

"No," Sheldon whispered, "I'm pretty sure I'm always going to find this cool-as-shit."

RELEASE THE DOGS OF WAR

Sheldon was waiting at the front door at fifteen minutes past seven when a darkened SUV turned into the parking lot. The morning sun reflected off the white dealership walls, highlighting the palm trees around the building.

He started jogging towards the back of the parking lot. The red garage door started rising, allowing the SUV to drive into the garage as Sheldon followed them in and the garage door closed behind them.

There, in front of the SUV, were three F12berlinettas all in the beautiful dark red Rosso Fiorano color Bethany Anne had specified. They were staggered like they had been staged for a calendar picture.

Which, interestingly enough, they had been.

Sheldon nodded at Mark Koeff, who had been setting up his camera and lights for the last few hours. When Mark arrived, Sheldon gave him the news just who he was photographing, and even Mark was impressed.

That was saying something for a man who had photographed luminaries like actor/governor Schwarzenegger, astronaut Buzz Aldrin, and had met others such as Christie Brinkley, Raquel Welch, Ringo Starr and Michael Caine as he shot exclusive events in LA.

Mark turned out to have a story for just about everything, but was kind and soft-spoken. If there was ever a more down to earth person who had survived working in the glitz and glamor of California's LA and Orange County, Sheldon was hard pressed to figure out who it could be.

Mark prepped the cars and explained how he wanted to set up the shots with Bethany Anne leaning on the first car, and her security on theirs.

The front doors of the SUV opened, and John, then Eric stepped out and nodded to everyone. "Morning guys," John said.

Sheldon had his team of three off to the side and TQB's people, Marcus, William and Darryl were standing with them.

Darryl broke from the ranks and walked over. "They're clean, and they are ready. Although, I have to call bullshit on you two getting this ride first!" He grinned.

"Kiss my…" Eric started. "Tell me you didn't make sure it went up and down correctly as a security measure," he challenged Darryl, who shrugged but didn't answer.

"That's what I thought," Eric said. "Besides, you get to take the SUV back to the house."

"Woohoo!" Darryl said sarcastically as he twirled his finger around in a circle. "Be still my beating heart. SUV or Ferrari with flight capability. Gee, I wonder which one I would pick?"

"The one you're told to." John interrupted them. "Let's make sure we get out of here guys. Enough horseplay."

Eric mouthed 'sorry' to Darryl for getting them off track. They separated, and Darryl stepped to the back of the three cars.

The SUV opened up, and Bethany Anne stepped out. She had on large dark sunglasses and ruby-red lipstick, with a short, tight leather jacket, red pants and mid-height white-topped leather red-soled shoes.

She could hear the photographer snapping images. That was all right, as Sheldon had held up his end of the bargain, and this was the start of her plan to give the finger to everyone who wanted her technology. She stepped over to Sheldon and held out her hand. "Thank you. This is exactly the type of service I was hoping to receive. You've done your profession proud." She turned to smile at the photographer. "Mr. Keoff, how are you?"

Mark looked up from his camera in surprise. "Fine?" he answered before smiling. "Okay, I'm a little sleepy from the red-eye and this atrocious time zone, but other than that?" he shrugged. "Fantastic!"

Bethany Anne walked over to shake his hand. "I'm excited that Sheldon was able to procure your expertise. I've seen a lot of your work under your Mark Jordan name and approve. Excellent work, wonderful eye." She looked back at the three beautiful cars. "Where do you want me?"

"Ahhhhh," Mark studied the beauty in front of him and the cars. He turned to the largest of her guards, "Is there any way I can get some sunlight in here? The fluorescents are going to wash out her skin tone." The big guy snorted, and she pointed a finger at him, but it didn't cause him to hide his grin.

"Sure," John answered Mark. "Let's get the paperwork done real quick and that way if anything happens we can leave in a hurry."

Mark spent the next ten minutes taking a lot of photos of Bethany Anne as she signed the paperwork and then with all of the guys who had worked through the night to prep her cars. When they each had their turn, they were respectful.

Bethany Anne walked over to Marcus and whispered, "Smartphone cameras?"

Marcus said, "Not a chance."

She nodded her appreciation and turned back to the team. "Hey, is there anyone who'd like to make a thousand bucks this morning?" Two of the guys who had worked on the cars threw their hands up in the air. "Great! We have an

SUV outside and we need it driven back to Key Biscayne." This caused Darryl, William, and Marcus to turn to her. "We have six bodies and six seats, guys. You think I wouldn't take you all with us?"

Darryl looked over at John. "You ass!" John chuckled.

Then it was time for Mark to get busy with his camera, and it was magic. The light streaming off of her fair skin against the beautiful blood red color of the Ferrari was going to get him bookings around the world if he was willing to travel from Southern California again.

I'm picking up chatter that there's an APB to stop you in the SUV.

Why?

Request to find out your whereabouts during the disappearance of Sean Truitt.

That ass?

Yes.

What do they think?

I have no data of any real evidence, it is just a request to apprehend.

Well... shit. I'd be more annoyed, but I did kill him. Bethany Anne mused as she winked at the camera.

No remorse?

Hell no, TOM. When have you known me to be bothered by death of the deserving?

I haven't, but they usually don't result in APBs for you.

Politics, probably. Oh well, let's get this done. Where are they?

Down on the 913.

Well, that would have worked for them about an hour ago. Tell you what, let's do this and have some fun.

"Mark?" she interrupted his shot.

"Yes?" he asked, not putting down his camera as he worked.

"You want some shots that will rock the world?" she asked.

"You mean more than this? Because I'm pretty sure I have some outstanding ones already." His voice was muffled behind his camera.

"I mean pictures never before occurring outside of Photoshop," she told him.

This time, Mark put down his camera and looked back at her as he considered what he knew. "Where do I need to set up?"

"Back seat of the SUV as it goes back to our home in Key Biscayne. You'll have to be quick, but if you do it right, these shots will be in on the front page of the papers in the morning."

"No one hurt?"

"Nope," she agreed.

"When?" He asked.

She turned to Sheldon. "Ready for your video?" He nodded, and after she gave him an enthusiastic recommendation video, she stepped back to her car and grabbed the keys. Her guys were already in their cars, with their driver's windows down as she slipped into hers.

John.

Yes?

How long has the SUV been gone?

Maybe two minutes, why?

They're going to be stopped on the 913 causeway to apprehend me. We're going to be right behind them.

You aren't stopping, are you?

No, but I want them to point to our cars before we pass them by.

Bethany Anne, there are only two lanes on that road, what if they block the causeway?

That's what I'm counting on, John.

Where are we going?

Back to Colorado, I guess. I need to store these somewhere before we take them to Australia. Too hard to put them on the Ad Aeternitatem and I'm not having them suffer the wind buffeting all the way to the other side.

You good with this?

I'm going to have to deal with these feelings at some time.

I got your back, Bethany Anne.

And I got yours, Mr. Grimes.

Thirty minutes later, two police vehicles pulled out on the causeway to stop a dark tinted, black SUV with personalized TQB license plates. The vehicle used to spot their SUV had followed them onto the bridge and blocked the SUV from backing up.

Four officers got out of their cars and stepped over to pull the doors open and asked everyone to get out. Including the photographer who had his camera around his neck. The police officers were in the middle of questioning the three men when the roar of supercars could be heard coming their way. Two of the men pointed at the three identical F12berlinettas screaming towards them when they all took to the air and turned as if on invisible roller coaster rails and headed back towards land… across the water.

Well, one thing was right. Mark's pictures were seen all over the world the next morning. By the time Bethany Anne and her team needed to land, her legal counsel Jakob Yadav had the APB quashed, and more than one countersuit fired off in her defense.

Not that it mattered. While the three Ferraris might be in residence at TQB headquarters in Colorado, the six people had already left.

CHAPTER THREE

WASHINGTON D.C. USA

The blond man pulled off his sunglasses as he stepped through the door into the little Italian restaurant. He nodded to the hostess and then told her he was going to the back. He walked past the fifteen or so tables and half a dozen cozy booths around the main room as he made his way to the rear of the restaurant.

He passed the restrooms and continued to the last door on the right and opened it to step through. There were two doors on each side of the twenty-foot hallway. He knocked on the first door to the right, and when he heard the lock click, he stepped into the room.

Inside was a nicely appointed meeting room with a couch and two chairs, coffee table, bar, and a kitchen table for six in the back where one man waited. He stepped past the coffee table to pull out a chair. "Hey Johann, we're claiming TATP—triacetone triperoxide."

Johann reached across the table. "Damon, damned glad to talk. Do you want anything different? I ordered tea, but I can get anything."

"No," Damon replied as he pulled off his sport coat and draped it over the chair next to him. "You ordered the cheese manicotti, right?"

"Yes, of course. That was the best dish we had last time," Johann said. "Even better than the lasagna which I didn't think possible. I'd marry the sauce if I could."

"If I could take it to bed, then it would be a match in heaven," Damon agreed. "But let's get back to talking about Colorado."

"Yes. Isn't TATP the shit the terrorists used in France?" Johann asked as he buttered a roll. "At least that's what I remember."

Damon reached across to snag Johann's bread. "Delicious!" He grinned as he chewed.

"Ass!" Johann said, reaching for another roll. "For that, I'm taking this dinner out of your consulting fee."

"Done," Damon said. "Whatever your guys did to get me out of that hot water back in Georgia and pulled into this cush assignment here was fantastic. I thought the idea that real friends help you bury the bodies was just a joke." He reached for his tea and took a sip. "God, you even remembered to tell them I like it sweet."

"Sweet?" Johann chuckled. "You and your sister use half the sugar at the table to sweeten your tea. That was what, our first study group before finals our freshman year?"

"One for all…" Damon smiled.

"And all for us!" Johann replied as he reached across the table to bump fists with his college friend. "I'd like to claim it was a bitch to accomplish, and you owe me your firstborn, but for two things," he said.

"What are those?" Damon asked.

"I hate kids." Johann stated as Damon started laughing. "And the chick in the other car was so high that the discussion with the judge was easy. The lawyer showed how fucked up on cocaine she was, and it became a moot point. Judge saw it our way and tossed it. Then we pulled some strings, talked with a friend a little higher in your organization, and you became the appointed contact."

"I'm the cutout if it all goes to hell?" Damon considered.

Johann picked up his drink to clink with Damon's. "That's our assignment, my man. Until we figure out how to overthrow our masters and take their places we ride the risk," he said with a shrug.

"The Sith have nothing on us," Damon mused.

"Fucking pussies, those two." Johann agreed as he switched voices to mimic an old person. "Always two, there must be. A master and an apprentice." He switched back to his normal voice. "Anyway, now that we have you in position in the FBI, we can start to figure out blackmail material on those above you. If that shithead Sean Truitt hadn't gotten himself killed, I would have had enough to own his fucking ass."

Johann allowed himself a moment to feel the frustration of that situation. He had been so close when that ass had allowed his plane to bring in that backpack nuke. He got back on track. "How is blaming the explosion on TATP going?"

There was a knock on the door and a feminine voice said, "Food sirs."

Johann reached over to push the button that released the magnetic lock on the door, and it opened to reveal an attractive brunette in a red and white blouse and black miniskirt bringing in a cart. It took only a moment for her to refresh the drinks, the bread and lay out the food before retreating behind the door.

Damon picked up their conversation. "Really well. We were able to blame the size of the explosion and the plume on the walls in the canyon. Since the canyon layout did screw up the explosion and the explosion was so small, it wasn't a big deal. We still have it completely blocked off as domestic terrorism against TQB. We are so sorry that someone attacked such a valuable company, and how powerful TATP is but hard. They had a lot, but there's a reason the terrorists nickname it the mother of Satan and it got away from them, to blow so close to the base."

"You'd think the Chinese or Russians would say something," Johann said.

"I thought you guys might be involved in that." Damon said as he started on his second manicotti.

"Not us. I think someone in one of the black organizations might be doing something. Keeping the information that we had even such a tiny nuke explode inside the U.S. out of the regular news. That shit would scare the sheep all over the place." Johann answered.

"Well, somebody is putting a hard lock on the news. Fucking people in Denver would shit a brick if they knew anything nuke went off, no matter how small it was." Damon said.

"Probably," Johann agreed. "We're already having to deal with the whole sympathy thing with TQB being attacked by domestic terrorists using TATP. If I can, I'm going to let out that it was some new technology TQB has that actually exploded, but I'll let this die down first. So, since the terrorists blew themselves up, the worst we feared didn't come to pass."

RELEASE THE DOGS OF WAR

"What happened to the merc bodies?" Damon asked.

"Mostly all gone. What wasn't blown up was spirited away before any first responders arrived as near as we can tell. I'm not sure why TQB doesn't want stuff known, but they only left a handful of bodies shot outside to discuss with the police. It could be because their weapons made fucking hamburger of some of those guys. Plus, we heard something about a bear at the very end. I'm sure Stephanie Lee isn't sharing everything, but Phillip from South America had extra microphones listening, and he picked most of it up."

Johann looked up from eating and used his fork to point. "I can tell you one thing, those signs that talk about wolves that the newscasters mentioned are right. There were certainly wolves attacking, and we have no idea what the fuck happened there before we lost communications."

Johann went back to eating, "The weirdest fucking shit is on those recordings," he muttered, half to Damon half to himself.

———

QBS POLARUS, MID-ATLANTIC OCEAN

Stephen walked into the office that Barnabas was using as his judge's chambers. While the massive amount of data Bethany Anne's team was throwing at him was more than enough to assuage his curiosity, he had never felt this way in the last one hundred and fifty-two years.

He wanted a vacation.

He pulled the top manila folder and took a look at the name. "Clarissa Bernier, CEO." He opened the folder, and it was now in the agreed upon format. There was one page with typical information of name, age, location, and a two paragraph background, and the requested punishment. It was kind of a joke now between Barnabas and Bethany Anne. No matter the requested punishment, she would strike it out and write "DEATH" and add a happy face with fangs on it.

It told him that she was not giving up on her intention to make a lot of people pay for Michael's death.

The team had already executed six individuals across the world in the last three months. Sean Truitt was just the first.

Stephen interrupted him. "You look tired," he said as he took a seat in one of the two blue chairs facing Barnabas's desk.

Barnabas leaned back, keeping the folder open. "Is she serious?" He pointed at the document. "Even ADAM, using our agreed punishment matrix, is calling for this lady to be punished financially." He closed the folder. "She walks the line towards Michael all the time, brother."

"No, I think what she does is point out to you that your desire to be thorough when the data is all there and available is silly. You want to be lenient, and she is offsetting it with requesting death." Stephen shrugged. "How many times did you fail to arrive at the same conclusion as what's suggested in the folder?"

Barnabas thought about it. "Twice. Both went to death when new information was found in addition to what they had been a part of that got Michael killed."

"So, they weren't guiltless, then?" Stephen pressed.

"Hardly," Barnabas agreed. "I've read so many of these stories that I think it would have been better to stay in my madness."

Stephen pursed his lips. "You know, you've never explained that experience to me."

RELEASE THE DOGS OF WAR

Barnabas weighed the folder with the hundred sheets of paper in it and tossed it to the side of his desk so he could rest his elbows on top and clasp his hands. "That's because I'm not proud of that time, Stephen." He looked out the small window across the water. "I was insane for six months and six days." He turned back. "A woman I loved had been taken from me..." he sighed. "And I broke."

He leaned back and put his hands over his eyes. "Stephen, I completely robbed the world of over three thousand souls in the space of that short time between satiating my anger and sleeping. I researched my disgrace some years later. Fifty families have been erased from the Earth. None of their lines exist because they lived in the place where I lost my mind. The only reason I awoke was I had apparently been tracking something and got caught by a log that took me downriver and over some falls. Then, I mentally awakened as the sun started burning my skin. I needed my mental faculties to survive."

"That's when everything became a question to you?" Stephen asked.

"Yes. If intellect could pull me out of the Time of Disgrace, then I would make it my focus." Barnabas said.

"Are you fighting Bethany Anne or your memories, brother?" Stephen asked.

"Now... now I'm not so sure." He sighed. "I have to agree that she did not destroy everything in a violent rage as I expected she would." He crossed his arms and looked back at Stephen. "Is this where you tell me 'I told you so?'"

"For what?" Stephen replied. "For saying I trusted Bethany Anne?" He shook his head. "No. I know her well enough to know she's playing the long game, Barnabas. She's a woman, and they can all hold on to anger and react years later.

She's showing you respect, far more than she needs to, in my opinion."

"Yes, I get that now." Barnabas replied. "We've cleared maybe twenty names. Did you know," he asked. "That she had ADAM not only ruin one of the men financially, but she also ended up owning his company in the process? Then, she found malfeasance in his books and she had the company bring about a lawsuit, and he's now in prison?"

"I might have heard about that," Stephen said. "I think she said something about being able to find his ass when she needed it."

"That's powerful hate, Stephen." Barnabas cautioned. "It can eat at a person."

"You won't get to me by arguing she has very strong convictions and powerful emotions, Barnabas. But you need to see that she is passionate in all things, not only justice."

Barnabas lowered his eyes. "Why is it I cannot believe as you, Stephen? Why is it I cannot just trust and then... then all of this," he waved at the massive number of folders on his desk. "Would become so much easier!" He tried to grin but failed as he considered what he just said. "You don't think she would be so devious as to be dangling that possibility in front of me, would she?"

Stephen laughed. "Yes!" he swung a hand. "I'm not suggesting she's doing that. I'm answering your question that she could be devious enough to be doing what you fear." He continued chuckling. "But let's ask you the question that you need to answer, shall we?"

Barnabas drew his eyebrows together. "Why do I sense that you are about to ask something that I'm not sure I want asked?"

"Because it is time, old friend," Stephen said. "You need

to realize that intelligence and neutrality are not the paths forward."

"Oh? And what is?" Barnabas asked.

"Forgiveness, atonement, belief, and action," Stephen answered in a calm voice.

———

MANUFACTURING FACILITY 01, ASTEROID FIELDS

"There's the frame," William said to Bobcat as the two came closer to the large manufacturing hub that Jeo Deteusche, Head of IOS Mining and Manufacturing and Bandile Annane, his Chief of Mining had focused the teams on building.

"Damn, they really have got shit together out here," Bobcat said. He tapped the glass in front of him and spread his fingers to zoom in on a location in front of them. "I see they've used Jeo's design to build platforms between the ships for staging and additional manufacturing." He moved the camera angle. "Shit, they've completely enclosed an area with that canvas stuff and inflated it. Rigid, lots of space under it."

William was looking at the ship. "That is going to be one sweet ride when it's finished." He reached down to pull up his tablet and switched to another app. "Looks like the latest design calls for a hundred and twenty-one separate gravitational engines. Sumbitch, that's a lot."

"Yeah, they added some to the front and sides for rapid maneuvers. Another of Jeo's ideas," Bobcat said.

"Kid's been around too many video games," William muttered. "He should have focused on shooters."

"That's because you're just embarrassed you didn't think

of it first." Bobcat retorted. "Give yourself a little credit for the tweaks you suggested."

William shrugged. "That's from the modifications we did on Shelly and how she handled," he said. "But I'm completely taking credit for the 'stopping on a dime and giving you nine cents change' braking option."

"Gott Verdammt dangerous if you ask me," Bobcat said. "If the gravity modifications don't work out, someone is going to impale themselves on the bulkheads if they ever have to stop quick."

William put up a hand and waved two fingers up and down. "Someone get me out of this wall!" he chuckled. "Yeah, we'll test the gravity to push against forward momentum and inside the protective shell as well to hold stuff in place against their momentum."

"Fuck all, I don't want to be riding during the first test of that feature," Bobcat said.

"Yeah, that one does give me a few concerns, I'll admit." William said, then thought for a second. "But I can think of a few ways that would help a lot."

"That's because you watched Top Gun. It isn't like this ship is going into a dogfight."

"What if you come out of high speed right into an asteroid belt?" William asked.

"I'd suggest you don't come out at speed, then!" Bobcat argued. "That's why TOM's people always engaged the engines from standing still. It meant they were motionless wherever they popped out."

William watched a moment as the massive production zone grew in size. "Bobcat, all kidding aside. This is going to be Bethany Anne's ship for the foreseeable future."

Bobcat looked at the almost complete shell and thought a

moment. "We'd better make sure that gravity idea works and while we're at it, see if we can do a flipping maneuver." He sighed. "And whatever else we can think up because sure as shit she's going to want to do it."

"Worse than that, she's going to get into some situation where she NEEDS to do it." William retorted.

"Fuck," Bobcat replied.

CHAPTER FOUR

QBS POLARUS, MID-ATLANTIC OCEAN

Bethany Anne nodded to the two female Guardians as she and Ashur walked to her suite. Just a little earlier, she had told John that he and the Guardians needed to go blow off some steam. She would be a 'good little Queen' and stay here on the ship with Gabrielle and a bunch of protection until they got back the next day.

Well, so long as they got back by noon New York time. When she said noon, John made her say where noon was being counted from as he didn't want her to change the time zone on him.

She flipped him off while she laughed and decided New York would work.

When she stepped into her conference room, Ecaterina was already there, speaking with Barb in a hushed tone. She wanted to roll her eyes as she stepped over to the small fridge. She grabbed a glass bottle of Coke and dipped down to check no Pepsi had made it back into her fridge. She heard Ecaterina snort behind her.

She put a fingernail under the cap and popped it off. She tossed it into the trash before sitting down at the head of the table. "So, when are you going to fess up to being pregnant?"

Ecaterina's mouth opened and shut a few times as Barb snickered.

Bethany Anne smiled. "I get it, you think you're not making me face what's missing with Michael, but realize that hurt will heal with time. Well, it should fucking heal with time," she agreed. "But it hurts a little that you wouldn't trust me to be happy for you."

Ecaterina put her hands on her slightly expanded stomach. "I'm sorry, I can't say I'm thinking properly anymore," she said. "For what it's worth, Nathan argued that telling you would be better."

"Don't you hate it when men get things right?" Gabrielle said as she walked into the room. "Not that we can let them know they're right." She looked over at Ecaterina, concern clearly written on her face. "You didn't tell Nathan he was right, did you?"

Ecaterina rolled her eyes. "I said I wasn't thinking properly, not that I wasn't thinking at all."

"You haven't seen him in three days," Bethany Anne pointed out.

"Well... there's that, too." Ecaterina blushed.

Gabrielle sat down with a notepad and a pen. "You were so going to throw women under the bus. Dammit, centuries of training men are going to go down the tubes." She threw her hands up in the air. "What are we going to do with you, Ecaterina?"

Barb interrupted, "You mean besides playing with the new baby?"

"Well, of course!" Gabrielle's eyes lit up. "I get to be Auntie Gabby and spoil him rotten!"

"Her," Ecaterina corrected.

"Great!" Gabrielle rubbed her hands together. "The first rule of woman's club is we don't admit there is a woman's club!"

Ecaterina rolled her eyes. Her daughter was going to be the most twisted child in history.

"Any names?" Bethany Anne asked, smiling at Gabrielle's antics.

"We are agreed on the middle name, and we think that we have decided on the first name," Ecaterina said.

"Well, don't sit there and make us wait!" Gabrielle said. "I'll tell Nathan about your working out if you don't spill the beans!"

Ecaterina looked around. "Uh…"

Barb looked back at her. "What? You think we're worried that you're working out? Hell, my mom was seven months pregnant with my brother and skiing—smoking as well," she mused.

"Really?" Ecaterina asked. "He's okay?"

"Well, he turned out to be a writer, so I don't know if we can say all right, but he isn't mentally deficient," she allowed.

"Ma'am?" The four ladies turned to the Guardian at the door.

"Yes, Jasmine?" Bethany Anne asked.

"Captain says a call is coming in from Tabitha."

"I'll take it here," Bethany Anne said. Gabrielle reached over and pushed the phone towards Bethany Anne, who waited for the first ring before lifting it up, "Tabitha. Yes, hello. Wait, hold on one second. I get that. You have more dead people but this time inside the house. What did you do? Mmmhmm. Oh, got a little blood-thirsty, did you?" She paused as the ladies all looked at her with curiosity on their faces.

Bethany Anne continued, "Okay, it sounds like you need action to get something off of your chest. If you want to take care of business, you need more people that I will supply. No, it comes with strings, of course… Do you want to take care of South America, Tabitha? It's a massive undertaking and to be blunt, you may be killed." Bethany Anne paused to listen.

Gabrielle got Bethany Anne's attention and whispered, "Does she need me?"

"Do you need Gabrielle with you? No? Then Hirotoshi and Ryu have to be doing a hell of a job I take it?" she said with a little humor coloring her voice. "Mmmhmm, if you're going to do this, then you will come here for a discussion. You will be required to take martial art lessons from your team, and you will be expected to grow and be the leader for those of my elite you have with you. Realize they are not allowed to serve any but who have given their allegiance to me, Tabitha."

Bethany Anne listened for a moment. "We'll send a Pod to pick you up in thirty minutes. You can join us here, then you and I will talk after. Very well. Make it happen, Tabitha. Good, see you shortly too, bye." Bethany Anne hung up. "Seems Tabitha is also going through a life-changing situation."

"I wondered why we didn't see her in Australia," Ecaterina said.

"She couldn't handle the ceremony," Bethany Anne replied. "She doesn't believe Michael is dead. She's holding out hope that he turned to myst and is going to come back to us."

"Isn't this what you hope?" Ecaterina asked.

Bethany Anne breathed in deep and sighed. "Yes, but I cannot plan the future on that hope. God knows this universe owes me a fucking break, but I don't have the luxury of stopping our progress to rip through every conceivable option to see if he's there somewhere," she finished quietly.

The three other women wanted to reach out, but realized there was a gulf of responsibility between them as followers and Bethany Anne as the leader.

"Knock knock?" Jean Dukes stepped into the room. "Seems a little down in here, what happened?"

Bethany Anne smiled and the darkness lifted as she turned towards Jean. "Tell me, did the guys like your toys?"

"Seriously?" Jean asked as she sat down next to Gabrielle. "Those guys are in their own heaven at the moment. Those railgun rifles are works of art. I should know, I made them," she finished with a smile.

A moment later, Cheryl Lynn and Patricia stepped into the room and sat down. Patricia said, "Sorry, we used a Pod and then we stayed up looking down at this beautiful blue globe for a couple of extra minutes, which turned into ten."

"Not a problem, with you ladies we make a quorum," Bethany Anne said.

"Uh oh," Gabrielle said. "Sounding very official throwing around Roman Senate rules."

"It should," Bethany Anne agreed.

"I see we have no guys, so is the topic the guys?" Jean started. "Because you practically bribed them with those guns to go use them."

"They need to go get rid of some pent up aggression," Bethany Anne said.

"You mean they need to shoot people and fuck up others?" Patricia asked.

The ladies turned to stare at Patricia who looked back. "What? She can say fuck and I can't?" Patricia asked as she pointed to Bethany Anne.

"It's not that," Cheryl Lynn said. "It's that we nominated you the den mother of the group."

"I don't remember that vote," Patricia retorted.

"Well, I'll admit I nominated you since I have too much mothering with my two, and it sounded more fun to let you do it." Cheryl Lynn conceded.

"Was I even remotely supposed to be at this meeting when the vote occurred?" Patricia asked while keeping the woman in front of her directly in her piercing gaze.

"Can I confess we didn't have a vote?" Cheryl Lynn sighed. "In fact, I was rather hoping you would just do it."

"How about the rest of you?" Patricia asked.

"Hey, as the oldest female here, I just want to say that age should have nothing to do with role specifications," Gabrielle said.

"I think we can go without a den mother," Bethany Anne said dryly. "But I do have a mother question for everyone here, and it's important enough that you will not speak of it outside of those present. I expect obedience on this matter, is that clear?"

The women stopped kidding and nodded at Bethany Anne as she caught each of their eyes. After she went through the group, she started the official meeting. "As Jean suggested, this discussion is about the guys."

"What about them?" Gabrielle interrupted. "Other than getting some aggression out. They seem to be okay to me."

"That's because you're not looking at what they should be doing," Bethany Anne said.

"What?" Gabrielle asked, looking around the room. "I've trained them carefully, I'm not sure what they're missing here."

"Honey," Patricia started. "It isn't the training or the fighting that's missing."

Gabrielle looked at Bethany Anne, concern on her face. Bethany Anne shook her head at the woman. "You have done an admirable job as the Captain of my Own, Gabrielle. But you're used to vampires who have been alive for at least a hundred years. These guys haven't and they're missing something they need."

"What?" Gabrielle looked around before her eyes opened wider. "They need women?"

"Well, I might've said action," Jean said.

"I don't think it's just getting laid." Bethany Anne said. "We have a connection so that I can feel them to some degree. Sure, they might need to get laid, but they need to share feelings with that 'one other' that a female will give them."

"Or male," Cheryl Lynn said. All of the women looked at her. "I was thinking Akio, not John, Eric, Scott or Darryl."

"Oh," Jean Dukes answered, "I was going to tell a few women that they needed to get a dick addition if it was one of the four."

"Hey!" Barb asked. "Could the Pod change a woman to grow a penis?" Her question caught everyone off guard, and they all looked at Bethany Anne, who stared back at them.

"Seriously? This is the pressing question of the moment?" She got six women nodding at her. She rolled her eyes. "Un-fucking-believable," then put up a finger to tell them to hold a second.

TOM?

I heard.

What's the answer?

It's possible, but it will start changing a lot of internal organs for a long time before they come out. It isn't going to just sprout a new appendage.

God Bless America.

Why?

What? Oh, it's just exasperation on my part. Why I thought I could have a straightforward discussion with women is beyond me.

Tom decided to stay quiet.

"The short answer is yes, it's possible. The longer answer is it will take a long time in the pod, and nothing will be the same when you come out." From the looks on the ladies' faces, Bethany Anne could tell they each had something they didn't either care to lose or care to gain. "So, if we're done with the biology questions?" She looked around the table.

"I talked with Giannini after her date with Darryl," Cheryl Lynn started. "She could tell that she would play second fiddle to you in his mind, and she wouldn't accept that, so they parted with a kiss and as friends."

"That's going to be a tough sell." Barb allowed.

"Not necessarily," Jean said. "If the date is with someone committed, then they both are committed to the cause, and Bethany Anne is the figurehead for the cause." She thought a moment before blushing. "Sorry, didn't mean to call you a figurehead, boss."

Bethany Anne said, "No, I believe you are on to something there." She tapped her fingers on the table. "If a couple is committed to a cause above themselves, then they are joined in their efforts and both sides would be stronger in their commitment and understand what it takes. Or, at least most will."

"What about kids?" Ecaterina asked.

"What about them?" Bethany Anne asked. "Oh, you're asking what happens with kids?" Ecaterina nodded. "Well, it won't be an accident. The guys are all shooting blanks right now after the enhancements."

"But, they *are* shooting?" Jean asked grinning.

"As far as I know, Ms. Dukes." Bethany Anne raised an eyebrow at the woman. "Unless you need further research done?"

"Well," Jean said. "If I have to sacrifice my body on the altar of John Grimes, I'm just saying that …" Jean saw everyone staring at her. All were smiling except Barb, whose mouth was open in surprise. Jean blushed. "Can I just say that I'm used to working with men, and they tend to be a little more blunt?"

"You can," Gabrielle said. "But it won't erase what we heard."

"On the altar of John Grimes?" Cheryl Lynn asked. "That's erotically poetic, I think."

"You should have seen him snap that lock in his fingers," Jean said, twisting her right hand in the air. "God, what a turn on."

"I'd say you're still pretty turned on," Patricia smirked.

"What happened to the Chief Engineer?" Gabrielle said.

Jean made a face. "Well, I could say it was fun while it lasted, but it didn't last long enough to be too much fun. I learned that he admired me for a few years, but he has been in love with space for decades. Space is such a slut."

"Chose to go out to the Asteroid Belt?" Cheryl Lynn guessed.

Jean nodded. "Yeah, the new ship they're working on caught his imagination. Apparently, nothing we have down here is nearly as sexy as the first spaceship in existence. Thank God we never went to bed, I don't know if my ego could handle being second fiddle to a spaceship."

"Well, isn't that what we're asking anyone who is with the guys?" Bethany Anne brought the question back around. "To be second fiddle to me?"

Jean shook her head. "No, because you embody the future. That's what I meant by a figurehead. You are *you*, but you're also what we are striving to do all of this for, to save the planet. I'm okay being second fiddle to something that important, but a spaceship is just a huge vibrator. A technological plaything that has his imagination, and I can see that he is going to be infatuated with that bitch for a few years."

"Angry much?" Gabrielle asked.

"No. Well yes, in a way." Jean said. "Not so much about Chief Rodriquez following his dream, I think that's great. It's more that I knew that he admired me, and it felt really good after all of the other shit that happened to me. Now, I'm playing second fiddle to his space dream and my ego took a hit."

"Oh." Gabrielle said. "Just making sure you're not rebounding onto John. I wouldn't agree to that." She kept her face pointed at Jean until the woman nodded her understanding.

"No, at the moment I'll admit I don't want John Grimes for his intellect, which he seems to have plenty of if you ask me. I just want him for his body." She shrugged. "I just want to spend all night getting my brains fucked out. I admire and respect him for what he does, but it is the man outside that has me ready to load my weapons!"

Patricia put a hand over her mouth as she snickered at the blunt answer from Jean.

"So, how exactly did this conversation go into the gutter so fast?" Ecaterina asked.

"Sweetie, you must have had a very sheltered childhood," Patricia told her.

"My childhood was on a mountain," Ecaterina answered. "Or with my brother."

"Well, that answers that question," Cheryl Lynn said. "You need more girl time before it's all babies and diapers."

"Ladies," Bethany Anne interrupted. "And I'm starting to wonder about using that word now. I need you to focus!"

"Hey, did we ever get the baby name?" Gabrielle asked before looking back at Bethany Anne. "Oh, sorry!"

"She can tell you the baby's name," Bethany Anne spoke in a clipped fashion, "At the end of my damn meeting!"

Twenty minutes later, there was a knock on the door and Tabitha stepped in. She was wearing a pair of leather pants and an Under Armour shirt. This caused Bethany Anne to raise her eyebrows.

Gabrielle greeted her with a hug. "Hey shrimp! Those don't look too bad on you."

Tabitha looked down at the leather pants. "You mean you're jealous that my ass makes them look good, right?" She looked back up, grinning at the vampire. "Because, let's face it, European asses just don't got that slap!" She popped herself on the butt.

"Whatever," Gabrielle said. "C'mon and sit down before I slap you, you disrespectful cur."

Bethany Anne nodded to Tabitha. "One second, Tabitha. Okay, Patricia, Barb, and Gabrielle are going to take the next steps, and we'll talk again. Get with ADAM if you need to speak to me." The others stood up from the table and started making their way out.

Barb came around and gave Bethany Anne a hug and whispered in her ear, "What about Frank?"

Bethany Anne looked at Barb. "I thought you were going to deal with that. You aren't?"

Barb blushed. "Well, I'd like to. Perhaps not quite as emphatically as Jean."

Bethany Anne thought a moment. "You need to remember that while Frank looks in his late twenties or early thirties, he's a product of a century ago. You might need to take him in hand to get him moving."

Barb smiled. "Well, I think I can take something in hand and then I'll have his attention."

Barb turned to walk out with a smile on her face, completely missing Bethany Anne's look of total shock as her eyes followed the woman out of the room.

"What?" Patricia asked getting Bethany Anne's attention. "You didn't think she had that in her?"

"I'm not sure what I thought, but I'm wondering if Dukes is creating monsters here." Bethany Anne answered the older woman.

"Well kid, I've got to go jump your Dad," Patricia told Bethany Anne. "All this talk of manly men has my heart pumping and it's time he takes care of the home front," she said and started laughing as she walked towards the door.

"That's…" Bethany Anne started, but Patricia was already at the door laughing at the expression she suspected was on Bethany Anne's face. "Just not right…" Bethany Anne finally overcame a strong desire to stick her tongue out at Patricia's back.

Bethany Anne turned to regard Tabitha, who looked up at her. "And now, that leaves you," she told her.

CHAPTER FIVE

QBS POLARUS, MID-ATLANTIC OCEAN

Bethany Anne turned toward her suite. "Come on, let's go to my room." She grabbed her Coke off of the table as Ashur stood up and followed them. Bethany Anne grabbed a coaster from the writing desk to the left of the main door and walked over to her nightstand, dropped the coaster on it, and set her Coke down before getting on her bed.

She looked down at Ashur, who was looking up at her. "Yes, come on up. You better keep your shedding down, you four-footed rug." Ashur chuffed as he jumped up on her bed and lay down with his head next to her hand and looked up at her. "Yeah." She lifted her hand so Ashur could move his head underneath it and she dropped it back down to rub Ashur's ears.

Bethany Anne turned to Tabitha who was staring at them, surprise showing on her face. "What?"

"Do you and Ashur communicate?" Tabitha asked. "I

mean, I know he's intelligent, so maybe he just knows a little more than most dogs, but it seems like you two really communicate."

"What?" Bethany Anne looked down at Ashur. "What kind of bitches do you like?" Ashur chuffed again. "Seriously?"

"What did he say?" Tabitha asked.

"Well, if I believe this, he said promiscuous ones." Bethany Anne regarded Ashur further. "You know four-foot, we're going to have to do more testing to see if this is real, or if my mind is playing jokes." Ashur made a whining sound. "You and me both, needles scare the shit out of me, well they did anyway," she amended. "I imagine it's going to be the Pod for you soon." She rubbed his head hard then reached over and patted him on his side. "Damn, have we been communicating?" She wondered aloud.

Bethany Anne turned to face Tabitha. "Okay, sage of the databases, spill it."

"Well, you know about the first two attacks on Michael's house," she began before Bethany Anne put up a hand.

"Your house now. I get that you don't want to believe he's gone, but for now, let's call it your home. I went through this same thing already when he disappeared before. If he should ever make it back, you can give it back to him, okay?" Tabitha nodded.

"Okay, I told you about the first two attacks. Hirotoshi and Ryu took care of them, and it wasn't a big deal since they were in charge. This time, I answered the front door, and three guys I encountered were pushy. Something snapped in me, and I left the front door open and told them I didn't want company, but if they wanted to push it and come in, it would go bad."

"So, they took you up on your offer. Did they say who they worked for?" Bethany Anne asked.

"No, just that their masters would be there tonight." Tabitha shrugged. "That was enough to say vampire to me. Hirotoshi and Ryu have been kind and only drunk from mugs for me. This time, I offered the three men's necks to them."

"Did you watch?" Bethany Anne asked.

She made a face. "Yes, I did. I figured if I was in charge of the execution, then I should be willing to witness the deaths. I can't say I didn't have a moment in the bathroom re-acquainting myself with lunch, but I felt it needed to be done." She looked a little green remembering the episode.

"Good, that gives me hope that you have the stomach to do what your anger is driving, Tabitha." Bethany Anne said. "As a leader, especially a leader of mine, I expect your best and then I expect you to figure out how to surpass your best. You can't expect others to do what you can't do. That means if you decide people need to be killed, you need to be able to kill."

Tabitha sat quietly, thinking about Bethany Anne's words as the woman went on.

"Further, you know all about the intelligence and computers and hacking, and your body is in decent shape, but you're going to have to get into superb condition."

This time, Tabitha made a small face of disgust. Bethany Anne concealed her amusement and continued, "Finally, you'll need to learn how to fight and protect yourself. If you don't, there could be a time when one of those underneath you could use just a little more help. If you can't do it, they could die, and that is not the kind of leader I allow."

Bethany Anne watched as the realization of her not

wanting to put in the physical effort, and the possible death of one of her guards switched something in her brain, and her lips compressed in determination.

Good girl, you might just make a good leader, she thought.

"Finally, Hirotoshi and Ryu are protecting you under my orders. For you to start taking the fight to others, you will need at least six, perhaps seven. The answer to that I will leave with Akio, and I'll ask Gabrielle as well."

"Gabrielle joining me?" Tabitha asked.

"Do you want her to?" Bethany Anne responded.

Tabitha was quiet a moment. "No. I mean, yes I do because it would make me feel more secure. But I'd just start relying on her to make everything happen, and I would still be the Tabitha I don't want to be anymore."

"Which Tabitha is that?" Bethany Anne pushed.

"The weak one," she replied in a small voice. "The one that wasn't there to help Michael when he needed it."

MANUFACTURING FACILITY 01, ## ASTEROID FIELDS

Jeo walked towards Bobcat and William, who were both looking at the high ceiling above them. "Pretty impressive, isn't it?" The two men dropped their gazes and reached out to shake Jeo's hand. "We used the ideas from the BEAM module for ISS," he said as he shook their hands. "For the inflatable habitat, the transported compressed air allowed us to fill it up, and the new interlocking modules keep us from losing air as people come in and out."

"I noticed," Bobcat said. "Flying a Pod into a double-wide

and then spacewalking into the little booth was disconcerting. Hearing the air injected into the airlock was a great feeling, let me tell you."

"Speak for yourself," William complained. "You guys need to build a big and tall booth."

"Shit, lose a few pounds," Bobcat snickered and popped William in the stomach.

"You think that shit's funny, just wait until John Grimes has to use it." William retorted and laughed as he saw Bobcat's realization, "See! That shit's not so funny when you wonder what would happen if John got stuck."

Bobcat looked at Jeo. "My rotund friend here is right." Bobcat dodged a playful punch from William. "You're going to have to worry about bigger people. Shit, Scott would get stuck because of his shoulders alone."

"How many bigger people are there?" Jeo asked. "I mean, I guess I've seen the Guards, but…"

"Well, there's a few of the Guardians that eat a cow for lunch," William started then shrugged. "A bunch."

Jeo made a face. "I didn't want bigger because of the air loss, and another entrance is another potential leak."

"I'm sure you'll come up with a good solution. I'd recommend roping Adarsh into the mix," Bobcat offered. "There's more to him than meets the eye." He turned towards the main office and started walking. "I see the gravity measures keep us feeling like we're on Earth. That's convenient." William followed.

"And healthy, and a whole lot of other things," Jeo agreed as he turned to walk with the two men. "We modify the gravity depending on what we want to do, as you would expect."

"How's it going on the Angel project?" Bobcat asked. "I'm getting reports from ADAM, but that is a shitload of manufactured parts we're lifting out here for that baby."

"Hey, we're net positive cash flow." Jeo said. "I've talked with ADAM, too. The mining processes are netting us a ton of potential income, but getting it into the Earth's markets without killing the profit options is a little challenging."

"For who?" William asked as the men entered Jeo's office and sat down. "ADAM's dealing with that, isn't he?"

"No," came a female voice from Jeo's wall. A visual came up of an attractive blond from the waist up. "I am helping Jeo deal with the financial markets."

"Hello Samantha," Bobcat said. "I see you changed your outfit."

"I was told to turn into this business avatar for your meeting, yes," Samantha answered.

Bobcat heard Jeo mutter, "Oh God, no!"

"Well, it's just the four of us," Bobcat started before Jeo interrupted him.

"Samantha, please lock all avatar requests down for twelve hours," Jeo hurriedly instructed.

Samantha said, "I understand the avatar request change, Jeo."

Bobcat turned to Jeo. "Why are you so red?" he asked. "You know this isn't going to work, right?"

Jeo looked back at Bobcat, shocked. "What do you mean this isn't going to work?" he replied, suddenly nervous.

William chuckled. "Jeo, Bethany Anne has a handful of people she trusts with her life. There are also people who she trusts to make sure other lives are protected, and Bobcat is at the top. Do you think she would let anyone block Bobcat out of a system?"

"But...but..." Jeo looked at them, horrified. "I've made changes to Samantha's programming."

"I'm sure you have," Bobcat agreed. "And every one of them, all changes, in fact, that are made to anything even remotely intelligent go through one of ADAM's systems." He shrugged. "So, change her back."

Jeo looked embarrassed but spoke to the avatar, "Samantha, please change back to your avatar from this morning."

"I'm sorry Jeo, but I am blocked from accepting avatar changes for another eleven hours and fifty-eight minutes," she replied.

Jeo looked at Bobcat and shrugged. "I tried?"

"I'll bet," Bobcat snorted before turning to Samantha. "Samantha, implement this morning's avatar representation per Bobcat vocal approval and Level Five security code Delta Delta Kilo Gamma Three Two."

Samantha said, "I have an approval on Level Five approval Delta Delta Kilo Gamma Three Two. Implementing pre-existing G4 Avatar."

Samantha switched to an incredibly lifelike representation of Gabrielle in black leather with a sword on her back. Her voice even had a European accent. "Is there anything else you would like me to do, Bobcat?"

"God, now I know why he did it," William whispered to Bobcat, who nodded his agreement.

Bobcat viewed the avatar for another few seconds before turning back. "Jeo, do you know why I made Samantha switch back?"

"So I would be horribly embarrassed?" he replied, his hand covering his eyes with his fingers split so he could see between them.

"No, so you don't get an ass kicking from Gabrielle and then from Bethany Anne—among others." He pointed at the avatar. "I'm guessing you're infatuated with Gabrielle, and you think this harmless. But what you should be thinking is 'this is creepy.'"

"Creepy? No, I don't think it's creepy. So, I'm going to have to go with harmless." Jeo started before William interrupted him.

"Samantha," William said. "What can you do for me?"

"What would you like me to do for you, William?" Samantha asked.

Bobcat pointed at the avatar. "Seriously?"

Jeo was studying Samantha. "Well, to be fair I don't *think* it's Gabrielle, and I need something."

"Yeah, you aren't getting it yet." Bobcat said and turned to the wall. "Samantha, Implement Dobby G1." The avatar on the wall changed to represent a submissive elf slave, in old clothes with a large nose and brown, mottled skin.

"Harry Potter?" Jeo asked, shocked. "You changed my avatar to Harry Potter's elf?"

"Well," Bobcat asked, sweeping an arm up to the wall. "Isn't this what it does for you?"

"Well, of course not!" Jeo exclaimed, "Samantha is not a slave who does… does…" Jeo stopped then asked the avatar, "Samantha, what can you do for me?"

The voice came back as the elf in the movie had, very respectful and full of self-loathing yet helpful at the same time. "Whatever my master would have me do, Jeo! Please, tell Samantha what you would have me do so I can please you."

William said into the silence, "If Gabrielle ever learned that there was a virtual Gabrielle, who spoke even remotely like that, she would have your testicles pinned on a wall. That's if someone who respected Gabrielle didn't come here first and just cut everything off. Those guys don't fuck around."

Jeo nodded. "Samantha, delete avatars G1 through G7."

He looked over to Bobcat and flushed again, "In fact, delete all avatars except S1 through S17."

"I have deleted all avatars in the system, my master." Samantha/Dobby said.

"Yes," William agreed. "That other would have gotten you killed," he assured Jeo.

"You're intelligent and smart," Bobcat said. "But you're also young, dumb and way too far away from most women. Of the avatars you created, Gabrielle and Bethany Anne will be here in the future. Bethany Anne might, just might, have found it foolish but a little funny. I guaran-damn-tee you that the Bitches would not. So, be a little smarter about what you need to do to make your job happen and be very respectful because ADAM is always watching."

Bobcat exhaled loudly. "Now that we have that bit out of the way, tell me more about Bethany Anne's ship and how soon we can get it ready with all of the components we're shipping up here."

———

QBS POLARUS, MID-ATLANTIC OCEAN

"So," Bethany Anne asked. "You think that somehow you're to blame for Michael's death?"

"He's not dead," Tabitha replied, a little more strength in her voice.

"Maybe not," Bethany Anne agreed. "But perhaps he is. Either way, he isn't with us, is he?"

"No," Tabitha said.

"So, you're blaming yourself for his absence?" she asked a second time. Tabitha nodded. "And are you blaming me for asking him to go to Colorado to protect the children?"

"No!" Tabitha looked at Bethany Anne in alarm. "You can't possibly be in two places at one time and he wanted to help you. It's just," Tabitha slumped in her chair. "It's just that I should have known what was going on. I've tracked down some of the players, and they met in South America! Fucking Costa Rica. If I'd found that out, then we would have stopped them cold."

"We can't look into everything," Bethany Anne told Tabitha in a calm voice. "Even ADAM can't be in every computer casting about for clues to all the evil in the world."

Don't give me any lip, ADAM.

>>I wasn't going to reply to that, Bethany Anne. To accomplish what you ask would give me a headache.<<

"Okay, I understand the logic, but when does the hurting stop?" Tabitha asked.

"When you begin to live life again. For you, I imagine it started when you invited the three thugs into your home to accept their fates." Bethany Anne replied.

Tabitha thought about it. "Maybe. I've been doing something instead of just existing since I made that decision."

"Do you still want to take the fight to the Forsaken?" Bethany Anne asked.

"Not only the Forsaken, there are a few other people that need some cleaning up." Tabitha said. "Some politicians who are not happy with what Michael was doing with Anton's money."

"So, we have politicians doing what?" Bethany Anne asked.

"You name it, and we have it in South America," Tabitha said dryly. "South America, Central America, and North America."

"You know, I need to house some reporters and their protection detail, do you have enough room?" Bethany Anne asked.

"Who and how many?" Tabitha asked. "I'm sure I can do it for you. Hell, I meant what I said. You are my Queen, and I will get it done if we need to build an additional house or buy something. Just tell me what you need accomplished." Tabitha said, squaring her shoulders to try and mimic Gabrielle.

"Well, it will be two reporters, a videographer, and two Australian vampires that proved themselves in the base attack. I've changed their nanites to allow them to be out in the sun, but I'm keeping them away from Australia and the reporters need protecting."

"So, say eight in my group and five in theirs? The house can easily hold that many. Probably more like twenty to twenty-five, if they're a little friendly. All of the Elites are sunsafe, right? They don't need SPF1000 sunscreen?"

Bethany Anne snorted. "SPF1000? No. They're all 'sunsafe.'"

"Hey!" Tabitha jerked upright. "Did you know that not all of the Elite are gay?"

Bethany Anne cocked her head a little in question. "Yes. Why, is that a shock to you?"

"Well, um… I didn't." Tabitha admitted. "And so when I got off the phone with you I started undressing since I thought they were all gay." Her face flamed red.

"You undressed how much in front of Hirotoshi and Ryu?" Bethany Anne asked.

"Well, not so much when I left as I walked out with nothing but these leather pants on. Then I put my bra and shirt on right in front of them. They didn't move." Tabitha stopped and shook her head a little.

"Well, they moved even less than their usual statue-selves, as if that was a thing," she continued. "But I noticed just a little bit of facial expression and asked them and they said they weren't gay."

"They spoke to you?" Bethany Anne asked.

"Well, they have before, but no. They just shook their heads when I asked if the Elite were all gay."

"So, you asked two men that you had just flashed your tits at if all of the Elite were gay, and they said no. Do I have that right?" Bethany Anne asked, smiling.

"Well, yeah," Tabitha replied, confused.

"But you didn't think to ask the two in front of you, who had just had an eyeful of Tabitha's chest if they happened to be gay?" Bethany Anne continued.

"Well, no." Tabitha made a face. "So I don't know if they're gay or not."

"Why does it matter?" Bethany Anne asked.

"I don't want to be flashing straight guys!" Tabitha roared with alarm at Bethany Anne.

"Tabitha, these men have been around for a long, long time. Assuming they are straight, I imagine they have had their fill of nice racks. Plus, they are the Elite. You could go walking around naked, and you wouldn't get a rise out of them. NOT," Bethany Anne put up a finger. "That I want you to test that!"

"I wouldn't do that!" Tabitha exclaimed. "Oh my God. Walking around naked in front of all the men?"

"If you are on an Op, you might have to change clothes in front of them, but what's on the Op, stays on the Op. It's just another thing you're going to have to learn to get over. But just walking around the house nude is disrespectful whether they're gay or straight." Bethany Anne finished.

"I'm still trying to get over you telling me not to test getting a rise out of them," Tabitha said.

"After my talk with the women a few minutes ago?" Bethany Anne replied. "I'm not sure what I should expect."

Bethany Anne shook her head as if to shake out a thought that had lodged disobediently between her ears. She got up off of the bed, grabbed her Coke and started walking for the door. "Okay, this is what we're going to need to do before you can move forward."

The two ladies left her suite, with Ashur following behind.

Two hours later, Tabitha had sworn allegiance to Bethany Anne with Stephen vouching for her determination and Barnabas confirming she understood the details. Bethany Anne grabbed Ashur, and the three of them walked Etherically to the spaceship still stationed above the earth.

Ashur dropped on the floor in the main hallway as the two women stepped through the door into the medical room.

"Wow," Tabitha said as she took in the medical pod. "This is it, then?" She walked over to stroke the coffin-like device. "This is what changed Michael so many centuries ago?" She looked up at Bethany Anne, who was studying her. "And you?"

"Yes," Bethany Anne answered. "And it's going to modify your body a little. Not too much in the beginning, just getting you prepared with a nanite mix that is going to see what it might need to fix in the future, and maybe correct potential problems."

"Um, like what?" Tabitha's eyes grew a little larger.

"I have no idea," Bethany Anne said. "You'll have to go into the pod for us to figure that out."

Tabitha looked back at the pod. "What do I do?"

Bethany Anne clicked a button that lowered a seat from the wall. "Well, you start by putting your clothes here, and I'll prep the pod. Then, you lie down, and the pod will close over you. You'll go to sleep and wake up when you're finished."

"How long were you in it?" Tabitha asked as she pulled off her shoes.

"Somewhere between six and seven months," Bethany Anne answered while she focused on the Pod controls and what TOM was telling her to do.

"Six or seven…" Tabitha murmured before squaring her shoulders and started working more aggressively on her shoes. She removed her socks and dropped them into the shoes and then took off and folded her shirt and pants, and finally her panties and bra before standing up behind Bethany Anne.

"Kinda cold here," she said.

"What?" Bethany Anne said and turned around to notice the naked Tabitha behind her. "Oh. Here." She hit a button to open the pod. "Jump on in and your cold problem will go away."

Tabitha stepped up, sat on the bed, swung her legs in and then laid down. "Why is my cold problem going to go away?" she asked as the pod closed on her.

"Because," Bethany Anne said, "I'm about to hit this last button." She hit the button to start the medical review and Tabitha's eyes closed. "And you're going to go to sleep like that," she finished.

Do we have everything going correctly?

Yes, we do.

Great, we'll let her cook in here for a couple of hours and come back.

"Ashur?" Bethany Anne called as she walked out of the room.

Two hours later, Bethany Anne and Ashur came back and Bethany Anne read the readouts.

Bethany Anne, this isn't good. Tom said.

What is it?

She has a significant amount of cancer in her body and her genetics are such that she will probably suffer early neurological damage if the cancer does not kill her.

Bethany Anne thought for a minute. *Options?*

If we heal this damage, we are effectively messing with her genetics. She is going to be in the Pod for quite a while.

Days?

At least a week.

Shit, that's going to mess up South America. Bethany Anne considered a moment. *Fuck it, I'm the Queen. Fix her and upgrade her. I want her to have the enhanced package. We'll come back when she's healed to tweak her.*

CHAPTER SIX

So, we had a nuclear warhead go off inside of our borders, and you confirm it was tracked back to Russia via a Chinese purchase?" The President asked from inside the secure meeting room.

"Yes, Mr. President," General George Thourbourah admitted. "I've worked with all of the services, and I can tell you for certain it came in on Sean Truitt's personal airplane."

"I wish that asshole were alive so we could bring him up on charges and put him in front of a firing squad." The President said. "I cannot figure out what the hell he could have been thinking."

"What every large conglomerate is thinking, Mr. President. What does TQB Enterprises have that is going to destroy their company?"

"Yes, it seems like everything that derails an effort to move this country forward in the last half a year that damned company is somehow involved."

"Are they politically active?" General Thourbourah asked.

The President frowned. "No, they are not," he said. "But by being so damned neutral and focused on outer space, everyone is wondering what they're really up to here on Earth."

"And? What are they really up to?" the General asked.

"Believe it or not, they are really up to exactly what they announced," the President smiled. "Although they seem to be involved in incidents around the globe. I've got a meeting on TQB with the Joint Chiefs tomorrow morning over at the Pentagon. I'm going to have to deal with all of this shit including what to do about that little nuke over in Colorado. I've got the actual information locked down under codeword security, and I'll throw people in jail if they breathe a damned word. But that's going to only last so long before too many questions get asked and we need to understand how to handle that pretty quickly."

The President stood up to leave then paused. "George, see what we can do to plan a response. No one facilitates a bomb like this on our own soil and gets away with it. I don't care what jackass helped them. The Chinese purchased that son of a bitch and both of us know they want the same thing—TQB technology. I know that TQB have pulled all of their main people out of the US, but it would be a problem for us when it comes out the US didn't retaliate."

"How are we going to do that on foreign soil, sir?" General Thourbourah asked.

"I'll probably have a better answer for that after tomorrow's meeting, which I want you to join. Right now, all I have is a hunch," the President said, and then walked out of the room.

RELEASE THE DOGS OF WAR

QBS POLARUS, MID-ATLANTIC OCEAN

The bridge watch all focused on their jobs, but snuck surreptitious glances at Bethany Anne every little while. "So, we're still being shadowed, Captain?" she asked.

"Yes, by the U.S. and China, with Russia a little farther out," Captain Thomas said.

"I'm tempted…" Bethany Anne was tapping a finger on her lip. "Captain, what would happen if one of your major ships in a situation like this were to suffer a hole in a compartment?"

"Well, they would, of course, seal off that area and depending on their duties, they would probably return to get it fixed if a patch is not sufficient. If I'm the captain of a ship, I don't want to chance all of my men on a repair done at sea if I don't have to. However, those above me might make me."

"So," she continued. "If we punch a small hole below the waterline, it will flood a compartment and then?"

Captain Thomas started listing off the steps. "Well, lots of figuring out what went wrong, is it going to happen again, how bad is the problem, how hard to fix," he stopped and looked at Bethany Anne. "Do I need to get Jean up here?"

Bethany Anne looked in the direction of the Chinese ships. "Yes, I think you do."

PENTAGON, USA

The President stepped past the final check. With a moue of annoyance, he took off his fitness tracker and handed it to the sergeant who said, "Sorry Mr. President, no electronics inside the room."

"It's okay, Sergeant. I just hate the idea of missing my steps. It annoys the ever-loving hell out of me to be short of my ten thousand every day. I'm like a damned energizer bunny at the end of the night trying to catch up if I'm short." The President lifted his arms as the sergeant went over him one more time with a wand to confirm nothing else.

"Good to go," he smiled at the President, who stepped into the room; the door closed behind him.

"George," he nodded to his trusted go-between. There were times when he wanted communications to happen between his advisors, but nothing electronic and he trusted George to handle it for him.

"Gentlemen," he glanced around as he sat down at the head of the table. "I can't stress enough that I hope there's a silver lining in all of this mess. I understand that their capabilities cause a lot of people to be anxious. But I've heard rumors of things I don't support. So, what are your concerns?"

"Well," Chief of Staff (COS) Mark started. "From the Air Force's perspective, I can tell you that our planes can't touch them."

"Obviously, our ships can't either since ours can't levitate above the water," John COS of the Navy admitted. "We're also talking about a new type of weapons platform that took out two missiles and obliterated the attacking ship and one smaller craft. We have guesses as to what they are, but no absolute knowledge."

RELEASE THE DOGS OF WAR

The President turned to his Army COS. "Mark?"

"Not sure what to tell you there. We have some information gleaned from… sources," he started. "And I've gone over General Reynolds' jacket as well. They unquestionably had a much larger engagement in Colorado than those who responded in any official capacity understand. Now TQB has everything cleaned up too well for anything else to be reviewed without serious action on the legal side. The initial assault by the aggressors, we believe, was a feint to set up listening devices to sniff their networks. The mercs probably wanted to get in, create a diversion with the bomb, and leave. The problem is that it was Reynolds' home base."

There were many snorts around the table. You don't attack a person on their home turf when they've had time to set up defenses. "Yeah, that worked out as well as you would think," Mark said.

"How many dead on TQB's side, does anyone know?" The President asked.

"Sir," the Air Force COS responded. "We tracked eight outbound from their Australian base during what we believe was a funeral ceremony."

"How many attackers?" the President asked.

George took that. "We believe somewhere between fifty and a hundred. Probably closer to a hundred."

"Hell of a defense," the President commented.

"They have some railgun technology that is out of this world," the Army COS replied. "I bet the opposing group easily lost twenty or thirty men before the first encounter with TQB." He shook his head. "What I would give to know more about their weaponry."

"Have you asked?" the President inquired, but the Army COS shook his head.

"Well, it worked for my guy," COS of the Navy responded. "That's how we got the info we did on their Pods before they went screaming into the future. Right towards the oil production facility that was attacked in Iraq. ISIS was dealt a hell of a blow that night."

"Surgical, neat and precise," Bob said. "Damned nice. Can I get these guys?"

"That's the problem," George said. "We *had* most of these guys and gals. A huge component of TQB's people are ex-military. Mostly ours, some from other countries now."

"Re-up them?" the President asked.

"Only if you want to empower Congress to get involved. All of the officers resigned their commissions and some were on loan to a secret organization that, well, that could handle stuff our hardasses would rather sit out," COS of the Marines stated. "I looked into it."

"So, are they pissed at us yet?" the President asked.

"Doesn't look that way to me," COS Navy responded, "You respect them, they respect you. You attack them…"

"You become Sean Truitt," George interrupted.

The President held his breath and counted to three. "Is that confirmed?" he asked.

"No," George said. "But pretty damned likely. That was a surgical strike and executed expertly. We guess one of their Pods swooped down and that maybe they used a powerful magnet. We can't tell from his car as it has too many scratches from sinking and in the lake, but it looks like they grabbed it, went to the lake and dropped him in."

"So, they're into committing murder?" the President asked, testing the feelings of the men around the table.

"They were the victims of a sudden, unprovoked military assault," George answered. "I doubt they considered it murder."

"What would our courts think?" the President asked.

George shrugged. "That there isn't enough evidence to convict. You can't place any of them at the location or identify the method of killing him."

"But it's all plausible," the President said.

"Of course, but it's also plausible that the U.S. government did it," George explained. "It's not like we don't have some pretty hush-hush technology."

"Yes, but we had no reason to do it," the President responded.

"Yes, and neither does TQB. Remember, they hid everything. We would have to admit in court everything we know."

"They are such a pain in the ass," the Chairman of the JCOS said. "We want their technology, we're happy with what they did, we are pissed that's impossible to pin what we think happened on them, and did I already say we want their technology?"

"We could try to grab it," George tossed out. There was stony silence and he looked around at the faces staring at him. "Hey! I'm just throwing stuff on the wall."

"I wouldn't suggest it," the President said dryly. "You did show me the results of their actions in Australia. Something that can make those shockwaves is not something I want aimed at American soil."

"They don't seem to be focused on civilians, sir," George said. His job, apparently, was to be the bad guy and bring up everything he had heard from everyone sitting at the table at one time or another.

"And I'm not going to provide a valid excuse to test that theory," the President shot back. "I'm going to think about how we can use them, sure. But from the NSA reports, they've already started dealing with a lot of other corporations."

"What reports?" COS of the Air Force asked. "Is this something relevant?"

The President thought about it for a second. "TQB has used the financial markets to compromise something like sixty different companies around the world on various stock exchanges. Many of these businesses had been trying to attack them initially. The NSA has agreed that TQB probably has some sort of massively parallel computing system to be able to handle this. To date, twenty-six of the companies have been bought out, and all upper management has been fired. If there were any issues with how they ran the company from a legal standpoint, then the board and previous upper management have been sued. Seven are in jail, and one has committed suicide."

"They don't fuck around," CoJCOS Robert quipped.

"No, they don't," the President said. "Furthermore, they are now in a majority position in thirty-two additional companies and are petitioning to oust their respective boards."

"Keeping them busy looking at their jobs and stock accounts so they can't cause mischief with TQB." Robert agreed.

"That's one answer, the other is they're taking positions in additional companies in their sector and using their troubles to ride the stock prices and using the profits to procure larger positions to continue the financial warfare." George said.

"That is just scary," Robert said. "Were they doing this before?"

"No. They respond brutally when attacked," the President said. "So, research reports the lady at the top has an unyielding sense of justice. She's fine until she encounters something that isn't 'right'... then, well, all bets are off."

"Well, that explains why you don't want to push them," Robert said. "But what about talking to them? And what do we know about their CEO?"

"That you don't want to believe the tabloids," George took the conversation back. "You might be thinking she's a strikingly beautiful airhead who loves to wear expensive clothes. But from everything we have now been able to pull together, we have a thirty-two percent match on who she might be."

"Who is that?" Robert asked.

George looked down the table before answering. "A dead woman by the name of Bethany Anne Reynolds."

―――――

QBS POLARUS, MID-ATLANTIC OCEAN

Jean Dukes walked onto the bridge and raised her eyebrows at the Captain and a very annoyed-looking Bethany Anne waiting for her.

"I take it I am called and get to play?" Jean asked, getting right to the point.

Captain Thomas allowed a small smile to slip across his lips for a second before answering his ever-ready and ever-destructive gunnery officer. "Yes. Although this time it's surgical." Jean's look of disgust caused him to chuckle. "I'm sure you'll get to play with bigger explosions, Jean, but this time Bethany Anne wants to annoy the Chinese and keep injury to the sailors to a minimum."

Bethany Anne's voice was deeper than normal, controlled. "If they don't get the nice message, I'll send one they can't ignore."

Jean looked at her ultimate boss one more time. She didn't just look annoyed, she looked like she was trying to control something inside. Jean nodded her understanding.

"Tell me what you want done."

"Captain Thomas and ADAM have come up with a suitable target on the command ship, and I want to punch holes in it and flood it. Hopefully, this will cause them to go home. If it doesn't, do it two more times in different compartments. The third strike will hit three more of their ships simultaneously. If they're just that stupid, I'll decide if we're leaving, or they're sinking. I'll let the two of you finish this conversation. I've got a meeting with Barnabas that he wants to have in Australia for some reason. His shit had better be relevant," Bethany Anne finished before nodding to everyone and then stepping back and disappearing.

"That never gets old," Captain Thomas commented before turning to Jean. "You got the message?" He raised an eyebrow as he waited for her response.

"I understand. I'll see if we can set up a smaller puck and fabricate it to have a point. I'll have to use something damned hard and I'll…" Jean stopped talking as she noticed him staring at her. "I'll get you a plan," she finished.

"Good," Captain Thomas said as he sat back in his chair. "Let's see your first draft in an hour, and we'll go from there."

"Yes, sir." Jean turned to go back to what had been named the Den of Destruction. The current scuttlebutt was that Bethany Anne had modified it to Den of Iniquity and Destruction, and the guys in her command were wondering just what had been said about them. Jean had merely responded with, "Nothing's been said about you guys," as far as she had heard.

CHAPTER SEVEN

MANUFACTURING FACILITY 01, ABOARD NEW SHIP

How the hell are you able to get this done so quickly?" Bobcat asked Jeo as they walked down the main corridor from the front of the ship to the back.

"A lot of time on a new ship is design, tooling and then debugging," Jeo said as they passed a workman. "We have all of the specs in TOM's ship for this design. It was taken from one of the other species out there somewhere that is more aggressive than Kurtherians and are bipedal like us. They're about half our size, so ADAM, TOM and half the damned people that came over from the Navy side have been working like it's their new goddess to get it modified for humans and address any problems if Pricolici had to change to fight in here, as well."

Bobcat looked up at the higher than normal ceilings. "I was wondering why we had the extra height," he admitted. "I figured not even John Grimes was this big."

The two turned left to a stairway and went down a level before coming up to a door with a Guardian in front. The Guardian required their security clearances by scanning the back of their hands and confirming that they had approval.

"Good to see you're making sure this shit is all secured, Jeo," Bobcat said as they went in.

After his catastrophic failure in front of Bobcat and William earlier, Jeo was happy to get the compliment. "Thank you."

They walked into a room that was twenty feet tall and a mirror image across the middle. "Do I see double here?" Bobcat asked, looking from his left to his right. He had seen all of the plans and approved anything he could, but often what was going on was beyond him. Further, he preferred to play the ignorant boss. Jeffrey had been here two weeks earlier and come back so excited that Bobcat and William had decided the fourteen-hour trip would be worth it.

"No, you see eight command and control locations where we have four duplicated. Actually, any one of these stations can control any of the different ship's functions. Here in engines, we need two at a minimum. Normal watch is going to be two on engines, one on environmental and a watch lead that can run environmental, engines, or damage review. Duplicates exist here and if they need to replicate something elsewhere in the ship."

"Is that our design or the original?" Bobcat asked.

They walked up to one of the control screens that looked like a twenty-inch monitor in portrait mode at an angle in front of an acceleration seat. "The duplication was an original design, we modified it for how humans operate."

Bobcat sat down and looked down, he secured his legs into the holders. "These remind me of cyclist grips," he said.

The screen came up with an outline of a hand and the words 'Sign In.'

"Kind of the same concept, actually," Jeo said. "Everyone on duty has specific shoes specially fitted for them. They lock in and can use the pedals to operate certain controls if they want. The different layouts can be set up specific to the user. The logins are all kept in the shoes. So if I sit down and lock in, it will have my preferences, and when I step out, and you step in, yours are immediately good to go."

"Why didn't you just use a handprint?" Bobcat asked, pointing at his screen.

"We do have a manual override, but honestly, there's something about getting hooked in this way that rocks. I have to say, it's cool as shit." Jeo sat down next to Bobcat and clicked his shoes into the system.

The screen came up with Samantha in the upper left hand corner. "Hello, Jeo," she said.

"Hello, Sam. Are there any pressing issues at this time?"

"None, Jeo."

"Very good, how are we progressing on the ship?" Jeo asked.

"We are twelve hours and thirty-two minutes ahead of schedule. The next containers of ore have been distributed, and we had to skip India and move to Peru. Our last distribution to India has caused some government review," she told him.

Bobcat watched as Jeo leaned towards the screen and he noticed little movements by his feet as he touched the screen, quickly compiling windows from different screens into one overview. "Oh, that stupid-ass Kina dropped half his load in three days. Mark that company and any subsidiaries as undependable," Jeo said.

"Understood. That means we are now beneath our minimum one hundred companies to work with in India." Samantha responded.

"That's fine. Touch base with Frank and Barb and see if they can do the voodoo with ADAM to vet some more." Jeo told her.

"I am sending that request now," she said.

Jeo turned to look at Bobcat, who was watching the two of them work. "So, any thoughts on the weaponry?" Jeo asked.

"Yes, we have the railgun technology, which we've supersized as you know. The tests we've run against asteroids with and without protection both went well enough. Without protection, it was like shooting limestone with a nail gun except for the densest materials. William is working to deal with that right now. On the asteroids with the gravitic shield, it can be a bitch at times. We have a team playing defense trying to save the asteroids and they're getting smarter and smarter."

"That's good, right?" Jeo asked, "I mean, if I'm inside the ship, I want someone really good tweaking the shields to protect me."

"Yes, but that means that shooting the other guys can be difficult as well. So, we're creating new projectiles, including organic and organic with chemical payloads."

"Why, are you trying to eat into their ship?" Jeo asked. "Because that's going to take forever."

"Normally, yes." Bobcat said. "But we noticed when some dipshit sent out some trash because," Bobcat put up his fingers in air quotes. "'Try anything,' that something inside it sizzled the shield a little. Now, the theory is if we can hide the metal, that it might weaken the shield enough to allow the penetrators a little more kinetic energy as they slam home."

"Death by a thousand cuts?" Jeo asked and then rolled his

eyes as he saw Bobcat's eyes light up and a huge smile play on his face.

"Well," Bobcat smiled at him. "Funny you should ask that." He reached to put his hand on the screen in front of him. "Let me show you something."

———

TQB BASE, AUSTRALIA

"This had better be damned important, Barnabas," Bethany Anne said as they walked together over the Australian landscape in the dark.

"Yes it is, Bethany Anne," he agreed. "I think it might fulfill a couple of needs. One in me that Stephen so helpfully pointed out, and one for you," he finished.

"What, do I get to kill everyone?" She looked over at him, a patently false look of glee on her face.

Barnabas looked at her face and shook his head. "Nice try, but Stephen pointed something out to me. I am thinking your effort to 'kill everyone' is more of a ploy than a real desire."

"I'm going to neuter that son of a bitch," Bethany Anne groused. "That was the only fun I was having dealing with you."

"He meant well, will that help?" Barnabas asked, watching her face for any tell that she wasn't telling him the truth. He had tried previously to insinuate himself into her thoughts, and she not only slapped him mentally, but she also hit him physically and told him 'never to try that shit again!'

The physical slap had shocked him more than the mental one because no one had ever casually offered him bodily harm in the past.

He had finally realized it was rude. Once that realization was made and he decided that an apology was appropriate, one was offered and he had never tried to read her again.

Bethany Anne answered his question, "Well, it depends on why I'm out in the middle of the Australian Outback with a male vampire who is holding a cooler of blood in his hands. Is that supposed to be for me?" she asked him.

"No," Barnabas said and stepped a few feet away to put the cooler on a boulder. "I'm told that I'm going to need it," he said.

"Oh?" Bethany Anne asked, realizing that this was going to be some sort of challenge, and her anger screamed to be let loose, to be allowed to be truly free.

And the main pain in the ass in her life right then was going to allow himself to be her target. "Sure hope you have enough blood in there, because I can't say I'm too willing to let you drink from me," she said.

Barnabas smiled. "Well, I can understand that attitude." He turned to lean against the rock with the cooler next to him. "I have a story I need to share, and then if you are willing, I have a favor to ask."

Bethany Anne considered his request, his casual stance and how she trusted Stephen. Nodding, she indicated for him to continue.

This ought to be interesting, she thought.

———

MEETING ROOM, WASHINGTON D.C. USA

The President nodded to his Secret Service detail as he stepped in, knowing that they had already confirmed the room's security. "George," he said as he sat down. The door clicked shut behind him.

"Mr. President," General George Thourbourah replied.

"So, give me the scoop. What do we know and what are our options?"

"Well, sir, this time, we've stepped in it." Gen Thourbourah said, making an unhappy face as he started to talk. "It seems that while we suspect that Bethany Anne is a United States citizen, she has a legitimate birth certificate, papers, and various details from Romania. Furthermore, the little background info we have can be verified, but anything deeper and people start clamming up. Something is fishy, and it will take our people longer to confirm the validity of our suspicions."

"Well, if we're right, what does it buy us?" the President asked.

"It would explain why Lance Reynolds is working with TQB. If his dead daughter came back to life," the President snorted. "Ok, maybe resurfaced as this Bethany Anne, then we have something. But she is considerably changed, so she went through a lot of rework. Whatever was done, we can't duplicate it, and she's certainly not the same physical woman."

"I think I could tell that from the side by side pictures," the President said.

"Okay, that's fair," George continued. "And I know the genetics don't match, but the facial is at least a sixty-one percent match and her ability to get Lance Reynolds to quit…"

The President interrupted, "Which is your biggest hang-up I would say. You don't like how he left and jumped to TQB so quickly when no one knew who they were."

"Well, not only that, but we've been able to track down

the wife of Bethany Anne's last boss. We were only able to get a little information before she clammed up tight on us. She admitted she met Bethany Anne at her husband's grave. Now she lives close to the new Bethany Anne in Florida."

"Happenstance?" the President asked. "Coincidence?"

"I don't believe in too many of those, Mr. President," George stated. "I try to leave that out of my equations."

"I'm going to ask, George," the President said. "We're talking about the head of a thousand plus companies that have technology that could seriously hurt us. No reason to make an enemy here, not with someone gunning for them. Enemy of my enemy and all that." George nodded at him. "So, even if this is the same lady who has been miraculously healed and been put in charge of these companies for reasons that we cannot fathom, so what?"

"Well, how did she get healed? Why is she so focused on outer space? Did she get healed by alien technology, did she..."

"Hold!" The President put up a hand. "Are you about to tell me something about alien technology that I can sink my teeth into?" he asked.

George paused and thought for a moment. "Sir, assume that I look at all legitimate avenues where I need to question suspicious possibilities, and only legitimate avenues." The General looked at the President. "So, that would answer a multitude of questions, but it opens a can of worms or Pandora's box, take your pick."

"How so?"

"Assuming this question about hypothetical alien technology in use by TQB comes up, and assuming another hypothetical idea that a few governments around the world might have technology from off-world squirreled away as well. How is it that TQB knows how to use it, and these governments don't?"

The President's eyes narrowed as he thought about the question. "Yes, that is a can of worms, isn't it? You aren't supposed to make me feel worse when I talk to you, George."

"Sir, you asked me for the truth. Sometimes the truth is a bitch," George replied.

————

TQB BASE, AUSTRALIA

Barnabas sighed. "The story goes back a long time ago, centuries in fact. At one time I loved a woman dearly, and she persuaded me to change her to a vampire over my objections. I thought I would have to slay her if she failed. Fortunately, she survived." He paused, thinking back to his love. "Her name was Catherine. She had blue eyes and the blackest hair you've ever seen. I liked to say she was five foot nothing tall when I describe her now, but she was probably a little less. I found her fighting off two men who had happened upon her campfire way off the road. I could hear the little vixen fighting them a league away and more."

He looked at Bethany Anne. "I reached them when one tried to attack her from her right while another came around the fire from her other side and she dashed towards the fire and jumped it, coming straight at me. I slipped behind a tree to watch her pass, close enough to reach out and touch her. She smelled…" Barnabas lost focus for a moment as he inhaled in the night, reliving the memory. "Exquisite."

He focused back on Bethany Anne. "I mean to say she smelled fresh, alive! Not horrid and depressed. Even then, I could easily tell a person's mental state. The two men came after her, with lust in their minds and planning her death soon after."

His face became angry, his eyes drawing down, his mouth tightening. "They followed her and would pass right next to me. I stepped out and grabbed the first with my right hand, stepping towards the second one and grabbing him with my left. I pulped the man in my right hand with nails that had grown into daggers, and I pulled the second towards me to suck his life from his neck. He screamed for a few moments as loud as he could, piercing the night. Her horse was tied up, and I could hear it desperately trying to get away, pulling on the rope. It settled down as I finished the second man and silence spread through the forest night again."

Barnabas relaxed. "I pulled their two bodies towards the campsite and found a place off to the left to throw them, away from the horse. I gathered her things together and was packing her horse when I could sense her watching me through the trees. I called over my shoulder to tell her I would lead the horse about fifty yards away and stake it so that she could retrieve her belongings. It would be available in a few moments for her to pick up and continue on her way."

Barnabas turned to capture Bethany Anne's eyes in his own gaze. "She came to me out of the forest, walking brazenly, and told me 'that wouldn't be necessary.' If she would trust me not to be hiding in the bushes once I finished with her horse, well she could damn well trust me right then."

Barnabas paused for a few moments, lost in thought.

"What happened then?" Bethany Anne asked, caught up in his story.

"She became my world." Barnabas said. "She walked right up to me, pulled my face to the left and then to the right as she looked at me in the firelight and straight up asked me what kind of man I was. I was shocked that she would see all of the blood and not flinch." He shrugged. "I wasn't too gentle with the second man's neck. I might have had bad table manners."

Despite herself and the solemnity of the story, Bethany Anne snorted and then covered her mouth. "Sorry."

Barnabas grinned. "I was going for something besides doom and gloom, so I'm glad I was able to accomplish my task." He shifted his stance, crossing his arms, getting more comfortable leaning against the rock. "I told her I was the death in the night, and she might do well to saddle up and leave. She looked over to where I had tossed her attackers and told me, 'Not my death, but death to those who attack me,' then turned back to me and pulled my head down to kiss me. She was like that, very impulsive. Today, they would say that she wasn't all there mentally. For me, that was the first time someone had accepted me so completely since I had been turned. We were together for six seasons, a year and a half, when she came down with a sickness. She begged me to change her so that we might stay together and I did."

Barnabas's voice was quiet now, reliving the life that he had tried so unsuccessfully to hide. "I knew that her chance of a successful turning was low, but I did it anyway. She made it past Nosferatu, but only just past plus a little more. She didn't have much strength, and her mental disabilities became more pronounced after the change. She was like a young child at times, trusting anything I said without question. Three months later, I was out foraging for sustenance when she left our cave and was caught and killed. I found her right before the sun would break through the mountains and took her body home with me. I remember bringing her to the safety of the cave and finding there was nothing to do for her but give her to the sun. Nothing else do I remember for six months and six days until I awoke on a riverbank. I was tangled in a large tree limb that had gone down the river, the sun about to hit me. My skin felt on fire."

Barnabas paused, then turned to Bethany Anne. "I found out some time later I had taken over three thousand souls and obliterated fifty-two families during my Time of Disgrace. The sun saved more people, I'm sure. I chose to change to a life of seeking knowledge, and moved closer to Asia." He stood up, and clapped his hands together, knocking off any dust. "So, that is my history. Death and destruction is what I did, so it is what I expected you to do." He stepped away from the rock towards Bethany Anne. "I know that it could be your love was not as deep…" he started to say before he blacked out.

Barnabas awoke, his head droning for a moment or two before the buzzing slowed down and he could focus. Barnabas could see the stars above him. He painfully turned his head to see Bethany Anne standing near him, looking down at him in disgust.

He got up slowly, and then took off his monk's robe leaving him with a pair of pants and a wide sash where a belt might be on a typical guy. "I'm sorry, I'm not sure what happened," he said, a little groggy. "I was standing here, telling you my story and my worry that you were going to go into a rage. Then," he looked up at Bethany Anne standing four feet away. "I thought perhaps the reason that you didn't have the rage was that you did not love Mich…"

Twenty-two minutes later, Barnabas's eyes cracked open. His mouth was dry, his head on fire. He reached up and could feel an indentation slowly healing itself in his forehead.

"Here, you need this," a female voice said. Barnabas

turned to look towards the sound while the stars above him swam in an ocean of darkness. A pouch landed on his stomach and bounced off. He weakly grabbed for it and then more quickly searched for it when he smelled the blood.

He devoured the nourishment and laid his head back on the sand, waiting for the energy to flow and the healing to follow as he put his memories back together. "Bethany Anne?" he croaked.

"Yes?"

"Did you hit me?" Barnabas asked, trying to piece together what was happening to him.

"Yes," she answered.

"How?" he asked, slowly turning his head to regard the woman sitting on the rock next to the now open cooler of blood.

"Hard," she said. "You probably need another," then tossed Barnabas another pouch. This one he caught and then struggled to sit up before slicing it open and drinking the contents.

"I understand that," Barnabas said, touching his forehead, "But how?"

"Fast," she replied. "Do you need a third pouch? You don't seem to be able to think clearly."

Barnabas started to open his mouth before closing it again. "Why?"

"You dared to question my love for Michael. You do it again Barnabas, and you will need to reattach your head." Barnabas turned to regard the woman who now had red glowing eyes and fangs. "NO ONE questions my love for Michael!" she hissed at him. "And lives."

Barnabas nodded and held out a hand. "Please?"

Bethany Anne tossed a third blood pouch to him. "Why

did you bring five?" she asked, working to get her anger under control.

Barnabas grunted, "I wasn't planning on five, I had packed two and Stephen came up and dumped three more and told me 'don't be a jackass and you won't need them all.'"

"That should have been enough for you." Bethany Anne stated.

"I'm more of an experiential learner," Barnabas said. "Or I ask lots of questions."

"What have you learned?" Bethany Anne asked.

"Not to question your attachment to Michael," he said, then added, "And be careful of your right punch."

"Both. I hit you with my left the first time," she told him.

"Then, be careful of your left and be very, very careful of your right," Barnabas said.

"Other than telling your story, what was your reason for coming out here, Barnabas?" Bethany Anne asked, her anger finally pushed back into a mental box.

"Well, I was concerned if I leave my chosen path of neutrality that you would not be strong enough to cage and kill me should I fall into another Time of Disgrace. I needed to know that someone could stop me from committing another such atrocity to humanity," he said. "I think I have the answer." He looked up at her small smile and touched his forehead. "Experience."

"And what would I do with you, Barnabas?" she asked him as she moved over a foot and sat on a rock.

"Well, I can stay a judge, but I've finally realized the suggested punishments are all just. So, you are just guiding me to figure this out. I've never felt so disgusted having to learn about useless excuses for people in all of my very long life."

"Not everyone is an okay person, Barnabas. There are

Mother Theresas, and then there are Hitlers," she told him.

"How do you judge?" Barnabas asked as he worked himself to his feet and grabbed the empty pouches to drop into the cooler, "Maybe a fourth?" he said with a grin on his face. "No need to suffer the last little bit. I've had my ego handed to me, perhaps you knocked some sense into my brain."

Bethany Anne snorted but waved him to the cooler. "Drink up, and one can only hope." She stood up and walked a few steps away and looked up to the stars. "What can you do for me, Barnabas?" she asked, staring at the stars. "If you aren't being a patented pain in the ass, what can you do?" She turned back to him.

"My lady," Barnabas said. "I wasn't jesting with Catherine that first night. I might not be at your level, but give me a few weeks or maybe a month, but I promise you, I will be your death, your executioner."

Bethany Anne was quiet for a few minutes. "Barnabas, I don't need an executioner. If I have need of that, there are plenty who are ready and willing to deal out death for me. No, I have need of another role. What I have need of is a Ranger. One who is authorized to act on my behalf to dispense justice knowing how I think, how I feel with a core inside him that I trust to do what is right. Although you're a pain in the ass, I trust you to be just." Bethany Anne waited to see how it felt, this gut decision.

It felt right.

"This Ranger, it is one who does what, goes out on reconnaissance?" Barnabas asked, confused.

Bethany Anne shook her head. "No, you're thinking a military ranger. I'm talking about something like what in the U.S. is called a Texas Ranger. More of a law officer who will go and investigate and in the old times, they would dispense justice if necessary. My Rangers will be exactly that. Investigator and judge. Right now we're working on just one world. In the future, I think it will be required for multiple worlds. So, you are the first, and you will be the highest ranking. It will be your responsibility to build a core team as we find more. We'll send them out as we deem necessary."

Barnabas was letting his shock work itself out of his system. He was going to have to apologize to Stephen.

"Shall I give you my allegiance here or back in front of the others?" Barnabas asked as he finished the fourth pouch and dropped it inside the cooler. There was no way he was going to drink five of those. He had little room for anything at the moment.

Bethany Anne considered his question, thinking through the different permutations. "Back at the ship. I want to work on the wording first, but I will accept your personal word right now so we can get started. I have to check on how Tabitha is doing soon."

"You have it. What shall we do now, then?" Barnabas asked as he looked to see how many hours they had left of dark.

"Well, you're out of shape, no time like the present to start working out. Besides, you have another pouch left for later when you need it." She grinned wickedly at him as her eyes started turning red and her teeth grew.

Barnabas smiled. She was right, no time like the present to get back into shape.

Even if the form he was going to be in was probably a pretzel. There was always next time.

Fifteen minutes later, as he rolled off of his back to stand up again, he decided he might give himself two months to get back into shape. Because if he had to get his ass kicked every day, he might just beg to become chum for the sharks.

At least the pain would be over quicker.

RELEASE THE DOGS OF WAR

—

TOM'S SPACESHIP

You're going to make her a vampire?

I prefer the term Kurtherian Enhanced Superhuman

So, a vampire?

For a Kurtherian, you can be a real dick.

It's the company I keep.

Did you just get a zinger in on me? You titty fucking inbred barnacle fucker... Huh, actually, that was a pretty good zinger all things considered. TOM, make it so she can pull from the Etheric and if she wants to use the enhanced powers, she can make the decision to drink herself. God help me, I hope we don't create a monster.

How?

She's going to be able to kick the ass of the names she uncovers on her computer searches all by herself. Gott Verdammt... oh... wait a second, Barnabas is just going to love the fuck out of me.

Why? How is it I'm right here, in your own body and I can't follow you?

Because you aren't thinking about the new Rangers. We're creating the second Ranger in existence. Oh my God.

Bethany Anne leaned over the glass to see Tabitha, eyes closed as she slept in a Pod induced coma.

"South America, you just became my Bitch." Bethany Anne stood back up and started walking out of the Medical room.

TOM, tie her into me like crazy, but load her up. Those inbred fuckwad bastards in South America want to take over from Michael? Well, I'll send them my response and before Tabitha finishes they'll be begging me to call her off.

Or they will be dead. Bethany Anne grabbed Ashur and they disappeared.

CHAPTER EIGHT

WUHAN, CHINA

Stephanie Lee walked down the hallway in a proper businesswoman's suit. Her neckline was high. She wore pants, and her shoes had very low heels. She preferred the opportunity to dress less conservatively in Europe, but she needed to have a talk with the head of her clan. The one who stayed in the mountains and held to the old beliefs. The one who had told her that to leave was to forsake the path and she still had walked out on him.

Her father.

When she left eight years ago, she had told him in no uncertain terms her return would be as the head of a powerful organization without his help whatsoever.

Unfortunately, she had been wrong.

So far, two of the twenty-six leaders in her cabal had died under very mysterious circumstances, and their deaths brought back memories learned before she was steeped in the traditions of today. When mysticism was real to her.

From her childhood.

She had made a request through the proper channels, and had been told to arrive at two hours past noon on the last Wednesday of the month. In other words, arrive in three days at 2:00 PM. Biting down her annoyance at the old ways, she had replied politely.

Now, she was stepping out into the final place before she would be taken up into the mountains via helicopter. She hoped that this meeting went well.

She hoped that her father would accept her back, with as little disgrace to her as possible. Because if he didn't, she felt sure her neck was on the line. She had ignored Anna Elisabeth Hauser's advice about not attacking, and so far, it had not gone well at all. It felt like the calm before the storm, and that was with two mysterious deaths and military results that were… bad.

———

QBS POLARUS, MID-ATLANTIC

Cheryl Lynn was on the video wall as Gabrielle held up a dress to show her. "How about this one?" she asked.

"Do you want to say 'jump me?'" Cheryl Lynn asked, and Gabrielle pulled the dress away from her to look at it.

"How does this dress say 'jump me?' It's just a beautiful red," she protested.

"What color lipstick are you going to wear?" Cheryl Lynn said.

"Well, a red of course." Gabrielle looked back at the video screen. "You think maybe I should do black?"

"No, but I bet you ten dollars you pick a fuck-me red lip-stick," Cheryl Lynn said.

"Which color is that?" Gabrielle asked. "I don't remember that color in the choices."

"It's the color that says, 'your hose is going to be hot, and I've got the water to quench it,'" Cheryl Lynn said. She looked down at a box below her own screen. "It's the red on the far right second row in our case."

Gabrielle turned to look at the makeup boxes all of the women had procured and realized that she had taken that red out as a possibility to wear.

"Okay," she said as she walked back into her closet, talking a little louder. "How about a little black dress?"

Cheryl Lynn's laughter rang through her room as Gabrielle walked back into the video camera's view. "Stop laughing and start helping. I haven't been asked out in a while."

"Yes, you have!" Cheryl Lynn retorted.

"Okay, not by anyone intelligent." Gabrielle argued. "Like, rocket-scientist smart," she finished.

"You can break men over your leg, and you're worried he's too smart for you?" Cheryl Lynn came back, realization finally dawning.

Gabrielle put down the dress. "I'm five hundred, not dead. I've dated all types of men, but most guys of Marcus' character don't ask me out!"

"That's presumably because they're never around friends like Bobcat and William, who probably put him up to it." Cheryl Lynn retorted.

"I don't care. You should have heard his heartbeat, it was crazy. He was so embarrassed." Gabrielle said, looking into the mirror. "You're right, black is better. I'm going to wear my pumps with the red hearts on them, though." She turned to look from the side, "When I told him 'yes,' he got a dreamy look in his eyes like I had just made his life."

"Well, don't break him. Bethany Anne might have something to say about that," Cheryl Lynn snickered.

"It's a friendly date, you bitch. I'm not looking to break, or fix, anything on him." Gabrielle retorted.

"Well, I've had an earful from Jean wanting to know when she can hit up John, so maybe my mind is working itself into the gutter."

"Girl, Jean's mind would have to work a month to get up into the gutter from the sewers she swims in," Gabrielle said.

Cheryl Lynn thought about that. "Okay, you're probably right. I have to keep Tina and Todd out of range if I take a call from Jean. She comes on the video immediately talking like that and leaves the conversation talking like that. I swear she's half the reason the Navy has such a bad reputation."

Gabrielle spoke while laying the dress on her bed and looking through the makeup. She put the 'F-M-R' tube back in the box. "I doubt it. I'm pretty sure the Navy had the rap from before women were allowed on the ships."

"Well, it's funny is what it is. She almost makes me want to go take a swing," Cheryl Lynn added a little wistfully.

Gabrielle heard that note and carefully didn't change her tone of voice. She did throw out an, "Oh? Who would you line up for?" as she looked at the mirror and dabbed a little of each lipstick on before wiping it off.

"Probably either Scott or Peter," Cheryl Lynn said.

"Hey, which of these two lipsticks look better with black?" Gabrielle asked, getting Cheryl Lynn to change the subject and hopefully forget that she revealed anything to Gabrielle at all.

Because there was no way Gabrielle would be overlooking

that tidbit of information. One was an indulgence for a mother of two, the other a catch who had a need to protect others. Now, they had two guys with dates and two to go. Then they would start on the second group.

This was more fun than slicing up Nosferatu.

———

NEAR SHENNONGJIA PEAK, HUBEI

Stephanie Lee stepped off of the helicopter and ducked under the rotors as she walked from the platform and into the cement building. She could hear the engines ramp back up and shortly the helicopter left the landing pad to return to civilization.

Now she was stuck out here in the damned mountain wilderness she had tried to leave eight years ago. She resented the requirement to come here, but she was certain her father could give her information she needed. She might be prideful, but she wasn't stupid.

When she walked into the main room, she noticed a wrapped box with a flower on the top. The same flower her father gave her every Saturday.

She walked over and picked up the flower to smell it. It reminded her of peaceful times. Times in the mountains when the biggest concern she had was whether or not she needed to help get dinner ready, or if she was responsible for cleaning up.

She set the flower to the side. No one was here to greet her. She knew the way up the path, and this location was simply a way for those down on the coast to visit and ask, or petition, for favors.

MICHAEL ANDERLE

There were all sorts of clans in China. Many had worked their way into political power. But the clans that were powerful among those outside of the cities wielded much authority and a lot of power. Those that didn't respect the clan of the animal spirits feared them. For her father, the same was true.

She opened the box to find a beautiful dress and a pair of sandals appropriate for entering the sacred building up the path.

She sighed, there was no getting around it. So, she started taking off her business suit.

When you go to the mountain to visit the clan leader, you wear what the clan leader gifts you to wear.

As she stepped out of her pants, she reminded herself she was prideful, not stupid.

———

CAMP DAVID, USA

General George Thourbourah was allowed inside the retreat after he and his car were searched. He parked and walked up the peaceful trail until he arrived at his quarters. He nodded to the men protecting the President and went to the meeting room to get ready for his update presentation.

He was taking a long weekend, and they needed to meet. Since every meeting in the Oval Office was documented, and they had no desire to connect the two of them if it wasn't necessary, every attempt to avoid meeting in the White House was made.

Ten minutes later, the President entered wearing shorts and a polo shirt. "Hello George." He held out his hand.

"Mr. President," George replied, "You're looking rested."

"It's all of this clean air that isn't cluttered up with bullshit and ass kissing," the President said. "I swear we could get more done if half of Congress wasn't incompetent and the other half bought."

"Well, certainly on one side of the aisle," George said.

"Hmmph. I'm pretty sure that's both sides of the aisle, George." the President responded. "Maybe there are fewer idiots on our side, but that just makes the whole thing that much sadder. These guys are smart enough, and they're using it for personal political ambition."

"Make you wonder how you got in?" George said as he pulled up his PowerPoint presentation to review with the President. There wasn't much on it, just a few code phrases that reminded George what he wanted to speak about and in what order. He could have used notecards, but that just made him seem antiquated. So, one almost useless laptop later and he seemed up to speed on technology.

Hurrah for him!

"No, I got in because those who knew better thought they could manipulate me." He shrugged. "I wasn't too stupid to recognize that. I was just smart enough to make sure my eagerness hid any rejections of their requests until I got the job. Then they found out they could kiss my ass," the President said.

"Well, are you ready for the latest update?" George asked him.

"Sure, I popped two antacids before I came in here. I'm trying a new brand out," he joked.

George looked up at him. "Seriously?"

"Well, yes," the President said. "You give me a stomachache every time you leave. I might as well take the medicine early."

George turned back to his laptop. "Okay, Presidential Stomachache 022 is ready to go."

"Amusing," the President said.

"Well, if you've ever heard the axiom two problems are a problem, but three sometimes cancel out?" George asked him.

"I've heard something similar," he agreed.

"Maybe I have the quote wrong, but the idea is sound. Maybe when you have at least three problems, they can be used to fix each other." George replied as his first slide, 'China,' came up. "So, we have the matter of a group of companies based in China using mercenaries to attack TQB headquarters here in America using a small dirty bomb. The idea was probably to detonate inside the base and no one, except TQB of course, would presumably be harmed. Unfortunately for them, someone on the TQB side either caused it to detonate in the valley, or took it to the valley to detonate."

"Did they get away?" the President asked.

"Couldn't tell you. But the significant other of their CEO is no longer seen with her. We think he bought it in the blast."

"Who was he?"

"Again, hard to tell. We know his name is Michael and that he lived in South America. But we're getting a lot of runaround, and our computers seem to have a lot of junk data on him. So, he might remain anonymous." George said. "It's possible one of the caskets we tracked leaving their ceremony was him and a few others who died in the altercation."

"Why are they hiding the hits?" the President asked.

"Probably because they're a secretive bunch. They aren't using the opportunity to get a sympathy play with the public, so my best guess is it doesn't fit in with their strategy, or it isn't in the company's DNA to do so. Personally, I'm not happy not knowing."

"That's because your role is to know," the President replied.

"True, but when I unwrap TQB, all I get are more questions, not more answers."

"I'm on vacation, George."

"I was invited!" George replied, smiling. "Besides, we aren't even to the second slide. So, on the first slide, we have a group of Chinese conglomerates going after the technology in cahoots with American conglomerates. We've tracked down a couple of contacts, and they have fuzzy lines over to Europe."

"So, we have multinational companies who employ millions and millions of people all over the world implementing military operations in their zeal to steal TQB's technology. TQB bit back and slapped the conglomerates and has been fighting them on the stock market, and taking them out. Further, we have some very suspicious deaths, which you believe are probably TQB's response to the military action. Now I need to figure out how to respond to the Chinese allowing some of their industrial cronies to use weapons they shouldn't. Not only how to respond, but what assets we need to use, correct?"

"Well, ordinarily yes." George said. "I've spoken with the Chief of JCOS, and he's polled everyone. Some of them have dug up people who know people who either know TQB people or who've heard stories about some of those people. It's scary stuff, and I don't mind scary movies." George said.

"Are you going to lay it on the line this time, or are you going to hint at the answer, George?" the President asked him.

"Sir, one of TQB's men is Frank Kurns. I have confirmed an eyewitness to seeing him a few years ago." George hit the button on his laptop to bring up the next slide. "Here's a picture outside an ATM at that time and my contact confirmed this is Frank Kurns." The man pictured was older, healthy perhaps, but certainly elderly. "This is a picture of Frank Kurns today." The next slide was a thirty-something man.

The President leaned close and asked for the two pictures to be brought up side by side. George hit the next slide in the deck that showed them both. "NSA says seventy-eight percent likely the same man. We went back into our military archives. Check this out." George hit the next slide, and now three pictures were side by side. This time, the middle was a nice color shot, the far right a black and white.

"Son of a bitch," the President said. "How the hell?" He looked up at George. "The same man?"

"Yes, sir." George agreed. "Not only the same man but I did a little more digging. I'm pretty sure he's worked in a super secret group for the government since World War II. He's over a hundred years old I believe. There's some question of whether he lied or not to get into the service early, but that's him. I don't think we need to quibble a few years plus or minus when we're talking ten decades."

"What did we have him doing?" the President asked.

"Well, that's where it gets interesting," George said and hit the button to go to the next slide.

CHAPTER NINE

OUTSIDE PARIS, FRANCE

"I've always wanted to enjoy Paris," Marcus said as he and Gabrielle walked along a quiet road ten miles outside of Paris. "But I hadn't expected to have to walk the last ten miles," he said. "Some date I am."

Gabrielle laughed and slid an arm under Marcus.' "Hey, we're here to have a good time. I should remember that the French always have at least two strikes going on at any one time. I think there's a national law that says one of those that are striking have to be the taxi drivers."

Marcus was surprised that Gabrielle allowed the intimacy of slipping an arm in his. He didn't pretend to believe this would go anywhere, but he sure as hell would enjoy it. His time with Bobcat and William, and TOM as well, had made him a much more easygoing person. It had made his whole decade when Bethany Anne had supported the rumors in the media that he was the Marcus that had told NASA to kiss his ass. She had purposefully pulled Marcus into a meeting he wasn't expecting, so he was caught in a ton of photographs standing next to the world's most famous CEO.

He even had an old ex-wife try to call him. Just in case boredom set in, her message got saved on his voicemail group for later replay.

"Gabrielle, do you think Bethany Anne would allow us a little fun?" Marcus asked, thinking aloud.

"Like what?" Gabrielle asked.

"Like landing a Pod where we can be seen?" Marcus asked, a little concerned he was pushing the envelope.

"Hell if I know, let's ask her," Gabrielle said. "If you get a scratch on you, I'm going to get my ass kicked the next time we spar, so I'm not going to cheat on this one." She pulled up her purse and retrieved her phone. While it looked ordinary, the insides were not. It took half a second for the security to confirm it was Gabrielle, and she hit the shortcode to speak to ADAM. "Hey ADAM, I need to know if I can interrupt BA. Mmmhmm. Okay, I'll wait." She leaned over to whisper to Marcus, "She's kicking Barnabas's ass at the moment, so we… Oh! Hi BA, Marcus the man and I are stuck outside of Paris walking the streets. The taxis are on strike again. What? Hell, ever since they had horses I imagine. If there isn't a strike going on somewhere in this country, we've switched dimensions. Either way, Marcus would like to drop a Pod with us in it right into town… Mmmhmm, oh, I guess that was rude. Hold on." Gabrielle handed the phone to Marcus. "Sorry, she wants to talk with you."

Marcus accepted the phone from Gabrielle. "Hello? Yes, hello, Bethany Anne. Right, bad research on my part. True, not exactly a way to impress a lady, but until this evening, I've only had Bobcat and William around for guidance and might

I point out they are dreadful instructors." Marcus pulled the phone away from his ear for a second and whispered to Gabrielle, "She's laughing!" He missed Gabrielle's smirk when he put the phone back up to his ear. "Yes, well, I suppose that's true. Okay, I'll ask."

He turned to Gabrielle. "Is Paris a requirement, or would you consider visiting another city?"

"Did you have one in mind?" she asked him.

"Actually, I was thinking Los Angeles. I know a few places there to take a proper lady."

"A proper lady, huh?" She looked at him. "Why not? I haven't been to Los Angeles anytime recently."

"Well then, my knowledgeable date, why don't we whisk off to LA and leave these strike-happy people to their own devices?"

"I'm a little overdressed for whatever time it is there, aren't I?" Gabrielle asked, looking at her evening dress.

"My lady, you are going to Shangri-La, where traditional left the city eighty years ago and never came back," Marcus quipped.

"Well, then. Yes, I think we shall," Gabrielle agreed.

Three minutes later, the phone was back in Gabrielle's purse, and the two of them were on a twenty-two minute Pod trip to Los Angeles, California for a lunch date.

———

LONDON, ENGLAND

Beatrice Silvers walked up to George, the doorman of her building, and nodded at him. Her building was a quaint four story where she rented two of the four penthouse apartments.

She had the north side with windows on the east and west. It allowed her to switch bedrooms since they were mirrored layouts, initially. She had a ten year lease and expected to be able to buy out the owner by the time her ten years were up.

Or she would find something on him and ruin him. Either way, she wouldn't be moving.

She walked to the inside lift, pressed the button and stepped into the marble-lined elevator to go up the four flights. While Beatrice would often take the stairs for health reasons, she'd had plenty of walking in the last few days as she had gone from one member to another to get them back on track.

That stupid bitch Anna Elisabeth Hauser had spooked half the committee. As soon as these children in adult clothes were finally settled down, she would see what she could do to that useless excuse for a woman in power who had run the first chance she had away from this whole situation.

Beatrice stepped out after the doors opened. She walked down the green carpeted floor and turned to her left. There were two doors side by side as the entry to her apartment. She kept the right one permanently locked and management had added a heavy-duty steel lock to that side.

A computer controlled lock secured the other door. It notified her any time someone entered her home.

She stepped into her apartment, turned, and reset the door. Setting her purse on the table just inside the doorway, she hung her scarf on the hook next to the door. She had walked fifteen feet towards the kitchen when she stopped and slowly turned in place to witness a woman sitting in a chair in the corner, staring at her.

"Excuse me," Beatrice said. "What the hell are you doing in my apartment?" Her brain put the lady and the CEO of

TQB Enterprises together. "Oh my," Beatrice said. "What are you doing here?"

"Living," Bethany Anne answered.

Beatrice took a step back and bumped into another person. She moved forward quickly, startled to find a man in a monk's robes behind her. "Who are you?" she asked, her heart pumping.

"My name is Barnabas," he replied.

Beatrice turned back to Bethany Anne, who sat quietly in her chair, just watching her. "What is it you want?" she asked.

"Well, what I want I can't have, Beatrice Silvers," Bethany Anne answered.

"What do you want from me?" Beatrice asked, stepping once more toward the door.

"Well, I would ask 'why?' But having spoken with Barnabas a second ago after he delved into your mind, he informs me it was all business. People are not people. They are chess pieces. Lives are not lives, they are numbers to you, Beatrice Silvers," Bethany Anne said, her voice cold, angry.

Beatrice took another step while they watched her, neither one moving from their locations. "What are you talking about? You aren't making any sense!"

"Beatrice, you might as well go over to the door and try it. It won't open." Bethany Anne smiled a wicked smile. "I'll wait right here while you figure that out."

Beatrice's heart raced even faster as she hurried to the door and punched her code and put her hand on the lock, then finally tried to use the override to get out. Nothing worked. She banged on the door, pleading for someone to hear the noise.

"Oh, that won't work either," Barnabas said as he wandered around her living room, picking up a piece from her shelves to look at and then setting it back down. "I've made sure no one is on this floor, and those on the floor below are sleeping, and won't remember anything for the next few hours," he finished, picking up a unicorn made of glass. "This is pretty," he commented before dropping it to the floor. When it shattered, Beatrice jumped and turned around. She was holding the doorknob behind her, still trying to turn it.

"You see, Beatrice," Bethany Anne said as she stood up. "Anna Elisabeth Hauser tried to warn you, but you failed to heed the warning." She turned to Barnabas. "I'll have to visit this woman to see if she warrants punishment, or an award, Barnabas." The man nodded. Bethany Anne turned back to Beatrice. "You were part of a group that put into place actions that killed my people as well as my love. Your group is going to be pulled apart but, not so sadly, you won't be around to see it."

"Why?" Beatrice panted, her eyes darting between Bethany Anne and Barnabas. "What is he going to do to me?"

Bethany Anne turned back to Barnabas. "See? This is why big brooding men are a pain in the ass, the assumption of who to fear is entirely wrong," she said as she stepped closer to Beatrice. Bethany Anne looked Beatrice in the eye when she was within reach. "It isn't what Barnabas is going to do, Beatrice. You are mine, and while ripping your head off appeals to me, it's so damned messy. Plus, there are problems with people finding blood and the whole cleanup thing. No, I'm going to send you on a trip."

"Where?" Beatrice asked, stealing a glance at Barnabas who was watching impassively.

"Where I send a lot of useless excuses for human beings," Bethany Anne said, allowing her eyes to turn red, finally capturing Beatrice's attention entirely. "To Hell. With a pit stop in between." She stabbed out with her arm and grabbed the woman. Beatrice barely had time to scream before Bethany Anne had pulled her away from the door and pushed her into the Etheric.

Beatrice Silvers disappeared.

"You know," Bethany Anne eyed the broken glass and said, "We're going to have to clean up that damned unicorn now, for when someone comes looking."

"Why?" Barnabas asked. "I wanted to get her attention. Now, when someone comes to the house, it will draw them into the question of what happened to Beatrice Silvers with the broken unicorn?"

Bethany Anne stepped towards Barnabas. "You're playing with minds already, Barnabas?" she asked.

"I find a particular joy in mental punishment," he admitted. "I'm curious, how long will she last in the Etheric?"

"Well, air isn't the problem, but water will be and so will the emptiness. I doubt more than a few days."

"Could she run into anyone there?" he asked, looking down at the broken unicorn. "Do you want me to pick this up?"

Bethany Anne said, "You know what? Don't. You're making the call on this. I don't know why she couldn't find someone in there, and then they have each other to die alongside. Now, let's go."

ADAM, fix the security on this apartment and the video for the building as well.

>>Yes, Bethany Anne.<<

She reached out to grab Barnabas and the two of them were gone.

———

MICHAEL ANDERLE

HOLLYWOOD, CALIFORNIA, USA

"How did you get us in here?" Marcus asked Gabrielle as they sat down at one of the tables in the Grill on the Alley. The restaurant was decorated in the classic bistro style with a black and white tiled floor, mahogany chairs and partitions.

"Mind-voodoo," Gabrielle answered as she took a sip of her water.

"Really?" Marcus asked, looking around to see if anyone was looking.

"Well, that and a hundred-dollar bill," she answered, smiling. "I always have another reason if I can give it. The money helps anchor the request to give us preferential treatment. Well, at least for me it does. Bethany Anne or the two brothers could do it just fine without something like that, I imagine."

"I see, that's fascinating," Marcus said. "I hope you find something you like here."

They picked up the menus and perused the choices. "I'll start with the crab cake and move on from there. What are you thinking?" she asked.

"I'm thinking shrimp cocktail and the filet mignon," he replied. "It's still dinner for me, regardless what time it is here." He turned towards Gabrielle. "I really am sorry. I should have paid attention to the local situation in France."

Gabrielle shook her head. "Don't worry about it. I'm happy to step away from everything for a little while. It was very sweet of you to ask me out." She took another sip from her glass. "So, was it a bet or a dare?"

Marcus blushed. "That obvious?"

She chuckled throatily. "A little. I can hear your heartbeat, you know."

Marcus stopped for a second before resuming his motion. "No, I hadn't considered that at all. But to be fair, I lost a bet with Bobcat about putting a donut on the moon. I failed to define what a donut was, and so he took one of our moon landers and videotaped it doing circles in the regolith." He made a face. "That was cheating. But I've only myself to blame. It isn't like I haven't been around them long enough to know they're lawyers when it comes to wager verbiage." He looked at her and smiled sheepishly. "But, I have to say I won the bet."

Then he winked at her.

Gabrielle could feel her cheeks flush just slightly. This rocket scientist was trying his damnedest to flirt with her. Well, give him an A for effort.

"Oh, you did, did you?" She smiled back at him. Marcus had lost a lot of years with his body changes, and his hair had grown back nicely. She was about to respond when the two were interrupted.

"Excuse me?" They looked over to see a well-dressed man in a dark blue fitted Italian suit and white shirt next to their table.

"Yes?" they answered simultaneously.

"I'm sorry, but I couldn't help but notice you. I've seen you on television. My name is David Silverstein, and I'm a producer here in LA," he said.

Marcus turned to Gabrielle, who, he had to agree with the man, was stunning in her black dress that hugged her body so well. "Please," he said to Gabrielle. "See what the man has to say."

Gabrielle was about to respond when the man interrupted, "Not to be rude, but I was going to ask you if you're Marcus Cambridge? The Marcus from the 'Kiss my Ass NASA' slogan that works for TQB?"

Gabrielle wanted to pick her jaw up off of the floor. She hadn't necessarily expected anyone to approach her here in Los Angeles for acting, but she was accustomed to being accosted because of her looks over the decades.

Now, she was being upstaged by a rocket scientist. Gott Verdammt! She grinned to herself. Teach her to assume, wouldn't it?

"Well, yes I am," Marcus agreed. "But as you can see I'm in the middle of an excellent lunch with my date here. I'd be happy to contact you some other time."

The man seemed a little shocked and took another look at Gabrielle. He smiled agreeably and pulled out a card that he handed to Marcus. As Marcus accepted it, the man patted him on the back and leaned towards him. "Good choice." Then he stepped back and made his way to his table. Marcus looked up to see Gabrielle smiling mischievously at him.

"That sir," Gabrielle said as she leaned towards him. "Just got you a good day kiss!"

CHAPTER TEN

WASHINGTON, D.C. USA

"Sir, we are going to have a problem." George started immediately when the President stepped into the room.

The President shook George's hand. "Well, good thing I've had my antacids, George." He pulled a chair and sat down. "Okay, take it from the top."

"Sir, I've uncovered evidence one of our operatives in South America freelanced his services to the Chinese contact to pull together a merc group to hijack the TQB students' bus."

"What?" the President exploded in shock, demanding, "What the hell was he doing freelancing against Americans!" The President slammed his hand down on the table, "Who the hell did this?"

"Phillip Simmons. He's been a top lead down there for over two decades," George said.

"Why would he do this?" the President asked.

"The short answer, when I leave names out and ask those in the profession, is because he is probably looking to exit on his own terms. He has money squirreled away somewhere, and this would add to his retirement," George answered.

The President didn't speak for a few moments, as he pondered this information. "So, other than the fact he's broken I don't know how many laws and our trust this means... " he asked.

"It means he's on TQB's list, I'm sure." George said. "These people are damned good. The NSA guys are starting to look for weird stock manipulations as a way to hone in on where the likely players are attacking each other."

"Following the smoke signals?" the President asked.

"Yes," George replied.

"So, you think that TQB is going to do what to Phillip?" the President asked.

"Personally? He's probably in the same column as Sean Truitt. Hell, he would be for me. Hiring mercenaries to capture kids?" George said. "If it wasn't for the cops having been called already, we might not have known about that. They got there the same time as the TQB people. Weird stuff is going on with them as well," George reminded the President.

"Yes, but not one child hurt," the President said softly. "These people are good."

"They are probably the best," George said. "I've done more research into Frank Kurns. He was a contact that was only whispered about amongst the military. If your team found something weird out in the sandpit? Well, you called Frank. He would ask you some questions. If he told you it was your problem, then cinch your nuts up into a sack and get your ass back into gear. But," George said as he tapped the table with his finger. "If Frank told you to step back? Then the choices were listen to him or lose your men. You never questioned him twice."

"What would he do then?" the President asked, curious. "I'm assuming the situation didn't just magically disappear."

"No. His team would come in, usually ferried to their location by another group of military. You didn't get in their way, and they didn't get in your way. They came in. They took care of the problem, they left. Occasionally, they would carry out one or more of their people in a body bag, and many of the people would be wearing bandages," George said.

"So, they aren't supermen." the President said.

"Maybe not, but there's the Syrian event a couple years ago."

"Remind me? Syria is a constant powder keg of so many events I forget them."

"I'm not sure how much you know, but there was a situation with a crooked Colonel Nickelson, who had taken money to sucker a special black ops group into an ambush. He lost almost two complete fireteams getting the trap set for them."

"What happened to the black ops team?" the President asked.

"We think they got out. We don't know for sure because the valley was fortuitously hit by a meteor. It obliterated the whole valley along with any evidence," George said. "For a long time we couldn't figure out how something could be pushed down right into the correct orbit to come down on that valley, now we know."

The President leaned back in his chair. "You're talking about a group that effectively has kinetic bombs of mass destruction." He thought another second. "And this Colonel Nickelson?"

"Shot in the knee coming out of a bar here in Washington. Then, a mysterious package of evidence showing how he was responsible for sending those men into Syria and withdrawing all support from them along with supporting documentation of him receiving money." George answered, "Then, he was killed in prison."

"TQB?" The President asked.

"I don't think so," George answered. "No concrete reason except my gut says if they wanted to kill him, then they wouldn't have shot his knee out."

"So, you are attributing them the kneecap?" the President asked.

"That and the evidence, yes." George agreed. "Which brings me back around to Phillip Simmons." When the President just nodded, George continued, "We have a few choices. We can bring him back to the States and arrest him, or we can leave him alone and let TQB take care of him. I'm pretty sure based on what I've uncovered, he's marked. What are your thoughts about that?"

The President's eyes focused. "If Phillip Simmons had done something we asked, even if it was something a crooked superior asked, then we would pull him back and protect him. That's true for any of our people." The President's voice went a little darker. "But mercenaries attacking American children? Well, if TQB needs to know where he is, I'm for sending them his address," the President finished.

"Okay, I'll strike that problem from the list," George said, making a mark on his tablet.

———

RELEASE THE DOGS OF WAR

NEAR SHENNONGJIA PEAK, HUBEI

The presence of the trees and the cooler mountain air brought relaxation as Stephanie Lee walked the path up the mountain. As a girl, she would go up and down this path and never think about it because she was in condition and able to handle the exercise very well. That gave her a shape that looked very good as an adult.

That conditioning had eroded over the time that she had been gone. By the time she made the top step and entered through the ceremonial temple, she was breathing hard. Approaching the brazier, she dropped a small amount of incense in the ashes, allowing the smoke to waft up. She used her hands to pull the smoke across her, cleansing senses and mind.

She wanted to snort. It would take so much more smoke than this to cleanse her, but that was for another time.

Waiting there in the room for an endless seeming time, more peace came to her. It was the calmness that was always present, but too often easy to miss unless you allowed yourself the option of experiencing it.

Stephanie Lee turned to walk further into the temple and noticed the candles that both offered light and marked time were down thirty minutes from when she walked into the incense room.

Allowing the peace of the temple to embrace her, she decided to forego the little child in her that wanted to run away after throwing a fit.

There was another flower in the middle of the floor two steps from the altar. It was a not-so-subtle declaration from her father that she needed to meditate.

She knelt down behind the flower, bending down and inhaling the fragrance. She sat back up to view the many candles on the wall in front of her. They seemed to have a larger glow around them than they had a moment before.

Slowly, she closed her eyes as a voice called from the shadows, "Dream…"

———

TOM'S SHIP

Bethany Anne watched as the Pod door slid back and Tabitha opened her eyes. She blinked a couple of times before turning to focus and moving her head towards Bethany Anne. "Hello!" she smiled. "God, I feel great!" She lifted up and put an elbow out to brace herself. "So, what did the diagnoses say?"

Bethany Anne pursed her lips. "Well, you should stay put for a second while you learn what's happened in the last three weeks."

"Three… weeks?" Tabitha asked, confused. "I thought I would be down only a couple of hours?"

"Yes, that was the plan. But two hours after we talked, we found out you had a vicious cancer and other genetic problems, so I made adjustments." Bethany Anne answered.

"So, you took care of the cancer, right?" Tabitha asked, alarmed. "And what problems do I have?"

"None anymore, Tabitha. But all of these corrections come with a price," Bethany Anne added. "So, I chose to make the decision for you, in accordance with our agreement that you are to clean up South America and your allegiance to me as your Queen."

"Well, certainly. Why would that change?" Tabitha was

feeling battered by the whipsaw of information coming at her.

"Because you are now the second Queen's Ranger, ranked only below Barnabas. As such, I've told him your area of responsibility for the short term is South America."

And you have other perks, Bethany Anne said.

Wait? What! Are we mind speaking? How fucking cool is this shit! Tabitha's face lit up with a smile.

Bethany Anne grinned. *I guess you're right, it is fucking cool. The difference is I've had TOM tweak you. You can now reach through the Etheric to contact me directly. The Queen's Rangers will be able to communicate with me through mind speech. So, don't abuse it.*

So, no asking you what I should wear to go out? Tabitha started, *or asking you what I should eat or asking you…*

Bethany Anne growled, *Maybe I was a bit too quick to make this adjustment, TOM.*

NO! Tabitha stopped, alarmed. *I was joking, I won't abuse it, Bethany Anne, I promise.*

Well, I can always adjust it, TOM interrupted.

Who is that? Tabitha asked

That's TOM.

Holy fucking slut jumping on a stick! Tabitha squealed in their communication. *Am I talking with an alien?*

"Stop!" Bethany Anne commanded with a hand up in a stop gesture. "You are going to have to get a grip on this. Whatever the hell you just did to pierce my eardrums with a mental squeal—don't ever do that again."

"Sorry," Tabitha said. "I get excited still."

Bethany Anne reached down to the new set of clothes she had brought up to the spacecraft. "I get that," she replied. "We'll get that beaten out of you."

"Wait, what?" Tabitha's eyes grew large with alarm. "Beaten?"

Bethany Anne smiled. "Well yes, you're three weeks behind in your martial arts practice and your team is anxious to help you learn." She smiled deviously, adding, "And pain is universally considered an excellent teacher."

———

"So, sir, that makes Beatrice's disappearance the fourth person in the European theater since we struck," Johann finished. "And I'm pretty sure she didn't just disappear to keep herself safe. For one, she was seen going into her apartment in London, and she never left. Furthermore, we found a broken glass unicorn on the floor when we entered. The few times I've been in her home, it was always spotless."

"I understand," the deep voice came out of the speaker. "I will touch base with additional resources in Europe to track that. What are you doing to continue the effort to harass TQB for our members?"

"Sir, the congressman in Florida did about as much as he is willing. He's a sniveling coward. So, the lawyers are trying to tie them up them in court and require TQB to confirm that their technology is not infringing on any patents from members and others we can financially support. If we force TQB into court, the legal system can require them to explain how their technology is not the same. So, we have that."

"What's happening on that front?" he asked.

"At the moment, it's a stalemate between our teams and their lead counsel and the legal teams to which he is outsourcing the individual rebuttals," Johann answered, noticing that the three security bars on the top right of his screen were solid.

"What about his support person in Washington? Weren't we going to take care of her?"

"Well, we tried." Johann said with frustration. "We sent a total of three groups of thugs against her. The first two were soundly beaten and left on the side of the road. We haven't heard from the third."

"Hmmm," Mr. Escariot drew out. "So she has physical protection and with the third strike they took them out. I wonder if that is a weakness we can use."

"How is that?" Johann asked. "Strike more quickly?"

"Yes. They might allow one hit to test their defenses and then on the second respond more forcefully. You never know what little piece of information is going help, Johann."

"Yes, sir." Johann was happy he wasn't on video as his face clearly showed his confusion. None of the individuals he spoke to ever acted as if he was anything but a lackey and go-between. Here was arguably the highest and most secretive member treating him as if he was taking him under his tutelage.

The deep voice continued, "So, I want you to take the next private plane to Las Vegas. From there, you are going to go see a man that I want you to talk to, and leave a box with him. One I'll have waiting for you to pick up in the city. The combination will be sent to you when you arrive. He will know what the box is for, so do not open it at all, understood?"

"Yes sir," Johann answered. "Do I need to update anyone else, sir?"

"No, I will let them know the changes from my side. For now, you answer to me, Johann. Contact me again when you reach Las Vegas."

The connection was canceled.

As Johann closed his laptop, he failed to notice the warning that his connection was not secure.

CHAPTER ELEVEN

S on of a bitch that hurts!" Tabitha tried to bring her practice sword up after rolling backward only to have the flat of Ryu's blade pop her on the side of her knee and cause her to fall to her left. She rolled a few times before a 'hold' was called. Tabitha was on her stomach in the exercise room of her home. Anton had it built underground, and it was sufficiently large enough to hold a practice inside.

Or a good beating.

She looked over at Hirotoshi. "How did I do?" she croaked out. "Does he have any sweat on his forehead?" When Hirotoshi shook his head, she murmured, "Dammit." She could feel her pain recede as her body healed. When Bethany Anne told her that pain was a great teacher, Tabitha didn't realize how quickly she would come to understand that lesson and then hate the knowledge.

Barnabas had informed her before she got home that they

had moved in the reporters and their two vampire guards. She spent a total of ten minutes with Giannini, Sia, and Mark and talking with the two vampires on their team, Samuel and Richard. Those two had enough personality to fill the whole house. The two reporters and their videographer had arrived the day before she had, and the rooms they chose were fine with Tabitha.

Especially since two of them were her old rooms. Bethany Anne had asked the Elite guards to move Michael's stuff out and put Tabitha's stuff in while she was in the Pod-doc. So they had packed up Michael's belongings and moved them to storage. Ecaterina and Gabrielle had then come in and set up the rooms for her.

It was obvious that both women had helped, considering how it looked. It was tasteful enough that Ecaterina had to be involved and yet practical enough for a new vampire that Gabrielle had a hand also. Tabitha now had a rack with one sword on it tagged with a signed note from Bethany Anne. The katana was a gift, but it could not be removed from the rack until Hirotoshi approved.

Which, apparently, wasn't going to happen today.

Barnabas had told her that the two of them now represented Bethany Anne's Rangers group, it would grow, but for now it was just them. Tabitha had quipped that they were Bethany Anne's versions of Judge Dredd and Barnabas had just stared at her in confusion.

Then Tabitha had to explain the whole story and by the end, Barnabas said he preferred the Texas Rangers story.

"What, the Lone Ranger?" Tabitha asked. "Weren't there five Rangers originally and they got set up in an ambush? So, he ended up with an Indian sidekick who helped him back to health, and they went around doing good deeds?"

"I understand it was something like you are telling, yes." Barnabas agreed.

"Great, Ashur is spoken for, who's going to be my Tonto?" she said.

"I don't know. I like what Bethany Anne says, and I believe we are going to implement this saying," Barnabas told her.

"What's that?" she asked.

"One problem, One Ranger," he replied, a smile on his face.

"What about all of the Elite I have with me, do I have to give them back?" Tabitha asked, successfully keeping any whine out of her voice.

Barnabas looked at the Pod-adjusted slightly taller woman. "I said one Ranger, I didn't say how many Tontos you could have." He smirked.

So, now Tabitha called her Elites her Tontos and Hirotoshi her head Tonto.

Apparently, one of them asked the vampire Richard about it and the very next morning they referred to her as the Lady Kemosabe. If she ever figured out which smartass had started that, she would beat him senseless.

Well, if she could even learn how to beat up a five year old first.

Mad hacking skills did NOT provide her any support for acquiring martial arts abilities. All of those computer games did give her quick reflexes, but they had nothing on a man who learned martial arts from when he could walk, and had hundreds of years to refine those skills.

Just so he could show Tabitha how bad she really was.

"Tell you what, Hirotoshi, if I beat Ryu hacking into the Pentagon can we call it a day?" The tiny shake from Hirotoshi confirmed Tabitha's guess. "Well, no time like the present to continue my ass kicking." She got up off the ground and pulled her practice sword into position to go through the beginning practice steps. "Just so you know, I will get good enough to kick your ass, Ryu."

"I count on it," Ryu said in his clipped English style.

Tabitha was so shocked that he spoke to her that his sword came in undeflected to painfully knock her on her ass.

"Fucking SHIT that hurts!" she yelled when she finally rolled to a stop. "You cunt munching malcontent," she continued. "You knew I'd drop my guard you cock kissing masochist!" She rolled over and started to get up, then her eyes flashed red, and she ran towards Ryu. When she was ten feet from him, he had to duck under the rattan practice blade she threw, but he realized too late Tabitha was not acting out of anger, but rather had used that emotion as a way to hide her cunning.

Her knee hit him squarely in the jaw as he started to come back up. He rolled with the kick and was on his feet as Tabitha was working to get back up off of the ground. Ryu got behind her and put his practice blade against her neck.

She stopped moving. "I yield!" she said, her hands in the air.

Ryu pulled the blade away from her neck and bent down to whisper in her ear, "That fucking hurt!"

Tabitha grinned as she pulled herself up off the ground.

CHAPTER TWELVE

QBS POLARUS, MID-ATLANTIC OCEAN

So, Mr. Brajorly has decided he would like to retire to his island which is now infested with all sorts of armed defenses," Dan Bosse explained.

He had Bethany Anne, Barnabas, John, Eric, Scott, and Darryl, plus Akio and Gabrielle in the conference room on the Polarus.

"Further, he seems to have a fair amount of illegal weapons and who knows what else," Dan continued. "My guess is he's hunkering down for a final fight. He brings in supplies once every three days from the mainland, and his little island isn't too far off a main data trunkline, so he has underwater connections to the internet backbone between Europe and the United States."

"Drop a meteor on them?" Gabrielle asked.

"Too obvious," Dan replied. "ADAM says that we're probably going to be the ones all fingers will point to if that happens. Plus, he does have other family and friends out to the island, and they aren't all targets."

Bethany Anne stood up and went to the screen. "Zoom in here." Dan manipulated the controls to zoom in on the roof of the house.

"Big sucker. So, he has an anti-air emplacement here plus men to watch most of the island. Walls around the house to keep out any sort of attack from the water. Everyone either stays by the pool or goes out the main gate to take the path to their beach and the yacht offshore." She tapped her finger on the viewer. "I'm thinking just two of us. Myself and Barnabas for the house. Then another team for the yacht. Let's drug them and pull the boat away for a few hours. We'll make those in the house believe that he left on the ship, and then drowned at sea." She turned around, "Barnabas, you change the memories, I'll take out the security staff. We go back up to the roof and leave."

"What about electronic surveillance?" John asked.

"They're already on the internet," Dan answered. "ADAM is inside their firewalls and has been causing their system to have problems for three days now. When it all goes down, so will the security."

"Not fond of you going without one of us," John told Bethany Anne.

"I understand, but in this case, we know who's there and where they are on the island. We've used their own surveillance to spy on them." She shrugged. "You guys have the yacht, and Gabrielle is a backup for the two of us. This prick is on the board of the group that hit us. I want him to know who kisses him goodnight before he dies."

John nodded.

"Let's go have some fun, shall we?" Bethany Anne asked.

Everyone closed their books or shut down their tablets and got ready.

Another enemy was going to bite the dust tonight.

SMALL ISLAND OFF THE EAST COAST OF THE UNITED STATES

Bethany Anne and Barnabas took a normal two-seater Pod with Gabrielle in a Black Eagle to fly as their wingman. The Guards were in their usual Bitches getup and had their own Pods to take over the yacht.

When they were about five hundred feet above the roof, Bethany Anne used the video cameras to check out the security along the rooftop. "I see emplacements and, son of a bitch, an actual missile launcher. That's some pretty high-tech shit. It's a shame, all of that effort and we would still survive the hit. But I'll give them a B+ for effort." She looked over at Barnabas. "I'm surprised you ditched your monk outfit."

Barnabas tugged at his black fatigues John had provided. "I'm trying to adjust to my new life. The monk outfit was so last century."

"I see you're trying to gain skill in the humor department, as well," she replied as she turned back to the screen. "Don't quit your day job just yet."

"I don't operate too well in the daylight if you haven't noticed." Barnabas said.

"I told you, all things in due time. I didn't push you to stop being a pompous ass with a cork up his butt when I met you, did I?" she asked as she dialed the camera around to view other places they had marked as security locations.

"Well, no. You dropped me on Frank as I recollect," he agreed.

"That's because you deserve each other," she returned. "Okay, they're staying on the schedule. We're going to drop in, take out the roof guards and move forward. You make sure everyone is either asleep or play with their memories so they don't remember us. I'll go see to our buddy, Mr. Brajorly."

ADAM, when we drop, make sure you answer for their security personnel when they call each other.

>>I understand, Bethany Anne. I can mimic forty-eight percent of their speech and ninety-two percent of the terms they use for each other. I can fudge the rest, usually, with static on the line.<<

Well, let me know if you have any problems.

>>I will.<<

"How are we going to drop in?" Barnabas asked.

"Simple," she told him as she pushed open the Pod doors and Barnabas's eyes opened a little wider. "I grab your arm and we take a little hop. Don't worry, it'll be fun."

"I sure hope Bethany Anne is having fun," John complained as Eric pulled the last of the yacht's crewmembers in. They had boarded the yacht and sleepy-darted everyone. "Because this was beyond careless and sloppy of the crew. Seriously, who plays tequila shot games when you might be attacked at any moment? By TQB desperadoes, no less? Our rep must suck." John continued bitching while he set the controls to pull up the anchor and started loading the destination they had selected. The target location was a common enough fishing area which the owner had visited twice in the last couple of weeks. Once ADAM was in their system, it was easy enough to find the sailing data.

Eric dropped the last crewmember, whose head rebounded off the deck. Eric flinched when he watched it happen. "I don't know if that's going to bother his head any more than the tequila already has," Eric commented as he walked over to John. "You're just upset you didn't get the chance to shoot anyone."

"Well, the guys' night out was a shot in the arm," John admitted. "Did you hear that Frank's book made it up to the top one thousand ranking?" he asked as he pulled the final release and the yacht started moving. "Damned good thing we had the review on how to operate these boats. Next time, I'll consider asking for someone on the Navy side to join us."

"We'd get a lot of volunteers, especially Jean Dukes," Eric said.

"Yes, but we need the boat in one piece," John said. "I have no idea what she'd do with a perfectly sound boat we don't want to sink."

"Only one way to find out," Eric winked and left the bridge to make another loop through the ship.

———

"Wakey, wakey," Bethany Anne poked Davey Brajorly in his shoulder a couple of times. When the man didn't budge, she grabbed his arm and forcefully yanked him off the bed and tossed him to the floor where he landed with a body jarring thump.

"I said wake the fuck up!" she snarled as Brajorly's eyes flew open. He looked up to see a black-haired woman in leather pants and obvious mercenary getup, two pistols slung low on her hips and a sword over her shoulder.

"What the…" He looked around his room. It was luxurious; his king-sized bed with a blue cover was in the center of a twenty-foot wide by twenty-five foot long room. He had a pleasant sitting area in one corner with its own television and couch. He was sprawled between his bed and the doorway to the master suite bathroom. "How the hell are you in here?"

"Your men are sleeping on the job," she retorted. "Or dead. Which is just a sleep you don't wake up from. Kind of like this moment right here. You see, you're dreaming, and you definitely won't be waking up from this dream, you sorry sack of selfishness."

"What are you talking about?" he demanded and was starting to get up when the woman kicked him in the chest. He rolled twice before hitting the wall with a grunt and a stream of epithets. "That hurt bitch, and this isn't a dream!"

"Well, perhaps I misspoke," she told him as she walked over and squatted down next to him. "It's actually the end of your dream and many people's nightmares. You've been a useless leader, and now you won't be making mistakes because you focus on your own selfish needs. You played your hand out and screwed over the wrong people." Her eyes started glowing red, and she hissed at him.

"Namely mine!"

Elsewhere in the large complex, Barnabas heard a man scream in fear. "Dammit. I wasn't finished knocking everyone out here, Bethany Anne." He bumped up his running and decided to forego the gentle effort to knock them unconscious with his mental abilities. Anyone with a gun got a club over the head and a fast mental command that made them think that they had made a mistake that caused them to fall and hit their head. Fortunately, that was only two people.

Barnabas started walking back towards the master suite. "Couldn't you have waited just five more minutes?" he murmured and then remembered his own feelings when his love was killed.

Never mind.

———

John watched the two Pods come down to the back of the larger yacht. One was a Black Eagle, which Gabrielle was flying, the other a standard Pod. The Pod descended then halted five feet above the ship and turned to face aft and flew backward to match the ship's speed. The front doors opened, and Bethany Anne tossed a body to John, who was there to grab Brajorly as she dropped to the deck herself. "Thanks," she told him. "Bad catch, though."

The Pod doors closed, it rose up and then it along with Gabrielle's Pod raced back towards the compound to pick up Barnabas, who was finishing any mind altering he felt he needed to sell the story they had decided to lay out.

"What are you talking about?" John asked as he tossed the comatose man over his shoulder and followed Bethany Anne. "I didn't fumble the catch."

"That's my point!" She turned to smile at him. "I was kind of hoping you'd drop him."

"I still can," he told her.

She waved a hand. "Nah, he might hit his head too hard and fail to be available for my final resolution."

"Kinda devious, this one." John said as Bethany Anne turned in to the bridge.

"I hope so. Where's the box?" she asked, looking around

before spying it. "Ah, never mind," she said as she went to an aluminum box and opened the two locks before selecting a vial, smelling salts and a syringe gun. She slotted the vial into the little gun and turned around to face Brajorly. "Let me have his neck."

John pulled the man off of his shoulder and turned him around. Bethany Anne felt along his neck and then pressed the device to it and pulled the trigger. Both of them could hear it push the serum out of the syringe and stop with a final 'click.'

Bethany Anne pulled the gun away. "Would have been more fun with him awake, but a bit more of a pain to deal with his squirming." She pulled the smelling salts out of a pocket, cracked them open and started waving them in front of Brajorly's face. "Wakey, wakey asshole," she whispered to him. "It's time for your final dream."

─────

Ten minutes later, the yacht was slowly turning in a circle a half mile wide. "You can't do this to me!" Brajorly screamed as John held him firmly, one hand on each of Brajorly's arms, "I'll pay you any amount of money you want, no one captures and murders people anymore!" he whimpered as the water slowly moved past them.

"Of course, they don't in *your* world," Bethany Anne told him. "You think agreeing to a military attack on a business which had children involved…" She started to say before he interrupted her.

"I didn't KNOW about that!" he screamed. "Why won't you believe me?"

"Oh? You didn't know?" Bethany Anne pulled out a

mobile phone and brought up an application that recorded and played back sound. "Here, listen."

A voice Brajorly recognized as Anna Elisabeth's came on. "As is my right, rarely employed by my country, I ask for a table vote on whether you intend to acquire TQB Enterprise technology through whatever means necessary?" She played the tape all the way to when Johann said 'all the way to force' before stopping the recording.

"That was the vote where it was decided to toss your own ass into the sea to drown, Brajorly. Be thankful I didn't choose to kill your children as well."

"What about my wife?" he asked.

"You don't even have your wife with you on the island, you dick. You don't love her. She'll just get all of your money. I'd keep her alive just to piss you off. As it is, she *is* actually a decent person, so she stays alive for that reason alone." Bethany Anne turned towards the water. "However, the nanites injected into your system are going to start playing with your muscles, slowly making them fail to work for sporadic amounts of time. You can, of course, just drown yourself. But if you make it the half hour it takes for the yacht to circle back around, you can climb back aboard."

"Think about all of the people who died when your representative voted 'all the way to force,' Brajorly, as you try to stay alive." He barely had time to yell in surprise before she grabbed his arm and threw him off the ship to splash into the water below, the yacht already leaving him behind.

Bethany Anne watched him as he tried to swim towards the ship and she put up a finger and waved it in a 'no no no' gesture and he stopped to tread water. Turning to see where he expected the boat to be he started swimming in that direction.

"So, the more he swims, the more the nanites work in his body?" John asked from beside her.

"Yup." She shrugged. "If he stays calm, cool and collected throughout the whole process, ADAM assures me there is a one in nine hundred chance he could get back on the ship when it comes around.

"And if he swims to meet it?" John asked as he watched Brajorly swim away.

"Not a fucking chance in hell," she said as she turned toward where Eric waited by the two Pods. As the three of them got ready to leave the yacht, she watched him swim. "He'll get about two-thirds the way to the ship before his muscles seize up. Tough shit, asshole."

CHAPTER THIRTEEN

WASHINGTON D.C. USA

When the President entered the room, he raised an eyebrow. George had already provided a full package of Tums on the table in front of the seat he usually sat in.

Extra-strength.

So he sat down and opened the package, took two of the tablets, and popped them in his mouth. "Fruit, the better-tasting kind," he said as he put his hands back on the table. "I take it this is another one of those meetings?"

"Afraid so, Mr. President," George said. "We have another death, a Chinese navy vessel under fire, two companies under hostile takeover on the stock market and our information assets in Asia are getting info that one of the three most powerful clans is starting to awaken."

"What's that supposed to mean?" The President asked, "How does a dormant clan waking up in China have anything to do with the Chinese government??"

"Unfortunately, we don't understand much ourselves. Until very recently, this clan was more myth and legend than reality. However, our assets are saying that word has gone out from central China that their name either brings fear or respect. Those in power are still people, and this particular clan has been quiet for decades, if not centuries. Why the rumors are happening, our assets don't know or understand at this time."

"Well, maybe there's smoke, but we'll have to wait to see the fire part." The President pulled down the paper and grabbed another Tums. "I love the fruit kind, I can eat these like candy," he said.

George picked up a piece of paper, and the President could see the remains of his own package of Tums. "Already finished mine waiting for you," George said, grinning. He put the paper back down. "Okay, next item is the strange death of Davey Brajorly, CEO of Atomis Energy and about sixteen other energy-based companies both here and in Europe."

"Drowned, right?" the President asked, eyeing another Tums.

"Yes, but no one really remembers the details of how he got on the boat, the security video had been on the blink for a week or so, and two security people both fell down and hit their heads. He was found in an area that he would normally fish, but the yacht was going in a lazy circle. Most of those on the yacht had been drinking and couldn't remember anything they had done. There's a lot of finger pointing and much confusion. The net is that another major owner of a company that we believe was involved in the TQB attack is now dead."

"How are they doing it?" the President asked. "I'm not

for a second going to ask you if you think they did it. The fact you're bringing it up says you believe it. So, how do you think they did it?"

"I'm not sure," George answered. "I've asked some of those on the Joint Chiefs, and they provided consulting time with some of their people. Using what we know of their Pods, they probably dropped people right on top of his compound, grabbed Brajorly and spirited him away to the yacht. Set up the scene and then pushed him overboard. The problem is that Brajorly was in a good enough physical condition to swim back to the yacht, but he didn't make it."

"They checked for drugs, I assume?"

"Yes, and found nothing. It's like he just seized up or gave up and quit." George answered. "I'm going with the opinion that their medical capabilities are amazingly able to heal people, so they have to be just as able to kill people."

"Keep talking like this and you'll find yourself on their list as well, George," the President said. "Assuming they killed Brajorly, we have proof he was one of those that approved the plan to go after them?" George nodded. "And what are we offering the others?"

"Nothing yet. The two of them that are quietly talking to us aren't admitting to any wrongdoing. So I'm told we're telling them unless they have some reason to be afraid, we can't see why we need to spend the taxpayers money."

"Why make them fess up?" the President asked.

"Those in the FBI believe if we are in the middle of bringing charges, then TQB will back off," George shrugged. "It's just a guess based on TQB sending others to jail."

"So, either choose our justice or suffer theirs, is it?" the President asked.

"Yes. I think everyone now knows that Brajorly's hiding

on an island with a small military force doesn't count for shit," George said. "This was a major operation done cleanly, quietly and without evidence. Just because we can guess how they might have planned the op doesn't mean they did the op. I'd bet my pension they *did* do it, but I can't confirm it."

"If those who want our protection try a bunch of legal hijinks, I don't think TQB is going to be satisfied," the President said.

"No, and believe me, that fact will be pointed out to them as well," George told him.

"I wonder if we can use TQB as 'the boogeyman?'" the President muttered. "At least with those in Congress that are annoying me. That would be nice."

"Let's not and say we didn't, Mr. President. I think we don't want to be anywhere near TQB when their powder keg blows up, and I'm pretty sure it will," George admonished.

"George, you're always sure something bad is going to happen," the President retorted.

"Well, Davey Brajorly isn't laughing right now," George pointed out.

"Okay, good point," the President agreed. "So, Chinese Naval vessel? How are you blaming TQB for this one?"

"I got this from the Navy. The Chinese type 052D Destroyer Xiamen was one of the vessels stalking the QBS Polarus and the QBS Ad Aeternitatem when it suffered a leak. They apparently patched that leak and then suffered another. By that time, it was assumed that the QBS ships were letting it be known they didn't like the Chinese around them. The Xiamen turned towards the closest friendly port and left the area. The other ships dropped back another ten miles."

"That's not so far," the President pointed out. "Their missiles can hit them from that distance."

"True, but we think that it was an exercise to let the Chinese know their ships aren't safe. We suspect they were using some sort of gravitic kinetic weapon when they destroyed the two ships before. Now, they have something that is striking and making holes in the ships below the waterline. If this is true, it's a little frightening. First, because we weren't looking underwater. True, we have SONAR, but their damned coating is screwing that up. We believed we'd gotten a blip of noise before the Xiamen was holed, and we know that there was something on the second, but there's little we can do about it. For all we know, they have ten of these little bastards around every ship, waiting in case of attack and then hole them all. We can't find the sumbitching weapons yet," George finally stopped.

"I think you need to realize that TQB isn't the enemy here, George," the President said. "You see dark desires behind technological advances that you can't defend against. At least not yet. Perhaps diplomacy?" The President laughed when George scowled. "I see the military still refers to diplomacy as the weaker brother, right?"

"Well, we prefer to know that if diplomacy fails, we can kick their ass, yes." George said. "And for all of this, TQB isn't even a nation-state. If it's annoying our military, just think about the Chinese. Hell, they stole half of their technology from our people, and I know for a fact the Chinese haven't been able to steal shit from TQB, and they're getting their asses spanked at the same time. I'm sure it wasn't lost on the Chinese when TQB made those damned big holes in Australia's Outback. Something like that has to concern them. Now, we have TQB over in the Asteroid Belt building God knows what. It's enough to keep a nervous person up at night."

"So, how is your sleep, George?" the President asked with a smile.

George eyed him and said, "Lousy."

The President laughed and pushed his half a roll of Tums across the table. "Now I know why you've already eaten your roll."

"Yeah, thanks," George said as he grabbed the roll and peeled out two Tums. "These are the best tasting." He pushed the remaining Tums back to the President, "I'm calciumed up for the day, I think. So, that leaves us with another two companies lost in the stock market."

"Anything unfair going on?" The President asked.

"No, just too damned smart by half. The NSA is now thinking it's feasible they have some sort of supercomputer focused only on handling the stock market. They have to be manipulating something, somehow but there's no evidence whatsoever." George said.

"Once again, anything illegal?

"No."

"So, is there any reason we shouldn't open up communications with TQB?" the President asked.

"Only my gut, Mr. President, only my gut," George said.

"Well, I'll give your stomach two more weeks to calm down, and then we need to consider how these discussions might move forward."

"I understand." George kept his reservations to himself.

***

CLAN TEMPLE NEAR SHENNONGJIA PEAK, HUBEI

Stephanie came back to consciousness lying in bed. She could feel the mountain air drifting through the room and the silence that nature always brought with her. She turned her head to see that she was a guest of the Clan's temporary living quarters.

So, not in her old room.

Her head was clear, but she could only remember a little from her dreams. The dreams spoke of mysteries, and magic, technology, and testing.

They spoke of secrets.

She sat up in her bed, the simple coverlet was warm enough. She dressed in the same outfit she walked into the temple wearing. There was a glass and pitcher with water next to her bed. She reached over, poured herself a drink and took a few sips.

She sought the meditative state, the level where she would be able to replay what her conscious mind could not. She reached over to put the cup back down before sitting back on her bed, folding her legs under her and closing her eyes to seek the answers within her.

It was time to find the answers that she knew were inside.

If she had come here with the attitude that the outside was the final answer, then she would leave with answers she would never be able to hear. But she had come with the knowledge she needed help, and help had been provided along with a test. A test to see what she remembered from her past.

Did she forget too much of her training when she left the temple eight years ago?

Stephanie Lee smiled slightly before composing her face in calmness.

She was hotheaded, not stupid.

———

RELEASE THE DOGS OF WAR

MANUFACTURING FACILITY 01, ASTEROID FIELDS

"Marcus should be here in a couple of hours," William told Bobcat as they sat eating in the cafeteria area. The amount of space under the inflated building was substantial. Bobcat felt like he was sitting underground, not millions of miles away from Earth near the Asteroid Fields.

"What do we have on tap for him?" Bobcat asked, chewing on his General Tso's chicken and rice dinner. The chef had come from South Africa, but he knew cuisines from most of the world, except he couldn't do pizza for shit.

Fortunately, he knew how to do a decent flatbread, and Bobcat had cans of pizza sauce, mozzarella, and Hormel pepperoni stashed on the next shipping container coming to them. The resulting pizza would have to do for him until he got back to Earth.

He hoped.

"We're going through the gravitic field mergings, so TOM and ADAM are dealing with a lot right now. Marcus seems to get it intuitively somehow, possibly because he's worked with them so often. I'm hoping he will help bypass some of the problems they're encountering," William answered as he sat down with a meal of chicken fried rice. "The extra engines we put all over the ship are even giving TOM fits in the math department. He and ADAM have to reprogram old calculations and inject the changes. It's taking time."

"Does he think it will work?" Bobcat asked. "Or is it just not working at all?"

"Oh, TOM says he's sure it can work, it is just his people never conceived of something so complicated for a spaceship."

"They never thought of dogfights in space, then." Bobcat shrugged. "To the new and creative go the spoils."

"Let's hope so," William said. "I can tell you when Bethany Anne takes control of this ship, she's going to put it through its paces, that's for damn sure."

"Yeah, that's true," Bobcat agreed. "What did Jeffrey say about his conversation with Captain Thomas?"

William put down his fork. "Um, it was a little tense," William said. "He didn't talk to you about it?"

Bobcat finished his bite. "I couldn't get on the call, Jeo and I were working some smelting issues out. One of the new ideas to use gravity exploded all over the smelting test platform."

"Anyone hurt?" William asked.

"Only superficially, when one of the stray chunks that broke apart holed the temporary building. The building was hidden behind another big rock, but the stupid chunk rebounded off of a rock waiting for testing. One in a million chance it could happen, and it happened. The idiot didn't have his helmet on, so he suffered some lung damage before the gravity tech slammed on his helmet and got him on internal oxygen. I doubt he'll make that mistake again."

"If being that close to death doesn't make him religious about safety, he needs to go home," William offered. "I'm surprised we aren't sending him there anyway."

"Oh, it was considered, but he was cursing himself out so much even Bandile Annane, the mining boss, felt sorry for him, so he got ten days of slag duty," Bobcat replied.

"Damn, Annane has a heart?" William exclaimed. "I thought when it came to safety, you were either perfect or gone."

"No, he just yells a lot. He cares for his people. Plus, in his language, it sounds like cursing." Bobcat shrugged.

"So, what's our first order of business when the team is all back together?" William asked.

Bobcat looked up at William and smiled. "Why, the name of the first bar in outer space, of course."

CHAPTER FOURTEEN

TABITHA'S HOME, SOUTH AMERICA

Tabitha reviewed the screens on the laptop in her office and spoke softly, but loud enough for her voice to be heard at the door. "Ryu, I need to speak to you and Hirotoshi for a minute."

A silent body stepped out of the shadows, and a few moments later, Hirotoshi and Ryu came into Tabitha's office. She turned the laptop around, and a map showed a small office building on the outside of a nearby town. "This is the location I believe the closest Forsaken are housed. I've tracked down some of the money transfers to our last visitors. Plus, there are now four missing people in the last two months on that side of town. Suggestions?"

"Daytime." Hirotoshi said. "There is no need to offer any advantage to Forsaken in this, Kemosabe," Hirotoshi's lips quirked slightly when he used the team's name for Tabitha.

"Fine, but I want to question the people, so make sure we

don't kill any who aren't Nosferatu," she told them, ignoring the name.

She would get them back.

"It's going to be a hit, grab and take away, then," Hirotoshi said. "We go in, kill Nosferatu and decide how to implement a cleanup after we grab Forsaken and then skip out. We will need sun protection for them between the house and a van."

"Damn, cleanup is such a bitch," Tabitha thought about it. "What's the normal procedure?"

"Burning in some places, Kemosabe," Ryu answered. "Although here it looks like we would be hurting others and I doubt the Queen would like us to do that."

"No she wouldn't," Tabitha agreed. "So, we need to consider creating our own cleanup methods. Heavy duty plastic bags, bleach, etc." She reached over and grabbed her phone. After handling the security, she punched a couple of numbers. "One second, guys."

She waited a few seconds. "Frank? Tabitha. I have a question on how to clean up a bunch of dead bodies. No, I don't have any dead bodies at the moment, but I'm expecting to have some shortly. Well, probably some Nosferatu and we're grabbing some Forsaken to have discussions if we can. Daytime. Yeah, well while it's true that daytime means others will be around, the vampires will probably be asleep. No, I can't have everything, or, well never mind."

She listened for a few seconds. "Really? That would be great. No, I'm not trying to get rid of any underground crime lords at the moment. They leave me alone, I'll leave them alone unless they get involved on their own." Another pause. "Okay, if you would find and make that connection, tell me what we'd need to pay for the cleanup. We'll supply the time and location once we're going in." She laughed. "I'm young, not stupid. Right, I do plan to be around for a few hundred years."

She hung up the phone. "Okay, we need to figure our own cleanup for the future, but we might have backup by the criminal underground. The sun could take care of some of it, and I don't want to burn it if the flames are going to hurt innocents. In the future, if we don't have to depend on criminals, I'd feel a little better. Stupid Forsaken are already making me connect with people I don't want to," she griped.

"Don't think about it, Kemosabe," Hirotoshi said. "You are the Queen's Ranger, not the local law. I would advise you to do what you need to handle your responsibility. You will need to be trustworthy to both those above and below the law if you are going to do your job appropriately. Even the criminals need to know that your word is your bond."

"Well, that rips it, I can't give my word," Tabitha said. "Or I need to be careful giving my assurance, or just be damned sneaky."

"See, already she has figured out a way around this conundrum she has, wisdom is quick for one so young, Ryu," Hirotoshi said as he pointed to Tabitha but spoke to Ryu, who was next to him. Ryu nodded his head like he was looking at the Emperor's young daughter.

"Wow, sarcasm is such an admirable trait Tonto Prime," Tabitha said. "I get it, always be truthful, but make sure my truth can cut multiple ways," she said. "Now that we have that little bit of wisdom dispensed, let's figure out how we're going to get there, what we need, and the particulars."

The three of them got down to planning their first operation.

RELEASE THE DOGS OF WAR

———

The dark gray van rolled up to the Rodriquez Carpet Emporium building that sported signs outside that said 'Going Out Of Business, Everything Must Go!' The signs looked like they had been there for a few years, half ripped in places and dirty. There were no people in the deserted-looking and rundown office park. Time had not been gentle to the buildings, some areas had cement patches, and many of the walls had graffiti sprayed on them. Even the graffiti had faded. The weeds were growing through cracks in the concrete.

The van's sliding door opened, and Hirotoshi and Ryu stepped out. He signaled the two in the front who understood their responsibility was to protect their egress and stop any from entering or exiting the building. Tabitha walked up to the glass door with the metal bars over it. Even to her less than well-trained eyes, she could see the footprints in the dirt.

"Well, someone is home," she muttered and looked at the lock. "Seems like it's a simple lock, but physical locks aren't my…" Ryu stepped up and pulled a small leather pouch from his shirt. All of the men were dressed in black military cargo pants and shirts that seemed to hide more pockets than should be physically possible. Tabitha asked them about their odd-toed boots, and Hirotoshi said that they preferred the design from the ancient times to the new boots that did not allow them to feel the sticks under their feet as they moved.

Less than ten seconds later, the lock was picked, and the small leather pouch disappeared back into Ryu's shirt. He nodded to Hirotoshi, who was backed up by Ryu and then three others. Hirotoshi put up three fingers, two, and then one before pulling his sword and entering the building. Ryu pulled his sword and went next. Tabitha could feel a little push and heard a tiny 'Kemosabe' from behind her. "Guess that makes me the one," she muttered as she followed Ryu.

In their getup, with faces covered, she could only tell that the one pushing her was one of the twins in her group, but not if it was Kouki or Shin, his brother. She pulled a knife. She had been informed that unless necessary, it would be better if she wasn't swinging a sword yet in a close combat situation. She had the sword with her, but as far as she was concerned, it was ornamental unless she had to pull it. If that happened, she was probably in deep shit.

Her heartbeat raced as she followed Ryu into the building. Whoever originally inhabited it had left without cleaning out the place. There were old desks with dust on them in some of the rooms and an occasional mess of papers. There was a small hiss from ahead of them, where Hirotoshi had a door open, and had his sword pointed down into a darker gloom.

The smell of rotting flesh hit Tabitha's enhanced senses, and she wanted to gag. She heard Ryu's nearly silent comment from ahead of her, "If you vomit, please miss me."

Tabitha bit down on her gag reflex, "Hai!" and continued to follow Ryu. She could hear one of the guys stay at the top of the stairs as the five of them went down. Hirotoshi was at the bottom. The only sound Tabitha could hear was her own steps. She tried to keep her steps quiet, but even the damned shoes she had on made some noise.

She looked at the Tonto's footwear made of leather and how their toes were split into two groups. Maybe she would have to try them after this operation. Leading as the last of the invading group came close to the end of the hallway, Hirotoshi pulled open a door, and Ryu slid into the room beyond.

There was an audible slap when Tabitha heard Ryu cut

something and then Hirotoshi went, and it was her turn.

One vampire came in with her, and one stayed in the room by the stair entrance as Ryu and Hirotoshi checked out the next room over.

There was a light coming from an electronic device plugged into the wall. Tabitha grabbed a small capsule from her jacket and cracked it, allowing the contents to merge. The merging created a bioluminescent jelly. She finished shaking it as it started to glow from the chemical reaction and threw the capsule up onto the ceiling where the outer shell broke open, and the jelly stuck, bathing the room in enough light for her eyes to see the disgusting festering dead bodies and the two newly headless Nosferatu.

She turned away from the display slowly. Both to show that she could handle the view, and also not to upset her stomach by turning too fast.

"Kemosabe," Hirotoshi said from the next room. She went through the door and found Hirotoshi and Ryu next to two others, both sound asleep. "They are weak enough for vampires," Hirotoshi said. "They are having trouble staying awake during the day. They probably think they can control the area with human thugs, so they possibly are capable of mind control," he told her.

She regarded the two sleeping. "Let's take them up. If they hit a little sun, maybe it will wake them. If they try to yell or fight, incapacitate them," she said. "I'll get with Frank's contact about cleanup." She slid her knife into the sheath. Turning, she walked out of the room and past the scene in the next room before taking the stairs two at a time pulling her phone out on the way. When Tabitha hit the top, she nodded at their guard and hit the number she had already entered to call her local contact.

"Mr. Jaminez? Yes, this is Tabitha. I'm going to send you an address by text in a moment. There are human remains, and recently dead humans at this location. The remains need to be removed, the evidence destroyed. No, I don't want the place burned down. Well, then use a lot of chemicals! The amount of money you're being paid is sufficient. If I need to get more, I'll hack your damned accounts to give it to you, so don't push my buttons. No, that isn't a threat, it is a tactical explanation of where I'll get the funds to pay you. And I'm going to charge your account a ten percent withdrawal fee for hacking it in the first place. So, feel free to adjust the price as much as you want, I'll wait for your final decision. No, not that long, I'll wait one minute."

Tabitha turned the phone's speaker on and opened a program that allowed her to view the screen on her laptop. When the interface came up, she hit the third tab on the application and started plugging in numbers into a form she had built. Finally, the voice came back on telling her she needed to add another thousand U.S. dollars to the account. She added a thousand bucks and hit send. "Okay, I've sent the money." She closed her connection to her server. "Got it? Good. When will your team be here? That's fine, I'll have someone confirm your results."

Tabitha clicked off her phone and muttered, "Ass. Chemical surcharge my butt." She walked to the front door while setting a reminder to pull the money out of the criminal group's bank account in three days before putting the phone back in her pocket.

A minute later, Hirotoshi and Ryu walked out with the two vampires over their shoulders. Unfortunately, the sun was being blocked by the building and the late afternoon sunlight wasn't enough to wake them.

"God," Tabitha remarked. "Talk about two useless excuses for vampires, knock them out harder, I have a plan for them." Tabitha and the men got back into the van and left. Hirotoshi would have someone come by tomorrow to make sure that the criminals they contracted did their job. "All right, let's go home."

———

Jaime woke up, his arms tight behind his back and tied to a heavy wooden chair. He was immobilized. His eyes snapped open, concern evident when he looked around. He was in a concrete room, and it had the smell of old blood.

"Ah, we have our first volunteer," a woman said, walking from behind Jaime to where he could see her.

"Who are you?" he demanded. "Let me out, or you will find I am your worst nightmare." Jaime tweaked his voice to put a level of fear into it.

"Oh, that's what that feels like," the girl said and walked up to Jaime. "Stop playing with your voice, or I'll slap the shit out of you."

Jaime's eyes went red, his fangs grew. "I'll tell you what is going to…" Jaime's face was blasted with a slap that took him and his chair off the floor to land a few feet away. Jaime's jaw cracked loudly as it worked to heal.

"Son of Satan's whore!" the girl cried out in pain. "That hurt!" She grabbed her right hand with her left and massaged it.

Jaime felt his arm painfully caught and he and the chair were brought back up to a sitting position. "Not a human, Forsaken, I'm a Ranger," she told him, stepping back, still shaking her right hand.

Jaime tried to speak, his broken jaw not helping him any as he asked, "Wath ith a Rangther?" He eyed the woman in front of him. She obviously had been around vampires, since she didn't even skip a beat when Jaime had tried to scare her and her strength was more than a human's.

"Detective, judge and occasionally executioner for Bethany Anne," she told him.

"That whore?" Jaime had just said the last word when he yelled in pain, looking down to see a knife stuck in his leg, and the woman holding a hand up to stop something from happening behind him.

"Shut up," she ordered.

"You have a knife thuck in my leg!" Jaime screamed, "How am I thuppothed to thop yelling?"

"Because if I pull this knife out, you lose your head, jackass," she told him and crooked a finger to someone behind him. It took Jaime a moment to readjust as he worked to focus on the person coming into his view. It was then he realized that he was seriously fucked.

This was a powerful vampire. He had a katana out, and although Jaime could only see his eyes with his mask drawn up over his face, they looked seriously unhappy.

"What is your name?" the woman asked him.

"Ja… Jaime," he got out before shutting his mouth again, trying not to move the knife impaled into the chair.

"Well Jaime, meet Hirotoshi from the Queen's Elite. He was about a second from taking your head off with that katana for disrespecting the Queen. Bad choice of words, I might add. They take her honor very seriously. However, I need information that you might be able to provide so I'm willing to deal. First question, why are you trying to take over Michael's area?"

"He is dead." Jaime got out. "Why should I answer questions from you?"

Tabitha's eyes flashed red as she stepped closer to Jaime and grabbed the knife handle. "Because I control the knife, asshole," she said and moved the knife back and forth a couple of times as Jaime screamed. "Keep talking like Michael is gone and we will be done here." She stopped playing with the knife and stepped back, looking at the man next to her who was carefully eying her. "What? He pissed me off." The two continued staring at each other a couple of seconds before the man broke the staring to look back at Jaime.

Jaime got his voice back. "If I tell you everything, will you set me free?"

The woman considered his question, "I will allow you a ninety-second head start. The front door of the house is up the stairs behind me, and then you take a right down the hall and then a left at the next room. We'll leave the front door open. If you fail to get out, you will be killed. If you try to do anything but leave, you will be killed. This, plus me pulling the knife out of your leg right now, is the best deal I will offer. You have seven seconds to decide."

He started to speak when she cut him off, "You accept, or you die, which is it?"

"I accept, I accept!" he groaned as she pulled the knife from his leg.

"Okay, no time like the present to tell me why you're trying to get into this house. You were trying to get into this house, right?"

"Yes," Jaime answered, trying to get past the pain as his leg slowly healed. "It's rumored that Anton left a fair number of valuables hidden in the house as well as books about his experiments into the serum. We wanted to look around."

"Hmm, we never found anything like that," the woman said. "Any ideas where it would be?" Jaime shook his head. "Damn," she spat. "What about your friend, what's his take?" she asked him.

"Marcus is in it with me. We would split it sixty-forty," he answered.

"Who gets more?" she asked.

"Me," he grated out.

"Well, that tells me who the smarter of you two is," she said. "How many more Forsaken are trying to get back into the business that you are aware of?"

He shook his head. "I don't know any in this area. They all left when Michael came in."

"Why didn't you two guys leave?" she asked.

"We aren't very powerful, and figured keeping our heads down and avoiding turning anyone would keep us off the radar."

"Not the wisest idea, but I suppose it was smart enough. You're still here," she said, thinking about his comment. "How did you get your blood?"

"Prostitutes in exchange for sex," he told her.

"Prostitutes traded their blood for sex with you?" she asked, surprised.

He tried to smirk at her, but failed. "Yes, the soporific in our bites turns them on when they can't enjoy sex anymore. It's one of the few ways they can still get an out of this world orgasm, and I speak very persuasively."

'That's just… well, cunning." she acknowledged.

"I am a cunning linguist," he said, and smirked at her.

Tabitha rolled her eyes. "Okay, time's up," she said as she looked behind him. "Ryu, would you open all of the doors leading outside and have our guys make sure he can find his way?"

Jaime felt his leg. It wasn't healed all the way, but he could probably get going. Once out in the night, he should be able to figure out some way to hide. Marcus would be on his own.

There was a nod from Hirotoshi letting Tabitha know it was ready. She walked behind Jaime. "I'm going to cut the ropes holding your hands. Then, I'll give you ten seconds to get out of the chair. If you make it out earlier than ten seconds, well that just works out better for you. Ready?"

Jaime thought she was a little too nice. "Ready for what? Are you going to stab me after you cut the ropes?"

"No, but if you besmirch my honor again with a question like that, I'll sever your Achilles tendon and then tell you to run, how about that?"

Jaime shook his head but kept his mouth shut.

He could feel a knife make its way between the ropes and then a quick cut, then another before a hand grabbed the ropes and pulled them off of his hands. "You have ten seconds," she told him.

Jaime pulled his arms around, biting back the pain he felt as his arms screamed from the torture of being so tightly tied. His hands, barely working, helped push and pull ropes. He was slowly getting his feeling back when she told him, "Nine seconds." He struggled up out of the seat and began pushing himself towards the door. Half walking, half dragging his body towards the stairs, he started his way toward freedom.

Tabitha and Hirotoshi started cleaning up the rope and chair as they listened to Jaime make it up the stairs and turn the corner.

A few seconds later, they heard him scream in horror and then pain.

"God," Tabitha stood up and stretched. "You would think he didn't appreciate the beautiful morning sun."

Hirotoshi grunted his agreement.

What seemed like an eternity later, but was probably more like half a minute, the screaming finally stopped.

"Okay, let's bring in contestant number two," she said.

Fifteen minutes later, there was another scream of horror and pain.

CHAPTER FIFTEEN

LAS VEGAS, NEVADA, USA

Johann stepped into the country club on the west side of Las Vegas near the Red Rock Casino and located the men's locker room. Walking in, he searched for and found locker one-one-four. On it was a six-digit lock. He found the code that had been sent to him by text message and used it to open the locker. Inside was a small aluminum lock-box about four inches wide, two inches tall and six inches long. Picking it up, Johann thought if felt pretty solid.

He closed up the locker, walked out of the room, and went to his rental car. Las Vegas was already getting hot.

———

Leonard pulled his cowboy hat off his head, wiped the sweat and put it back on. He was walking back to his two double-wide trailers on his own hundred and twenty acres of rock, sand, and cactus at the foot of the mountains when he saw the dust trail from a car heading his direction. He figured by the time the car arrived, he should be at the door waiting for him.

Leonard had received a text the day before that he should expect a man with payment today, and it looked like the messenger was going to arrive in about ten minutes. He was driving pretty slow.

Leonard pulled his .380 Colt Mustang and checked the chamber. No reason to be foolish.

He continued to the deck of the first mobile home and used the hose to wash off his face. He had been digging a large hole in the back forty, and it had been hot and sweaty work.

He waited for the rental car to come to a stop and a man to push open the door. The new arrival was holding an aluminum case in his right hand as he stepped from the car.

Leonard stepped off the porch and started walking towards the man. He felt a flash in his eyes and put up a hand to block the sun reflecting off of the other mobile home's window, not realizing that the sun wasn't hitting it.

"Hello!" he called out to the new guy. "Name's Leonard."

"Mine's Johann," the man told him while blinking his eyes, adjusting to the brightness of the sun. He pulled out dark sunglasses and replaced the set he had used for driving. "I was told to bring this package to you, and you would know what to do with it?" He held up an aluminum box.

Leonard put a hand out, and the stranger put the box in his hands. It felt full and didn't chink when he shook it, so Leonard told him, "Yes I do, young man." Leonard put the visitor maybe in his late twenties or early thirties, with dark hair. "We have some little way to walk, you want some water?"

Johann begged off from the offer.

"C'mon then, no need to waste time unless you want to.

We all have our parts to play in this little game, and your boss is going to want to know you did your job."

"I imagine he will," Johann said. "How do I tell him?"

"You won't, son. I'll deal with that. I've got something for you to do after you're given your next orders, capiche?" Leonard said as the two men walked away from the mobile homes and out into the desert. They stopped and talked for a few moments close to one of the forty-foot tall cactuses that grew on Leonard's land. The older man said, "That's why I like it out here. It tests you. If you forget who the apex predator is, then Mother Nature is going to kick your ass. Maybe kill you for your stupidity. Keeps you alive, it does."

Johann agreed, and the two men continued walking. They made it to a dried-out streambed before Leonard said, "Where we're going is just around the next bend. If you allow me a second to catch my wind young man, we'll get there, and then I'll give you what you need before you head back. I imagine you will be told what the fuck to do with it."

"Should I go ahead?" Johann asked.

"Well hell, if you need to be going somewhere fast, let's do this. You take the lead, and I'll carry the rear," Leonard said. Leonard held back just a bit so that when the young man turned the corner, it blocked him from seeing Leonard take out his .380. He held it up and walked around the bend holding it out in front of him.

But the area was empty.

What, did you believe that you were the apex predator, Leonard Martinez? a man's voice spoke into his mind.

The pistol shots could be heard for a half-mile in most directions along with the screams. The only problem was that the closest humans were twelve miles away.

Twenty minutes later, Barnabas walked back to the two

mobile homes and stepped into the second, a white one with green trim, heading for the safe that he knew to be hidden under the kitchen sink.

———

QBS POLARUS, MID-ATLANTIC OCEAN

"This piece of trash's name is Johann. Johann, meet Mark, Sia and Giannini." Bethany Anne was speaking to the four of them on the Ad Aeternitatem. Richard and Samuel were getting something to eat while the reporters had a few hours with Johann. "Johann has decided that he would like to be as helpful as possible so he's going to answer each and every question you have, honestly and directly." She nodded to the man, who seemed to show little emotion.

"What's wrong with him?" Mark asked.

"He's been under a lot of mind probing lately, and now he is under a compulsion to tell the truth, no matter how bad he doesn't want to do that," Bethany Anne said.

"Is this what you did to Silvens-Werner back in Colorado?" Mark asked.

"Yes, I gave him a compulsion to tell the truth."

"Can it be broken?" he questioned further.

"Not by him, not now," she said.

"Why?" Mark pressed.

"Nunya," Bethany Anne answered.

"What?" Mark asked.

Sia slapped him on the arm to get his attention. "It means none of your business. Don't ask." Mark put up his hands in surrender.

"Okay, so how long is he going to be like this?" Mark continued.

"As long as you have questions, then he's going to a penal colony without parole. I would suggest not leaving out any questions the first time since there will not be a follow up," Bethany Anne said as she walked out of the room. "Do ask him about his congressional contacts," she added as she slipped out.

Mark turned back towards Johann like Mark was a dog and Johann had just become a juicy steak.

———

"So, a dead end, huh? He was just a hit man to kill Johann and tie up that loose end?" Bethany Anne asked Barnabas as he flew back in a Pod. "No, I get it. He would take the contracts and handle them. Nice sum of money in chips, though. I should tell Johann he was taking twenty-five thousand and walking to his own funeral, so to speak. Hand the guy his money and then walk to the grave. You have to give it to the guy, a couple of dollars in rounds and some shoveling, and he'd be good to go. Then he drops off the rental car, goes into town on a bus to play for a while then change casino tokens to cash. Nice way to get paid and hard to track. True, okay, see you soon."

Bethany Anne slid her phone into her pocket and considered who was next on the list. Annoyingly, she couldn't find Stephanie Lee. The woman had gone back to China and so far, hadn't come back out. She had a list of people to go through and somehow, some way, was going to finish it.

Come hell or high water, her justice would be complete.

———

MICHAEL ANDERLE

QBS POLARUS, MID-ATLANTIC

The meeting room held Bethany Anne, Barnabas, Dan, Stephen, Captain Thomas, the Queen's Guard, Peter, and a handful of others. Most of them were sitting in the chairs in the back. In the front, in shackles, sat Johann.

He tried to glare at everyone and snarled, "You won't get away with this!" He had been given a nice dinner and had a nap. He could remember answering all of the reporter's questions with the truth.

It was infuriating, to tell the truth when the lies came into his mind first. He just couldn't speak them.

"Well, perhaps you might have thought of that when you decided to send a bomb into our offices?" Bethany Anne stated, walking in front of him before turning around and walking the other way.

"That wasn't me," he argued. "That was Stephanie Lee!"

"Johann, we both know you're part of the group that pushed to take whatever actions necessary to acquire our technology for your bosses."

"Yes!" Johann grabbed ahold of the idea. "Why aren't they on trial here? I'm just the…" He started before Bethany Anne cut him off.

"You are just the little parasite that wanted to move up the ladder. Remember, some of them have already paid the price. Or are you forgetting Sean Truitt?" she asked him.

Johann shook his head.

"Unfortunately, you have nothing with which to bargain. I know what you know, and now the reporters know who to go after as well. You don't know the main guy, although you suspect a lot. The evidence has already been placed before this court."

"Then why am I even in this jacked up setup?" he spat. "You have me, and are going to kill me. Why even put me through this?"

Bethany Anne turned and caught his attention. Her eyes went red, her fangs descended, and Johann struggled to push back against his ropes to move as far as possible away from the thing standing five feet from him.

"Believe it or not," she said, barely constrained anger coloring her voice, "This isn't about you, Johann. This is to show those that follow me that I'm capable of delivering justice when what I want is revenge. Hot, painful, ear-shrieking revenge, where it takes days to dismember your body. That is what I crave when the nights are lonely because you took my love away," she hissed at him. "What you get is justice and a sentence, not what I believe you deserve, but justice is what the future is built on!"

Johann heard everything she said and realized there were some things worse than a quick death. He wasn't ever supposed to meet up with those who were affected by what his group did. They were all nameless faces.

Now, the face had a name and red eyes and vampire teeth.

He was a dead man talking.

Fifteen minutes later, Johann was sent to the Etheric without the torture Bethany Anne's emotions craved, but her intellect argued was just.

This time, intellect won.

———

Captain Thomas handed the chair and the shackles to a seaman who took them from the room.

Bethany Anne took the front while everyone took a seat.

"Two of the three of what we are calling the Black Cabal are now sentenced and sent to the Etheric. We are missing one, Stephanie Lee. She has disappeared into China, and that isn't a small area to search. So far, she isn't sending any messages we can locate."

"What about Phillip Simmons, the US agent?" Gabrielle asked.

"This time, there was a Pricolici involved, so I had intended to have a particular Pricolici deal with it, but she's pregnant." Bethany Anne smiled. "So, it became a male Pricolici issue, and those two drew straws. The problem is that some shenanigans were going on between the two…"

Bethany Anne was interrupted by a snort and a 'go figure' from Eric and a 'wasn't me' from Peter.

She continued, "Okay, enough interruptions. So, I've told the two of them that they are to bring Phillip to Barnabas. As the Ranger on this operation, he has to make sure Phillip doesn't have more information we need to know. Barnabas, when do the three of you leave?"

"Tomorrow, late afternoon. From ADAM and Frank, Simmons has the weekend off, and he's going to go backpacking."

"Bad timing, that," Scott quipped. "I believe there is a one-hundred percent chance he's going to find his nightmare in the forest." He waggled his eyebrows.

"Or two," Gabrielle added.

"Well," Dan asked. "Any way we can put cameras on the guys and beam the video back to the ship? It would make a hell of a show."

"I'll pop the popcorn," Darryl said, as a huge smile lit up his face, and Bethany Anne turned to look at him.

"Seriously?" She looked around the room to a bunch of interested faces. She turned to look at Peter, "Are you okay with this, Peter?"

"No skin off my back, if we have something that will fit my head," he answered.

"Oh, hell yeah!" Jean Dukes interrupted. "I'll rig up something for you guys."

"You'll need a video team that can put the damned helmets on your monster heads," John said. "I'll volunteer for making sure the helmets are on tight."

"I'll go, in case they need adjustments." Jean kicked in quickly.

"Stop!" Bethany Anne put up a hand, and everyone stopped their chattering. "Barnabas, are you okay with this? It's your op."

Barnabas grinned. "Yes. It allows us to bring a little experience to those here on the ships that do not get to be a part of the operations for retribution. We probably need the practice with the electronics on the Pricolici as well." He shrugged. "I can see taking John and Jean, but I wouldn't want to keep adding to the group."

"Fine, provided Nathan is also on board, then Dan needs to deal with getting this set up before tomorrow. Darryl, you are in charge of the snacks," she smiled at his surprise. "Not just popcorn. You need to make sure everyone is having a good time." He smiled when Eric laughingly pushed his shoulders.

"What about the U.S.?" Captain Thomas asked Bethany Anne.

"As in, what if they find out we did this?" She confirmed to his nod. "Well, it isn't like we haven't done operations against their people before. While I hope they don't learn who took out their operative, we have created a substantial list of his crimes going back over twenty years. I'm pretty confident they will appreciate the quiet handling of Phillip Simmons."

She smiled. "It will be hard to pin a death by mauling on us for now, at least I hope it will be." She looked at Barnabas, who nodded. "Good. So, with Simmons taken out, we'll be focusing on two others that need to first be found, then brought to justice. Stephanie Lee and the guy at the top, whoever the hell that is. I've got Frank and ADAM working hard trying to figure out using any hint, but even the minds I've tried to view, as nasty as they were, did not have a name. He, or a seriously conniving she, is well hidden."

She looked across her group. "I suspect we're in for a fight when we find him. Make sure you're ready and that your teams are ready. Dismissed." She nodded to everyone and then took a step through the Etheric to her room for a few minutes with Ashur, alone.

CHAPTER SIXTEEN

MANUFACTURING FACILITY 01, ASTEROID FIELDS

The name Bar at the End of the Universe isn't going to work." Marcus told William. "For one, we aren't near the end of any universe, so it isn't in any way, shape or form, correct."

"Maybe, but for most people, it will be funny as hell!" William countered. "As far as they are concerned, here IS the end of the universe."

"No, the End of the Universe as mentioned in that book is the End of Time, the final explosion." Marcus argued, "Not the location like at the end of a block, you monkey wrench!"

Bobcat started laughing and pointed at William and then Marcus. "It's wrench monkey, brainiac!" He slapped the table a couple of times before the two other men started chuckling about the argument and grabbed their drinks.

"So, how was your date?" William asked.

Marcus shrugged and muttered, "Well, it didn't start off

well. I took her to Paris only to find out that the taxis were on strike."

"Ohh, there went the goodnight kiss," William said.

"Damn, sorry dude," Bobcat agreed.

"Who said I failed to get a kiss?" Marcus asked, perplexed.

"Ha!" William shouted, turning to Bobcat next to him. "You owe me a hundred bucks!"

Marcus shook his head. His friends would never stop betting.

"So, how was it?" Bobcat asked, his eyes bright.

"How was what, the kiss?" Marcus asked. "A gentleman doesn't kiss and tell."

"That's fine," William interjected. "So as a non-gentleman, how was it?"

Marcus frowned at William. "You sir, are not a gentleman."

William looked at Bobcat, then pointed a finger at himself. "Did he attempt to wound me?"

"Not likely, the truth is the truth," Bobcat responded. Both he and William shrugged.

"Despite your insane level of professionalism and effort to bring me to new lows in my life," Marcus started, but then paused to wink at them. "Which I do appreciate. Honestly, I am not going to kiss and tell with the fair Lady Gabrielle." Bobcat and William laughed and high-fived each other.

"You're scared," Bobcat said.

"Hell yes," Marcus agreed and joined the other two in laughter.

"Okay, we're even," William told Bobcat, who nodded his agreement. William turned to Marcus. "The bet was a hundred if you kissed, and another hundred if you would say how it went, so double or nothing. You did kiss, which I won, but you didn't tell, so Bobcat won the second hundred." He shrugged. "I have some more work to do on you, Marcus. It's supposed to be bros before hos."

"I'm sorry," Marcus said as he patted his chest a couple of times before pulling out his phone. "I missed that last part. Here, let me hit the record button where you called Gabrielle a ho." He smiled at William mischievously.

"On second thought, beautiful vampires before bros before hos?" William popped Bobcat's arm as he snickered at him. Marcus put away his phone, smiling.

"Okay, down to business and then on to the rocket stuff," Bobcat said.

"Business before rocket things?" Marcus scrunched his face a little, "I thought the rocket stuff WAS the business?"

"No, the bar is the business, the rocket stuff is work," William clarified.

"Rocket stuff is fun, with explosions and fire," Marcus pointed out. "It's every boy's dream to get to blow stuff up and send something to outer space."

"Mine was car engines," William said.

"Combustion engines, you were just playing with explosions contained inside the metal block," Marcus told him.

They looked at Bobcat, "What? Girls for me." He shrugged. "Ever since kindergarten when I played under the boat tarps with the girl across the street. Why the hell do you think I named my helicopters like I did?"

"You didn't, we did," William told him.

"Well, they were always a 'she,' and they wouldn't leave me," Bobcat groused.

"They also ate up your money," William told him.

"Just like a girl," Bobcat agreed.

They looked at Marcus who stared back at them. "What?

You expect me to add to this? I have two failed marriages behind me and my most recent date probably took pity on me."

Bobcat smiled. "That was one hell of a pity-date."

"Yeah, I'll take two," William said, as Marcus just shook his head.

"Pity date?" Bobcat asked.

The two looked at him. "What?" Marcus inquired.

"Pity date?" Bobcat said. "The name of the bar, something like A Pity Date?" He smiled. "So, when someone asks you where you are going, you say 'I'm going to A Pity Date?"

"Well, a little better than, say, 'Andromeda,'" Marcus agreed.

"I'm going to Andromeda," William said aloud. "I like it, but it gets old quickly."

"Well, we could also call it 'Be Famous,'" Bobcat continued.

"I'm going to Be Famous?" William asked and smiled. "That's kinda funny, actually."

"I got drunk at Be Famous?" Marcus said. "It doesn't quite work."

"Well, I can't work it all out, seriously." Bobcat complained. "You two offer something, and I'll be the critic for once."

"Cool your heels, buddy," William responded. "We're just getting our groove going. Remember, we need to have a good graphic so we can sell t-shirts back on Earth. Ours is going to be the most famous bar in the Solar System."

"Yeah!" Bobcat's eyes started glowing. "Drink the beer made at All Guns Blazing!"

William looked at Marcus, who looked back at him with a smile.

"All Guns Blazing," Marcus said, "I like it."

"Yeah, strangely enough, so do I," said William. "You can make it with guns, lasers and body parts."

"And rocket engines," Marcus said.

"Yeah, but the gravitic engines don't push out a flame," William retorted.

"Tell me about it. I already get shit from a few friends. They say that it takes away from pictures when you take the flame off of the spaceships."

"Tell them it's more Zen," Bobcat offered as he picked up his glass. "To All Guns Blazing!"

The three of them clinked their glasses together.

"Hell yeah!" the three of them joined, shouting, "All Guns Blazing!"

———

An hour later, the three of them were in Jeo's office, looking at the three-dimensional ship floating in the air in the middle of the room. "So, here are the railguns projecting out of the gravitic shield. They can either fire over the shield, and suffer no potential adjustments to the accuracy of the rod's direction when going through the shield, or we can try to shoot through the shield, and they are affected in some form or fashion. We don't yet know how to open a hole to allow the slugs to go through."

"You wouldn't want an opening that the other side can exploit," Bobcat explained.

"True, but that leaves our guns exposed," Jeo said.

"Can't be helped in this case," William replied.

"What happens to the gravitic shield when you push the gun through?" Marcus asked.

"It warps and weakens for a few seconds before connecting

back around the metal," Jeo answered.

"What happens if you just put a barrel through?" Marcus asked.

"Tried it," Jeo responded. "It works well enough, but as soon as you traverse the barrel it screws up the shields horribly. The shields are not happy and can't snap back quickly enough. So, we have to put the whole gun up, so the parts that move are above the shield, exposed."

"I wonder if any aliens have figured out a solution?" Bobcat said.

"None that we've found in the designs in TOM's databases." Jeo said. "We looked. We did see some hard designs where the ships had big-ass guns through the shield, but they have to be aimed by pointing the whole ship."

"Kind of like a Kamikaze run, or you were shooting from the hip," Bobcat murmured. "That isn't a bad idea for the Pods."

"What Pods?" Marcus asked.

"The ship can hold a total of twenty-four Black Eagle Pods along with a slew of other craft," Bobcat answered. "Not enough to stop an invasion, but they would be a significant force multiplier and more than sufficient to handle anything back on Earth."

"Are we looking to save the world, or subjugate it?" Jeo asked.

"Yes," Bobcat answered to the confused Jeo. "Look, we're here to make damn sure that the Earth can make their own decisions, except when it comes to allowing us to figure out a way to save their sorry asses. I don't trust them to make that decision. Look at what happened in Colorado."

"Sorry, I didn't know those who died, and I'm kinda out here," Jeo said.

"It's okay. You haven't been dealing with this as long. The politics are as much a pain in the ass as everything else. Fucking trust me, it's a lot easier knowing where the bad guys are and bringing the pain to them."

"Another good shirt quote, write that down Marcus," William motioned to Marcus, who nodded silently as he jotted a note on the side of his tablet's digital page.

Bobcat ignored the byplay. "So, politics aside, we need to be sure we're free to build and do what's necessary. That means some powerful people want what we have and are obviously willing to take it. This ship is going to make damn sure that Bethany Anne has a hammer to bring down."

"What about the other designs I've seen, and that we've built?"

"The puck destroyers and the puck battle-cruiser?" Bobcat asked.

"Yes, those."

"That rounds out the fleet for now, but we can't have the Queen riding in those ugly sons of bitches, that's just so…" Bobcat looked around at rest of the guys. "A little help here?"

"Plebian?" Marcus offered.

"Good enough," Bobcat said and turned back to Jeo. "Plebian."

"Fine but with that black coating those things have on them, you can't see them for shit out here," Jeo said.

"Well, the battle cruiser is Captain Thomas' ship. He wasn't happy learning that he wasn't getting this one, but the teams felt that this one needed someone more in tune to how we expect her to be fought."

"So, don't make me wait! Who's getting the ship?" Jeo asked.

"Lieutenant Commander Paul Jameson," Bobcat answered.

"Is he excited?" Jeo asked.

"Well, he might be if he knew about it," Bobcat said.

"Wait, we have a ship nearing completion, and the captain doesn't know about it yet?" Bobcat shook his head. "Why not?"

"Because Jeff took his sweet-ass time with Captain Thomas and made the man happy about losing this ship to take over the puck battle cruiser. Really sucked his nuts, too," Bobcat bitched. "I prefer Bethany Anne's method of just telling them, and they're happy. But I get where Jeffrey was going. His method was just too political for me."

"It's not like Jeff has Bethany Anne's assets," Marcus said. Jeo's eyes got large when he looked at Marcus, starting to shake his head 'no!'

Marcus looked at him, perplexed, "Why are you shaking your head? She's the one with the scary red eyes and sharp teeth. Whenever she talks like that, I'm willing to become the team's janitor, and I'll like it."

Bobcat and William both winked at Jeo as they chuckled.

———

Five hours later, Marcus bolted upright in bed. "Swarms!"

———

SOUTH AMERICA

Phillip Simmons grabbed his backpack from his car and slammed the trunk. He double-checked his Gen4 Glock G20 and his Smith & Wesson M&P10. Both weapons were larger and heavier than some people would want to carry. But the

RELEASE THE DOGS OF WAR

10mm in the Glock and the 7.62x51 in the M&P10 had a lot more stopping power than someone with a 9mm and a 5.56. Being a good shot, Phillip was willing to carry less ammunition to have the extra stopping power the heavier weapons offered. While he hadn't seen anyone tailing him, he didn't want to be too lax with his safety.

For a month, he figured this would be the first time in nineteen years he missed a trip out to the mountains. It honestly didn't matter which mountains, whichever ones were close to where he was stationed. He always planned it for the nights of the full moon. The one before, during and the one after.

He pulled the backpack on and locked it down, adjusting the straps for comfort. While his car should be safe, he had made sure that there was nothing he valued in it and left it unlocked. If anyone wanted in, they would get in. Hopefully, with the car open, he wouldn't deal with having to replace broken glass.

He started walking at a slow pace and took the first trail back into the forest. He was looking to get away for a time, away from all of the politics, the troubles, and the people.

He needed to clear his head.

He made it ten miles by the time he found an out of the way location to camp. He decided that a cold camp was best for the night. After setting a couple of sensors around the campsite facing the most likely directions anyone or anything might come at him, he went into his small tent and got comfortable.

Just to think.

To think about his life and his decisions. Some good, some bad, most of them in the murky gray of the middle. Coming to the conclusion that the world could go fuck itself.

He had signed up to fight for the red, white and blue only to decide the red that was running was his men's and his own. And the blood of the other sides as well.

That had caused him to start considering what was ethical. Was it ethical to do wrong for your country because it covered one's sins or did the actions actually land on his head? If they fell to him, were his hands so red with blood they could never be cleansed? If they could not be cleansed, then what was the point? He was being judged for the sins of those above him, who were probably washing their hands in something he couldn't.

The bastards. Well, bitches too. He'd had some female bosses over the years.

So, in the end, it came down to having a job he was good at. It was also time to think about his own future and since his hands were already red? Well, so be it.

He did moonlighting work that added more blood to the mix. Once coated, it didn't matter anymore how much blood your hands were soaked in.

It only mattered what you got paid for.

With those pleasant thoughts, Phillip Simmons went to sleep.

―――――

"I'm telling you," Jean Dukes told John as they prepped Nathan and Peter in the forest. "This fabric would hold even if those two tried to bite it."

"I fucking doubt that," John told her.

Barnabas smiled to himself, shaking his head. The two of them had been quietly arguing this whole trip about weapons, armor, and munitions.

She reached into her bag and grabbed a square foot of gray fabric. "Here, smartass, see what you can do with it." She tossed it to him.

John caught the fabric and pulled on it. He took his knife out and slashed at it, but it didn't cut. Walking over to a tree, he held it against the trunk and tried to cut it a few times, top to bottom and left to right. "Well, I'm impressed so far," he told Jean. "What is it?"

"It's made by PPSS in England. Harder than Kevlar for cutting and slashing, but would probably need a second material for biting, maybe." She smirked at him.

John rather liked that grin and the challenge. He put the fabric in his pocket, "Okay, we'll test it. Where is this headgear your mad scientist mind put together?"

"What the hell..." she groused as she turned to bend over and go through her bag muttering softly to herself and finished, "... does a girl have to do to get her body noticed, not her mind?" Grabbing the two headpieces for the Pricolici with the connections for the video cameras, she straightened up.

Don't worry, John said to himself, staring at Jean's ass as she was getting into her bag. *I see it, but it was your ability to enjoy wanton destruction that caught my attention first. The body is just icing on the cake.*

———

Moments later, Simmons' eyes popped open. There was something nearby. He had heard a soft footfall. He grabbed his Glock and looked at the readouts from his sensors. Nothing showed as tripping them along the paths.

There it was again! Setting down his pistol, he grabbed

his clothes and quietly put them on, making sure to tie his boots. He didn't want to be stumbling around out there without foot protection. He grabbed his Glock and his M&P10 and cautiously looked out of the tent, using the rifle's barrel to move the flap.

Nothing.

He put a foot out and tried to keep his clothes from making too much noise as he eased out of the tent, his eyes searching in the dark for whatever woke him up. He put his pistol in its holster and gripped the rifle with both hands as he turned, looking around to see what tripped his awareness.

Once again, nothing.

Phillip Simmons.

Simmons looked for the voice. He saw nothing. He stepped into the darkness under a tree to escape the moonlight near his tent.

Ah, the heartbeat doesn't go much faster, are you a trained killer then, Phillip Simmons?

What the hell? Simmons thought. He turned to his left and his right, but caught no colors, no eyes, not a thing that shouldn't be out here with him.

Suddenly, a wolf's howl echoed in the night, and Simmons' blood ran cold. There shouldn't be wolves in this forest!

Ah, Phillip Simmons, the first has called the start of the hunt. Well, I see you are armed, you will need it.

"What the FUCK!" Simmons blurted out.

Oh, I'm so sorry, I hear your heart beating a little faster now. Didn't you know that tonight your sins have caught up with you? Or, rather, they ARE catching up with you?

Suddenly, shockingly, Simmons could hear the squealing of alarms going off in his tent.

Simmons bolted.

Fucking shit! He ran the opposite direction of where he had set the sensors and worked to keep his heartbeat down, but if the other team was capable of pushing thoughts into his head, then he was in for a fight.

But, intelligence typically meant a body, and a body always could be shot. At least, it always had been true before now, but usually, the other team didn't project thoughts into his head. He jumped a downed tree and skidded to a stop to turn around and scramble back close to the tree trunk, his rifle aimed back the way he came.

And waited, his heartbeat suddenly loud in his ears as the blood pulsed through his body. He willed his body to relax as best as he could, and it started to work.

Then another howl, a deeper one from behind him.

Simmons turned to face behind when the first howl came again, this time, closer, along the trail he had just run down.

Fuck!

He scrambled up and considered his options quickly before deciding that between them was not a good strategic location. He slid back across the tree and started jogging the way he came, his gun aimed out front as he jogged back. He didn't know which wolf was bigger, but his crocodile brain was telling him that a deeper howl meant larger wolf.

A wolf, once again, that wasn't supposed to be anywhere near here.

Simmons was searching to his left and his right down low, looking for a wolf that would be stalking him from the shadows. He was not looking up when an arm with a clawed hand snaked down to grab his rifle and about yanked his arm from its socket as it pulled it out of his grip. The gun fired twice before it came free. He spun around and landed in the dirt.

Simmons rolled quickly to the side and pulled his Glock, breathing hard as his eyes frantically searched the limbs above him.

Fucking shit! That was no wolf.

I'd run, Phillip Simmons, the Wechselbalg aren't known for suffering idiots that lay there waiting for them for very long.

Simmons got up and ran. He didn't look in the brush anymore, and he hoped to God there was nothing in the limbs above him. He just ran.

A few moments later, his sensors beeped again as he passed them running in the opposite direction.

Seconds later, a dark body, with yellow eyes gleaming, bolted through the small clearing, jumping across his campsite in a leap of over twenty feet before disappearing into the darkness. A second ran in around the tent and followed the first.

The chase was on!

Simmons heard both howls behind him, and a few moments later, they were closer. He aimed his pistol behind him and fired off two shots in the direction of the howls before turning back around and watching his footing.

Damned dead fool he would be if he slipped or tripped.

He holstered his pistol and started to use both arms to climb a small but steep incline when he heard the growls behind him. He was almost to the top, so he pulled hard and rolled over, glancing behind him for just a second.

That second was enough for him to see two beings from folklore, werewolves, here in South America. This time, their howls assaulted his ears. He yanked his pistol back out and turned towards the lip, moving forward to aim over the side.

But they weren't there.

Phillip Simmons knew utter despair. He knew he wouldn't

be making it out of this forest alive. The enemy had come for him, and he wasn't prepared. He snorted to himself. Who the fuck was going to prepare for werewolves to come after them anyway? "It's just me, and I'm all out of silver bullets," he mumbled.

Phillip Simmons pointed the gun towards his head. "Hell if I'm going to suffer…" His gun hand was grabbed in a clenching strength he couldn't fight, and a guttural voice spoke behind him, "Yesss, You willll suffferrr Philllippp Sss-simmonnnnns." The pistol barked once into the night, whizzing off into a tree some distance away. "Besidesss, sssillverss burnns but isssn't deattthhh sssentannncee."

Phillip screamed as the bones in his hand were crushed between the anvil of the gun and the fist holding his hand.

"Yyyou wonnn't beee neeeding thiissss." The pistol was pulled from his broken and crushed hand. Simmons was in agony as he tried to cradle the pain-wracked hand and turned around to see three figures standing above him. Two with yellow eyes and one with red that made Phillip Simmons forget his hand for just a moment.

"Welcome to Judgment Night, Phillip Simmons," the vampire said. "My name is Barnabas, and I am your judge."

CHAPTER SEVENTEEN

CLAN TEMPLE NEAR SHENNONGJIA PEAK, HUBEI

Stephanie Lee allowed her mind to rest, to block out the thoughts of the outside world, the fear of seeing her father again after the long absence.

The failure she felt in her bones.

I come, her inner voice spoke.

And I am here, a pair of voices spoke back, in harmony but also separate. She could sense a higher voice and a deeper as if she was talking to both a male and a female at one time.

Why do I sense two? she asked, confused.

Because we are two in one, but we speak as two until you decide which works for you. With a decision, the voice will become one.

I choose then not to decide, as I prefer to remember always that there are two, she said. Confident in her decision.

Yes, you are the one, the voices replied back, *and we have been waiting for you.*

The one what? she asked.

The one to take up the mantle, and none too soon. We sense the five have a champion, and it is strong, perhaps too strong. We need to move forward, but we have not had a vessel to pour ourselves into yet.

Why? What about my father?

Too attached to family, the voices said, *and we thought we had time yet, centuries. Yes, if we had centuries, you would be unstoppable.*

I do not live for centuries, she argued.

Oh, but now you will, the male voice said, as the female voice added, *With us to guide you.*

What do I need to do? Stephanie Lee asked, *and what am I giving up?*

You give up nothing that you would not give up already to seek that which was waiting for you here when you left. You surrender your freedom to be a nobody in order to rule all that you see, the two voices said together.

No longer, the male voice said, *will you bow before others. Never again.*

Agreed, the female voice added. *You are the Leopard Empress and all will bow before you.*

Stephanie Lee's lips, composed in her meditation, still cracked the barest of a smile.

———

WASHINGTON D.C. USA

When the President stepped into the room, the door closing behind him, he noticed two rolls of Tums waiting for him. George didn't bother hiding the trash from his, already eaten with the empty wrapper on the table.

"I take it by the Tums sacrifice waiting for me here, and the roll that already died for you, this is not a good update?" the President asked as he sat down and started unrolling the Tums, grabbing the top two.

"Well, maybe," George waffled. "Depends on whether you are okay that Phillip Simmons down in South America is dead."

The President stopped chewing and looked at his secret liaison. "By the way you're telling me, I take it the death isn't cut and dried?" he asked, grabbing a third Tums tablet.

"No, it isn't," George agreed. "He went on an annual backpack trip and found himself dinner for a pack of carnivorous creatures."

"So, no bullets, no knife wounds?" the President asked for confirmation.

George made a face. "No, but the injuries he suffered aren't natural, Mr. President, not at all." He tapped a finger on the table. "Plus, one of his arms had been pulled damn near off. No carnivore with the claw marks that were found on his body would have the appendages necessary to do such a thing."

"Why not?" the President asked. "Grab his wrist in their teeth and pull, right? Or shake his body around?"

"Yes, that would work, but there aren't teeth marks to support that theory," George said.

"You know, you're starting to get a little weird about this whole TQB thing," the President said. "Are you really suggesting that they have modified wolves under their command? Genetically changed to be super-animals or something?" The President looked at George like maybe he was going a little too far in his seeking to blame everything on TQB.

RELEASE THE DOGS OF WAR

"Why would you say wolves, Mr. President?" George asked, trying to get back on track with his discussion.

"Because you mentioned them before, outside the TQB complex in Colorado."

"Well, you're right. The marks might have come from a wolf and if so they were really, really huge." George decided to skip the part of walking on their hind legs, and added, "Frankly wolves don't exist in that part of South America, so…" He let his comment drop. Better to plant a seed of doubt at this point.

The President nodded his understanding.

George continued, "Second on our list, we have a strange occurrence out in the desert north of Las Vegas. A Johann Pecora rented a vehicle in Las Vegas, which was found at a small ranch next to the mountains. When the car wasn't returned on time, it was located via the transponder. The cops went out to check and found two empty mobile homes. They looked around, found a trail and followed it. At the end of the trail was a dead older man, with a pistol that had been fired, laying half in and half out of a shallow grave. His throat had been torn out by something with claws. Johann Pecora was nowhere to be found. The car hadn't even been turned off, it ran out of gas. The police found a small aluminum case with twenty-five thousand dollars in casino chips lying on a kitchen table in one of the mobile homes. It had been opened but left there. They also found the kitchen sink door open and a safe. The safe was closed and locked. We don't know what's in it, yet."

"So, tell me why this is TQB?" the President asked as he gave up trying to be reserved and just opened up the rest of his Tums and started chewing the tablets. "Next time, you might bring me the original flavor so I don't eat them like candy, George."

"I hear you, but I think I'll disobey that suggestion, Mr. President." George smiled. "I bring it up because we have what may be a hit, but the original target left his money and left a car to sit there, idling, while he walked out into the desert. That seems fishy to me."

"Everything is fishy to you. It's your job," the President said dryly.

"Then I'm perfectly suited to it," the general smiled back and said, "So, moving on, we have Johann missing and the presumed hit man dead. No one walks that far out of the desert anymore."

"Helicopter?" the President asked.

"Possible, but he would have had to have walked a distance away. There wasn't enough dust thrown around to suggest a chopper had been nearby."

"Your gender stereotyping is showing, it could have been a woman," the President teased.

"Great, a black widow among us. Wonderful!" George replied, rolling his eyes. He closed one folder and pushed it aside to open another. "So, we also have some images from the spy satellite we put up last week aimed out to the Asteroid Belt to check on what TQB is doing out there. The few half-assed shots we've been able to take so far with all of the damned interference show that they have a few assets. Plus, a pretty disturbing shot of what could be a big-ass spaceship."

"Define 'big-ass' if you would?" the President asked his liaison.

"As big as an aircraft carrier?" George answered. "Larger, perhaps. We don't have a full shot of the body."

"What the hell do they need an aircraft carrier in outer space for? No countries have one that TQB needs to worry about."

"Well, not yet," George said. "But if TQB has one, it will be another arms race for us to get our own."

"Dammit, George," the President said, his voice rising a little. "This better not be another backdoor effort to increase the military's budget."

George chuckled. "No, although I thought about it. I realized I won't need to push you. If this huge son of a bitch shows up, I won't need to ask you for anything, Congress will be throwing money our way to build something."

"And trying to get TQB to give up their technology," the President mused.

George's eyes widened, then he reached across the table to the President's surprise to grab the other roll of Tums. The President watched the general break the roll in half and put one portion back in front of him before opening the other and eating two tablets. George looked up at his ultimate commander. "I hadn't thought about that. If those idiots up on the hill do something catastrophically stupid, I'm going to my bug-out hole in the Ozarks."

"You really fear TQB that much?" the President asked his advisor who had just grabbed two more Tums and popped them in his mouth. "Guess so," the President finished while grabbing his remaining half-roll to pull closer to himself. "Okay, what else is on your agenda?"

"Cargo," George answered him.

"Say again?" the President asked, surprised by the change in topic.

"Cargo," George said. "We're having a bitch of a time tracking everything they're shipping off-world, but if we assume that we're catching even fifty percent, then they are sending an enormous amount of cargo."

"Where is it going?" the President asked, surprised that

this topic wasn't causing him an ulcer. "I mean, they are a business so buying and procuring cargo isn't a strange or terrifying turn of events, George."

"Maybe, maybe not," the general answered. "We see what looks like a really large spaceship being built. How the hell did it come about so quickly? It takes us five years to build a Gerald Ford class aircraft carrier. That's with highly trained people doing it. What the hell are they using to get something together so fast and how the hell are they designing it? How long have they been planning this?"

George grabbed another Tums. "TQB is over a thousand companies, some of which have been in business for hundreds of years."

The President laughed. "C'mon George, you're talking as if they're the Illuminati or something!"

George laughed with him. "No, no they aren't the Illuminati, sir. I'm not saying that." He smiled at the President, waving both hands back and forth in the air in a no gesture.

Because I would know if they were part of us, he thought to himself.

CLAN TEMPLE NEAR SHENNONGJIA PEAK, HUBEI

Stephanie left her room, walking towards the sanctuary where she was sure she would find her father, finally.

The voices had decreed it.

She took the turns through the rock tunnels, since most of the compound was inside the mountain, hidden from the outside world for centuries. Only those in highest ranks of the clan ever knew of the inner complex, unless you were in the family of the clan leader.

Stephanie used the back hallways to make it to the temple. She exited out of a little-used door into a darkened hallway that turned left for ten feet before entering the main hallway into the temple. She walked into the large room again, the incense and candles reminding her of her dreams.

The dreams of people, and animals, spirits and voices.

The Leopard Empress.

She strode forward, sure of her destiny while also trying to still the child's fear inside her. The images she remembered now that she was back in the temple were frightening. Changelings, people transforming from human to animals, stalking through the night, killing foes and retreating. The power of the clan disappearing as technology and cities took over her country.

Not retreating, she corrected herself, waiting. Awaiting the right time, the right person.

Her.

The voices had decreed the message and she had accepted it. It was time her clan rose from the shadows and fought again before it was too late. Before they lacked the power to make a choice in the future.

She walked past the main altar and around it, to the small area behind where her father would occasionally stand to fill up the incense burners. There was a lever where her dream said it would be. Moving the catch, a small part of the wall disengaged, allowing her to pull it open. There was no one in the temple so there was no witness to see the young, attractive woman slip into the wall and disappear.

It took Stephanie at least ten minutes to feel her way down the pitch-black hallway. She would step, make sure her foot was secure as she reached out, keeping the wall to the right under her hand. Finally, she saw a small bluish glow ahead of her. In another minute, there was enough light for her to see the gray floor and her feet.

She was able to move faster then.

In another thirty seconds, she let her hand drop as she strode forward, aware that this was the hallway from her dream. She entered a stone room, some fifty feet long, twenty wide and maybe twelve tall. It was glowing with a blue phosphorescence that came from the walls.

"Beauuutiiffuulll, isn't it?" A voice, harsh and raspy, coming from her right. She jerked around quickly and took a step backward when she saw a… being. A man, yet a tiger staring down at her, its eyes sizing her up but not aggressively. Her brain tried to keep her from running in fear.

He was almost six and a half feet tall, much taller than her normally shorter countrymen. Stephanie noticed that he was as handsome as he was deadly looking. She looked into the eyes as he stood there, arms crossed, looking down at her.

There was something about his eyes, those dark eyes that reminded her of something, or someone. Her eyes widened in dawning understanding.

"Father?" she asked the being.

"Yessss," the Tiger man bowed his head slightly. "To you, my daaaughter, but alllssso your Prrriest and nowww yoo-ourr Aaahddvisssor."

Stephanie walked up closer to the figure who stayed still as she approached. She put a hand out and felt his arm muscles, the hair slick under her touch. She moved her hand to his chest when he suddenly started cough-grunting, and she yanked her hand back quickly. "No," he said, "thhhat ticklesss, notthhing morrre." There seemed to be an amused glint in its eye.

She smiled. "I think that's enough, I don't want to be touching my own father like this, but this body, your body is exquisite!" She smiled. "Is this what was hidden from me, for those many years? This is what I ran away from?"

The being opened its arms. "Yesss, my daughter. But you have returrrned, and returrrned as my Empressss," he said. "Be hhhappy, allll happennned asss it was forrrretolld. If my Emmmprrress allowwws it, I will chaaange baaack to my hh-humann body?" he asked. She nodded and turned around. She wasn't slow to figure out that her father would be naked when he was human again.

She'd wait until there was another person to watch change from this form to human before she satiated that curiosity.

A few moments later, her father's usual voice greeted her. "How is my flower?"

She turned with joy to see him, clad in a simple robe and smiling at her, the blue light reflecting from his eyes, his arms open. She hugged him, feeling his touch for the first time in eight years and it felt good.

It felt right.

It felt like the first chapter was over, and now the next chapter had begun in her future.

CHAPTER EIGHTEEN

MANUFACTURING FACILITY 01, ASTEROID FIELDS

Okay, can I be the first to say this thing is fucking huge," Bobcat said as they walked from the front of the ship towards the back. "I need a damned cart."

"We have those," Jeo said looking at the astonished Bobcat. "I figured you'd want to see everything and stick your nose in it, so why bother with a cart?"

"Bother already, man!" Bobcat told him. "Shit dude, my legs are going to… well, do nothing, actually. I guess I'm fine physically, but I'm bored out of my mind at the moment. Grab us a scooter and let's go!"

Five minutes later, they entered the bunkroom. Bobcat got off the scooter and stretched. "Next time I drive. You drive like my grandmother."

"Hey, in my defense, I'm not a pilot," Jeo argued.

"I know, you're an engineer, and you drive like one, too." Bobcat retorted as he stepped up to the door and stopped, perplexed. "What, isn't this going to swoosh?" Bobcat looked at Jeo, who was rolling his eyes in exasperation.

"No," Jeo replied. "You get no swoosh." He placed his palm on a circle next to the door, and it split down the center to open. "No automatic opening right now except in a few really trafficked areas that still need closed doorways unless someone is walking through. Otherwise, all doors stay closed all the time in case we get a hole somewhere."

"Bring those doors back out, but halfway," Bobcat asked. Jeo played with the controls, and the two doors slid halfway out. Bobcat looked at the connections, "Nice work. So, if you get a depressurization from inside the room, they pull this way, compressing the seal on one side. If the depressurization comes from the hallway, then the reverse is true. Sweet." Bobcat slid between the doors to enter the larger room. It was an oval. "Why an oval?" Bobcat turned back to Jeo, who had fixed the doors, and they slid shut behind him as he entered.

"The plans called for a more organic feel. Research suggests that humans need to live in places that aren't all straight lines and corners." He shrugged. "Not my area of expertise, but it allowed us to alter the plans. Plus, the few non-engineers who have been in here say it has a nice feel."

Bobcat looked around the room. "Needs a few potted plants," he remarked as he counted the doors. "Eight rooms?"

Jeo shook his head and walked over to one of the doors, "No, sixteen. Dual sleep chambers. The area out here is for general socializing." He hit the circle at the top. The door slid open, while a small hole also appeared on both sides of the wall with a rod. "This is for the person who uses the top. The step here is for a shorter person who wants to step up. Otherwise, they can grab that bar above and slide in, or crawl in, their choice."

Bobcat walked over and said, "Seems like a pain in the ass to me." He put his right foot in the hole and easily grabbed the pole to slide into the cubicle. His voice came out a little muffled, "Fucking nice, though! Shit, you can sit up in here. Shelves, hell, even a place to stand if you need it."

"Yes, that's blocked out of yours for the person below. If you need to do some sort of standing, you have eight square feet of space." Jeo stuck his head in. "This way, we barely use more space than a shared compartment, but it works to keep it private."

"Works until you need three," Bobcat said. "Then what?"

"We build a bigger ship?" Jeo answered. "Hell if I know. We're just proud of the small things we're doing here."

"Yeah, you really should be," Bobcat said as he played with a small door. "Holy shit, a six-pack altar."

"What?" Jeo asked, trying to see around the corner to find Bobcat pointing at something out of his view.

"A six-pack altar," Bobcat said before shutting the door. "A fridge you philistine!" He started sliding on the bed again as Jeo stepped back as Bobcat slid out of the cubicle. "That's actually a nice little cubbyhole," he admitted.

"I like to think so," Jeo agreed.

"What does the Captain's room look like?" Bobcat asked.

"I should have shown you when we were near the bridge, but it looks very executive."

"And Bethany Anne's?"

"Palatial," Jeo said.

"Her special room?"

"For at least two hundred pairs of shoes," Jeo agreed.

"Not that room," Bobcat snorted. "Although if we can increase that, we might want to. I mean her appearing room."

"Yup," Jeo said, "Room for eighteen if they're friendly."

Bobcat thought about that for a second. "We need to see if there can be a backup room, just in case we need more. I'd hate to be the eighteenth son of a bitch and find my elbow or something else in a wall when we rematerialize," he said.

"Ah, good point," Jeo said. Neither wanted to find out what would happen if the molecules merged.

"Ok," Bobcat stopped looking around. "I've seen everything I want to see, when can I take her out?"

"Come again?" Jeo asked, surprised.

"Take her out? You know, sea trials?" Bobcat responded before rethinking his comment. "Okay, space trials?"

"But half of her insides are still open. We haven't confirmed all of her gravity engines are connecting properly, and we have no supplies!" Jeo told him.

Bobcat barked, "Samantha?"

Samantha's holo-video head showed on the port wall, "Yes, Bobcat?"

"Can we take this hunk of metal out right now?"

"Negative, Bobcat. It will take a minimum of seventy-six hours on our projected timeline to be able to move."

Bobcat looked over to Jeo, "You have seventy-two." He winked at the stupefied man and walked out.

Jeo heard him yell from the hallway, "Hey, I'm taking your cart!"

Jeo waved towards the disembodied voice and turned to sit on the floor, "Samantha, bring up the project plan, we need to adjust some things."

"I understand, Jeo. How many levels of padding do you want me to pull from the plan?"

"If we pull all of it, how many hours does that buy us?"

"We can make minimum requirement to get underway in forty-seven hours," she told him.

"Ok, let's see what we can add back in so we aren't at a minimum when we hit seventy-two hours."

"Yes, Jeo."

"And Samantha?"

"Yes?"

"Transfer your core intelligence to this vessel, leave a copy behind for me. You are now the E.I. of this ship until Bethany Anne overrides it."

"Yes, Jeo."

———

TABITHA'S HOUSE, SOUTH AMERICA

"Sneaky?" Gabrielle asked Tabitha.

"Yes, sneaky!" she replied.

They were down in her workout room. She told the Tontos to leave them alone when she told them Gabrielle was coming for a visit. It was going to be girl talk. She snickered when the two men looked at each other, and she could see the agreement in their eyes to be somewhere else.

Probably anywhere else.

Tabitha had called Gabrielle and asked her for advice, and help. So, Gabrielle jumped in a Pod and came over an hour later with Ashur.

Tabitha had met them out on the lawn as the Pod came to rest. "Heya big guy!" Tabitha smiled seeing the big German Shepherd, who chuffed his greeting and allowed Tabitha to hug him before continuing to the kitchen. Tabitha watched the quickly receding dog before turning to Gabrielle with a question on her face.

"He hasn't eaten in a while. He was waiting for dinner

when I asked him if he wanted to come visit you. So, he's probably heading for the kitchen."

Tabitha grabbed one of the two bags that Gabrielle had brought along and gave her a quick hug. "And a heya to you too, big sis."

"Watch it, punk."

"Hey, it wasn't older sis!" Tabitha grinned, then added, "As in older, older, really much older…"

"The beatings only get worse as your disrespect continues," Gabrielle told her.

"Did I say older?" Tabitha stopped. "I meant wiser and charming, and let's not forget forgiving, too," she finished and Gabrielle snorted.

"I'll bet, so what's eating at you, Grasshopper?" she asked as they walked towards the house while the Pod disappeared back into the sky.

"I'd rather wait to tell you inside," she said. "Downstairs in the workout room."

"Ok, works for me. Let's check in on the four-legged trash compactor and then we'll get settled in," Gabrielle agreed.

Sure enough, Ashur had two of the Elites, the brothers Kouki and Shin, offering him food and he was eating what they were offering. "Make sure he's not being a glutton," Gabrielle told them as the women left Ashur eating.

Gabrielle unzipped the two bags after dropping them on the workout room floor. "So, you're continually getting your ass kicked. What did you expect?"

"Oh, I don't know, a draw maybe?" Tabitha said. "Look, I get that I'm not anywhere near their skill or awareness, but I know I've got the potential. I've studied like a whore on crack. Believe me, when you're constantly healing, it becomes an obsession to get better, fast. One of the reasons I was such a good hacker was it mattered to me for protection." Tabitha sighed in exasperation. "Now, my teammates are doing it to me."

"It's for a good cause," Gabrielle said as she pulled out two smaller swords. She casually tossed them both to Tabitha, who reached for them but realized they weren't going to be hitting her hands correctly and jumped out of the way.

"What the hell?" Tabitha said as the swords landed on the soft flooring behind her. "Are you trying to cut my ass up already?" Tabitha glared at Gabrielle.

"No, just testing you, Grasshopper," she said as she went to retrieve the blades. "It's what I thought. You haven't tapped into your true speed yet. Probably because these guys aren't pushing theirs either. Although, I'd wait a little while until you tell them that," Gabrielle said.

"How long, and what am I not telling them?" Tabitha asked, confused.

"Don't tell them until after you kick their ass a couple of times to get their attention, then you need to let them know, or you suffer the chance they could need the ability in an op and not have the benefit. So, you should tell them soon." She set the two swords down by one of the bags to pull out fifteen wooden dowel rods, each nine inches long. She turned around to Tabitha and said, "Here, catch." When the rods were tossed right at Tabitha, the startled target froze for a second before doing her best to catch as many as possible.

Which was five.

"Hey!" Tabitha exclaimed holding up her five rods. "Five isn't bad, right?"

"I swear, I owe Bethany Anne a huge apology," Gabrielle muttered to herself. "Yes," she told Tabitha, "It's bad. You have the ability to catch all fifteen and even throw them back at me. Now, pick up the sticks you missed and toss them back."

Tabitha frowned but turned around to pick up the sticks that were scattered about, asking, "Okay, are you about to pull some sort of Bethany Anne juju on me?" She grabbed the last stick and held them in a bunch in her hand. She was standing about twelve feet from Gabrielle and asked, "Ready?"

"Yesterday already," Gabrielle answered.

Tabitha frowned, and her hand shot out, tossing all of the sticks at Gabrielle, who seemed to blur into action, and three of the sticks came back at Tabitha who yelled, "Ow! Fuck! Shit!" and then continued hopping around thinking she needed to be dodging some more. When nothing came at her, she finally looked again at Gabrielle, who had the twelve remaining in her raised hand.

Gabrielle's frown was on full display. "How are you supposed to learn how to do this if you aren't paying attention?" she asked Tabitha. "I told you, you have it in you to catch them and throw them back."

Tabitha pressed her lips together and nodded once. "I've been acting like friend Tabitha, not student Tabitha." She walked over to Gabrielle. "I apologize. I was hoping that you had some mystic words and a spell to cast on my head, and all would be complete."

"Fat chance," Gabrielle said. "I'm going to show you an advantage which will help you out against any but the top vampires and most Weres, except the Pricolici for a while until your fighting skills get better. If you have to fight some of the best, then use your speed to run like hell, got it?"

Tabitha nodded. "Got it. So, is there a beginner's stick throwing class?"

Gabrielle smiled. "Why, yes there is." She dropped fourteen sticks on the floor, "So, let's start with speed enhancement 101."

"Wait, what did you make me do?" Tabitha asked.

Gabrielle scrunched up her face. "Well, since throwing shit at me was one of the first things Bethany Anne did when I didn't listen, I consider that class zero, or better yet, class get your shit together," she replied.

"Oh," Tabitha said. "So what's really going on?"

"Well, has anyone told you about the energy, the Etheric, running through you?" Gabrielle asked. Tabitha shook her head. "What wicked plan is Bethany Anne concocting now that she didn't mention that much?" Gabrielle wondered aloud.

"She told me I wouldn't need blood if I didn't extend myself," Tabitha offered.

"Yeah, there's that, too. I'd call and ask her, but I don't know what she's doing at the moment..." Gabrielle stopped when Tabitha put up a finger. Gabrielle raised an eyebrow when Tabitha tapped her head.

My Queen?

Tabitha? You can call me Bethany Anne, the my Queen stuff can be for public events or something. What's up? Tell me this isn't about an outfit.

No, I have Gabrielle here, and she's wondering why I wasn't told about the Etheric running through me?

Oh, that's because I wanted to wait until you were so frustrated that you asked for help. It's much easier to teach someone when they have an incentive to learn. Have you had your ass beaten enough? Bethany Anne's amusement colored the connection.

Yes! Thank you very much. Tabitha's grouchiness colored hers.

Good! Gabrielle will teach you, and I'll double check later. I'll have to ask Akio if he wants the Elites with you to also be taught. Once you improve, it will be tough for you to continue learning with such a huge advantage over them.

Oookay? Tabitha was confused. *Just how much faster am I going to be?*

Than a human? A lot. Than say, Ryu? Still significantly faster. Enough that it will be tough for him once you get it under control. But you need to be careful when you hit at speed. The changes in your structure allow you to handle it, but it can still be pretty painful.

Great, with every positive comes a negative, Tabitha said. *Whatever happened to only positive effects?*

Not a clue. If you figure it out, come and tell me, Bethany Anne replied. *Because I'd like to know the same thing. Remember to watch your energy usage, unless you want to learn how to drink blood.*

That's still not high on my list of shit I want to do today, Tabitha replied.

No? Okay, then you won't be able to stay at speed for very long. So make sure you pay attention to how much power you have. The more you retain, like a battery, the more you'll be able to use before either quitting, or sucking blood.

Okay, thanks. Tabitha said.

The connection dropped.

"Bethany Anne said it had to do with a willingness to learn. Until I was highly motivated, I didn't need to gain the skill," Tabitha told Gabrielle.

"Yeah, that sounds about right. She had to kick my ass to get me to want to learn. So, Ryu has done the same for you."

"Say instead that he kicked it over and over again," Tabitha replied, rubbing her butt. "Day and night." She pointed to three spots in the room, "There, there and over there. Fucking everywhere. I'm ready for some Ryu-ass payback."

Gabrielle chuckled. "Well then, Grasshopper, it's time you learned speed and got a little of your own back." Gabrielle put her stick up in the air. "Now turn around and when I say now, I want you to turn around as quickly as possible and grab this stick. Ready?" Gabrielle asked. Tabitha nodded as she turned away and prepared herself.

"Go!"

CHAPTER NINETEEN

PLA GENERAL STAFF HEADQUARTERS, BEIJING

Four men stepped into the darkened and quiet room, nodding to each other. No names were to be used, but any agreement reached would be put into effect.

After the appropriate respect had been shown, the naval representative spoke, "It is not acceptable that we not respond to this intrusion to our vessel," he hissed. "Why has no command been given?"

The one who represented the political side acknowledged the complaint and turned to the cyber-command representative.

"We have tried, multiple times, and various ways. They are using technology we cannot reach, much less hack," he said. "We hope they have weaknesses in their systems, but we need to get into them for anything to work."

"What happened to our agreements with the commercial group?" the intelligence representative asked the political one.

"The attack was a failure. Just like the ship they purchased from us, the men sent in with the nuclear bomb were ineffective."

"We should not have trusted those in business with a military solution," the naval representative responded. "I am still unhappy with the loss of our ship and the supposed way it was defeated."

"We have video," started the cyber representative before he was cut off.

"We have secondhand video. We do not know if it is raw or not, nor do we have a proper test against this group."

"They have ships that fly," the political representative said. "How is it you wish to test them?"

"I'm not sure yet. I think we need to bring a submarine under their ships. The torpedoes can be sent out and aimed upward. That should cause a response if we are going to receive one." The naval representative continued, "If they do not respond, then I suggest we bring our ships back closer to theirs. We have them at that point, forcing them to let our ships in or threatening to hole them from below."

"You would try to sink them?" the political representative asked.

"They are trying to sink us," the naval representative snapped back. "This is yin and yang."

"How exactly is this yin and yang?" the intelligence official asked. "They have already been attacked by a Chinese ship. I understand that it wasn't a Chinese Navy ship, but it does seem logical they might not want your ships that close."

"This attack on our sovereign ship cannot and should not be allowed to occur without response," the naval representative stated. "I would rather give up my commission than allow this. Our sailors need to know they have the backing that is willing to see the fight through to the end." He emphatically knocked on the table with each of his points. "No one, not even the Americans, dare do this to us!"

"So, you are not suggesting this is just an American group, now?" the political representative asked. "Before, you were sure that it was just the Americans using it as a front."

"No. I admit, I was misinformed," the naval representative said. "Both of the leaders on the business side are American military or American intelligence, we believe. There is much argument between U.S. and Romania about the head, Ms. Bethany Anne. She is also the one we suspect was in the leading plane in the French battle."

"Where is she right now?" the political representative asked.

"We believe on one of the two ships, but with their Pods leaving frequently, and at their exit speeds, it is impossible to keep track. Now, she has cars that can fly, too. Ferrari F12berlinettas."

"Bitch," the intelligence representative said.

The men chuckled in agreement for a moment before resuming. "If you undertake to strike this group, if it does not go as you say, you will suffer much and will leave the service in disgrace. Do you feel this is the path the navy must take?" the political representative asked, his hands folded together in front of him.

Three men looked at the naval representative, who eyed them all, then sharply nodded his head in the affirmative.

"Then we are done here until your action is completed." The political representative stood to leave while the three others bowed slightly until he was out of the room.

Once the door shut the naval representative said into the quiet of the chamber, "I need information."

Ten minutes later, the naval representative nodded to the two others and stepped out of the small room. The cyber representative turned to the man from intelligence and asked in a whispered tone, "What do you think?"

"I think," the intelligence representative replied just as quietly, "We are going to have a new naval representative soon."

The cyber representative nodded his agreement.

————

MANUFACTURING FACILITY 01, ASTEROID FIELDS

Bobcat strode onto the bridge, seeing the fifteen faces around him. "Thank you all for showing up for our little ride," he said. "Take a seat, any seat."

"For this episode, we are going to have Samantha, the Electronic Intelligence, guide everything. So, we are touching nothing, and if you do touch something, it won't work. What it will do is piss me off and the walk home is a bitch. So don't touch anything."

He looked around. "I've built, and rebuilt, helicopters and other ships all of my life. If you want to find out what's good and what's hokey? Well, turn on the engine. Not that I would usually fly the bird, mind you, but in this case, we aren't going very far, and we sure as hell aren't going to have a gravity problem."

He looked over the bridge. "I've asked you all here because you are in charge of the different departments on this ship. So, you should have the opportunity to say you were here when the first spaceship, an actual big-ass spaceship, was ever tested. Your names will go down in the history books." He looked around finishing with a smirk. "One way or another."

"Samantha?" Bobcat said.

Her face came on the forward viewscreen. "Yes, Captain?"

"Take us out using preprogrammed locations under Gemini, Gemini Alpha. Minimum power after making sure everything is disconnected and all personnel are safely away from the ship except those who are on station."

"Yes, sir. All personnel are safely away except for the ten Tug Pods stationed around the ship."

"Good." Bobcat said. "For everyone's edification, those Tug Pods will be with us the whole trip. If something goes wonky, you can bet my ass, and therefore your ass, is not walking back." He smiled to the chuckles around the bridge.

"Let's go, Samantha," he said, and the screens lit up with outside views from all around the exterior of the ship. Everyone watched as the ship ever so slowly started moving into space. The ship was turned and aimed for a straight shot out of the dock with no asteroids for a hundred kilometers in any direction.

Two minutes later Samantha said, "We are at Alpha one location, Captain."

"Good, please synchronize with the Pods so they can keep up and let's go to minimal power." Bobcat switched over to another channel. "How are we doing, Marcus?"

Marcus came on. "Bobcat, or Captain, whatever, we're fine. The engines all seem to be connecting well, and the tuning effort was accomplished easily."

"Very good. How fast are you comfortable pushing the engines?" Bobcat asked.

Marcus paused a second. "I'm okay to twenty percent power. There's a hiccup at thirty-three percent, and I'm not sure what's going to happen. We still have the math to figure out."

"I understand, keep it below thirty-three," Bobcat clicked off his connection.

"Okay Samantha, the maximum is twenty-five percent. Take the acceleration up in one percent increments each minute until we reach twenty percent. At that time, switch to three-minute increments per percentage point."

"Understood. It will take us thirty-five minutes to reach twenty-five percent power." Samantha responded.

"That's fine, let's see what this baby can do, shall we, Samantha?" Bobcat smiled.

———

The lights in the bridge were at half-power. "The fluctuation, Marcus, happened at twenty-eight percent, not thirty-three," Bobcat said. "I was well under your thirty-three percent cut-off!"

"Well, we wouldn't have lost power out in space if you hadn't pushed it," Marcus's irritated voice told him over the speaker. "Now we've been towed back to the shipyard in disgrace!"

"Look, get over yourself, Marcus," Bobcat said. "My job is to make sure this ship is safe. I'm going to risk a little to make damned sure Bethany Anne isn't risking a lot. We're safe, the ship is safe, the only thing bruised is your ego. Don't be so proud you can't see the goal, man."

There was a huff on the other side of the line. "Okay. Maybe there's some truth to what you're saying. But, dammit

Bobcat, this isn't rocket science."

Bobcat smiled. "That's why I have the Solar System's only human gravitic engine expert working on it, not a rocket scientist!"

"I…" There was a pause on the line. "Sometimes Bobcat, you are a pain in my ass."

"Count on it, Marcus, count on it." Bobcat clicked off the speaker.

———

Six hours later, Bobcat was with William in what was nicknamed Destruction Alley.

William turned to Bobcat. "So, they have a few ideas about a swarm concept Marcus came up with."

"I understand he had a bad dream or something and woke up thinking about it?" Bobcat said.

"Hell if I know. Who can say, strange is the mind of a scientist and all of that." William replied. "But the concept is interesting. We took a few pucks and started playing with the gravity when they got close and started trying to disrupt the gravitic shield by alternating the gravity fields on the pucks."

"How the hell do you do that?" Bobcat asked, scratching his chin. "I mean, gravity is used to move yourself in a direction. If the puck starts to change its gravity, wouldn't it go in a different direction and fly off into space?"

"Yes, and no," William answered. "We have to pull multiple pucks together and connect them. For example," William pulled over four three-inch diameter pucks, each about an inch thick on his desk. "If you put one in the middle, and connect three on the outside, then the three can keep it on track while the center throws a different gravitational pulse."

"Does it work?" Bobcat asked looking at the circle with the three pucks around it. "And how many can you put into a circle?"

"Depends on the diameters. We're still working on the whole answer, but the short answer is, it does fuck up the calculations and mess up the shield."

"Enough?" Bobcat asked. "Enough to get a slug through?"

"Maybe, but watch this video. We just did this while you were out gallivanting around."

"Hey, I could have blown up out there," Bobcat argued. "So, my life was on the line and all of that. Oh, and Marcus' too, and others, come to think of it."

"What was the chance of that happening?" William asked while raising an eyebrow.

"Significant," Bobcat replied.

"Significantly how much?" William pressed.

"Well, somewhere between being bitten by a dog and a lightning strike, I'm told." Bobcat said. "But it sounded a little more dangerous when I would say our chance of becoming rapidly expanding atoms was one in a hundred and twenty-five thousand."

William grinned. "Fine, Captain Danger. Keep your numbers. But first, watch this video." William hit a button on his screen. Bobcat watched as a thirty-meter metal asteroid was first hit with a couple of regular rods, the ejection of rock in the harsh lights showing the strikes.

Haze enveloped the stone, followed a few seconds later by three small, almost lightning-like, glitches appearing on the hazy shape close to each other. "That's the first test, three rods. We do another five tests with up to fifteen rods next. The lights are pretty, but we don't get any further into the rock." William hit a couple of buttons, "Here, you see the four pucktards come close to the..." William tried to continue, but Bobcat interrupted. William stopped the video to turn around and look at Bobcat, one eyebrow raised.

"Pucktards?" Bobcat asked, "You're going to call these new devices pucktards?"

"Well, one of the mental midgets in defense was telling Marcus it was like the reverse gravity was causing the field to become fucking retarded," William said.

"Not very PC," Bobcat said.

"Well, I'm not trying to say he was raised properly, I'm merely explaining how the term pucktard came up," William told him, a little exasperation coloring his voice.

"Cheryl Lynn is going to roast us alive if we keep that name," Bobcat said.

"Twenty bucks says I can come up with another story, and we not only get to keep the name; she tells the whole world the story if she ever gets the chance."

"Okay, but that kind of bet requires a timeline. We can't wait forever to close the bet out."

"Um, say six months?" William offered. Bobcat fist-bumped to seal the bet.

Bobcat turned back to the video. "Ok, pucktard for now, but I'm pointing at your ass when someone comes looking for an explanation."

William turned back to the video as well. "I'm changing your name to Captain Throw-My-Ass-Under-The-Bus," William chuckled. "So, start watching the asteroid in the upper right hand corner, see the first land?" He pointed to a little disturbance in the haze. "Here, here and here. There's the last one," he said as he tapped the video screen.

"I could see better if someone's sausage for a finger wasn't in front of the damned screen," Bobcat said. William pulled his hand away and used it to flip Bobcat the bird.

"Classy, just how I like my women," Bobcat smiled as William lowered his hand.

"Watch… now!" William called, and Bobcat saw the haze substantially reduced in the square area of the four pucktards when four rods slammed into the asteroid.

"Woohoo!" Bobcat yelled, clapping his hands. "Hot damn! Nailed that hunk of rock!" He slapped William on the back. "That is all sorts of awesome. Now, can you do that if the rock is moving back and forth and shooting at you?" he asked in a slightly calmer voice.

William put his hand and middle finger back up as Bobcat chuckled and left the room.

CHAPTER TWENTY

GREAT FALLS, VA, USA

In the darkened room, the man known to very few as Joshua Guildenstern reviewed his portfolio. Two years ago, it was a source of joy, a source of pride.

His father's, father's, father's legacy, passed down, built upon and passed down again.

The companies he wielded with complete authority numbered in the hundreds, he had a sizeable portion of hundreds more and, with the boards across the world, he, through them, ran thousands.

They were the Illuminati.

Or, to be accurate, they were an *offshoot* of the Bavarian Illuminati or the Enlightened. One of the splinter groups that could trace their secret history back to May 1, 1776. Joshua would admit the original intent of the Bavarian Illuminati was to be the power behind the scenes, to help the unenlightened.

Not any longer. Now it was to control as much power as possible, to be one of the most powerful forces behind the world's governments and activities, without having to deal with the sticky issues of government itself. Using their individual and joined power to sway opinion and public sentiment, to confirm the tactics together to forge the right future for the globe, minimizing the explosive nature of nationalism.

Why? Because it was bad for business. If it was bad for business, it was bad for them and their companies. Unless, of course, the portfolio of companies included some in the defense industry. So, at all times there were hotspots around the world, and forces in those conflicts to offer guns and bombs to. They had wielded control of local, national, and international events for decades through the simple times and the tough times; helping the countries move forward under their deft guidance, their gentle hand.

Their firm hand.

Except now they were in disarray as they had never been before, brought on by an unexpected and powerful foe who had caught them all, and especially him, unprepared. Unprepared to repel the massive onslaught of attacks against their members happening at breakneck speed.

Many of the attacks were in the stock markets, which was normally their untouchable domain. Others were more direct and executed against them privately. The attacks leaked information to the legal authorities who would raid their offices. Finally, the most feared attacks were covert actions marked by the disappearances of high-level people.

Members gone, without a trace, without a note, without a funeral.

Just gone.

RELEASE THE DOGS OF WAR

The members' hysteria was getting out of control. At no time in their history had the boards across the world had to deal with this level of primal fear.

They had six boards, and every one had fights during the meetings. The Asian board was the least contentious outwardly. They were the ones who had the most to lose. No one believed they had gotten away with anything.

Everyone was just waiting for the hammer to drop on them. In fact, most were secretly waiting to see what happened to the board that everyone blamed for the present crises, the Asian group.

Except Joshua. He looked through the catastrophic results of his latest stock portfolio review, turned off his monitor in disgust, and sat thinking.

He was down one hundred and one companies. His net wealth and controlling power, as he calculated it, was at sixty-two point eight percent from twenty-four months ago. He had been on track to be up twenty-two point four percent before they bombed TQB.

He was barely holding on to his rage at the bitch he blamed for it all. For having the technology, for ignoring their offers, for failing to fall to their power.

For killing his hit man and getting so close to him.

He wiped the dampness off of his forehead as he considered how close they had come to fingering him. Joshua had no doubt what would be his future if they found out his name. He would fail to have a funeral as well. He would be just another missing persons case.

Joshua considered his options. It was time to call in a few chits, a few favors, from his highest placed sources.

It was time to take out the bitch.

Joshua reached over and turned his monitor back on. He

hit a switch to jump to another computer located here in his basement. It had no internet connection and used no Wi-Fi signals. It was all wired from the room below with only the video signal traveling to his office. He used a finger reader next to his monitor for security and logged into his archive, his records. The names of the people his group had helped through the decades and families through centuries.

The network was extensive. Over twenty-two thousand highly placed individuals owed favors. Yes, there were congressmen and congresswomen. Military and civil authorities. But there were also the mothers, the fathers, the sisters and brothers to these same people. Those that would have influence on the powerful as well.

They also had blackmail. Joshua wasn't fond of blackmail as a rule, but he wasn't above using it, either. Sometimes, the greater good needed to win, no matter the tools used. When you operated with the aid of generals close to the President, he could, and would, use all of the options at his disposal.

He wanted that woman, dead or alive and what Joshua Guildenstern put his mind to, Joshua Guildenstern achieved.

QBS AD AETERNITATEM, MID-ATLANTIC

Jean Dukes, Cheryl Lynn, and Patricia got together on the Ad Aeternitatem in the captain's private meeting room.

Patricia started, "Spill it, Jean," she told the spunky gunnery officer as she lifted her water to take a sip.

"I think he's on the hook," she said. "I was my usual demure self when…" Jean had to suddenly push back from the table as Patricia's drink spewed out of her mouth and nose, as the woman tried to cover her mouth and quit coughing.

Jean grabbed napkins from the coffee bar and started cleaning up the table while Cheryl Lynn pounded on Patricia's back.

"Holy hell, woman!" Patricia said as she got her coughing under control. "Warn a person the next time you're going to throw out such a whopper!"

The women laughed as they finished the cleanup and tossed the wet paper napkins into the trash. Jean smiled, starting again. "Okay, I did everything but jump him right in front of everyone."

"Now that we can believe," Patricia said. "Although you might need a trampoline," she amended.

"Funny ha ha. I'm not short, he's just a mountain," Jean shot back. "A mountain of rock and hard muscles and…"

"Enough!" Cheryl Lynn gasped, putting up a hand. "Of the three of us, I'm the manless or non-man-focused one in the group and I don't need a reason for a cold shower tonight."

"Well, then go grab a piece of one of them and take him to bed," Jean said. "Hell, if John's member were velcroed on, I'd just borrow it, and I'd bring it back happy," Jean smiled at the two of them as she finished speaking.

"Bullshit, you'd miss the muscle rubbing," Patricia said. "And the heavy breathing and then the…"

"Enough!" Cheryl Lynn called out again. "You two need to tone it down a little."

Patricia winked surreptitiously to Jean and replied, "Well, little chickie, you might need to just fan yourself. This group is to focus on how we might do a little matchmaking. Every little girl's dream. Jean here has graciously offered to sacrifice her lust, sorry, her body."

"In lust," Jean added.

"Fine," Patricia nodded to her. "Her body, in lust, for John Grimes. Until that matchmaking opportunity goes away, we are calling him spoken for, at least for now."

"Don't make me hurt someone," Jean said, a nasty tone working its way into her voice, "I don't like to share my man spoils," she finished to a snort from Cheryl Lynn.

"Your man spoils?" Cheryl Lynn asked.

"Yes, my man spoils," Jean agreed. "The spoils of the man I capture."

"How well did that work out with the chief engineer?" Patricia asked.

"If space weren't such a slut whore, I would probably be able to say pretty well. Seeing how space is such a slut whore, I can't." Jean shrugged, adding, "I have some morals, the space bitch doesn't."

"I see," Patricia said.

"The slut," Jean griped, one last time.

"So, does John have any aspirations about space?" Cheryl Lynn asked, digging just a little.

Jean's eyes opened a little wider. "No, thank God! If I lost the second guy to that hussy, I'd have to hang up my singles card and just get a lifetime supply of Energizer batteries for my bunny."

Cheryl Lynn's face went red as she put her head in her hands. "I cannot believe you just said that."

Jean looked at Patricia with a 'what did I say?' look on her face. Patricia put up two fingers, flexing them like bunny ears. Jean burst out laughing.

"Oh my God, did you see the Sex In The City episode?" Jean asked Cheryl Lynn, who shook her head no. "I thought every woman was required to see that. I had three friends make me sit down and watch it when I got off my ship after it aired. Crap, I think I've seen it like five times."

"That good?" Patricia asked.

"Hilarious," Jean agreed. "I'm pretty sure Cheryl Lynn needs to see it. We need a girls night in to get her in the mood first."

Cheryl Lynn opened two fingers to look at Jean. "Do you even do a girls night in?"

"Sure, why not?" Jean asked.

"Um, because you're so brash?" Cheryl Lynn said as she took her hands away from her face. "It seems like you wouldn't go for the pink and frilly."

"What, I like to paint my toenails like any girl," Jean said. "Just because I want them to curl excessively because of John's…"

"AND HERE WE GO AGAIN!" Cheryl Lynn broke in, rolling her eyes. "I'm going to have to get my own." She noticed the two other women looking at her. "Never mind!" she said, raising her hands in the air before putting them back on the table.

Patricia reached across and patted Cheryl Lynn's hand. "I understand, dear. I waited a long, long time for my man to get a clue. I'm making up for it now." She winked at Cheryl Lynn and allowed a satisfied smirk to cross her face.

"So, let's take a guy and figure out who we might match him up with, shall we?" Patricia said. "I actually have a simple one."

"Oh, who?" Jean asked.

"Stephen," she said.

"Stephen?" Cheryl Lynn said. "Does Stephen even want a girl?"

"Well, he isn't gay if that's your question," Patricia said.

"This is a direct request from Bethany Anne. She has noticed two reactions, one from a female Guardian, Jennifer Ericson."

"She's the one that was hurt on the bus trip, right?" Cheryl Lynn said.

"That's correct," Patricia agreed. "She was hurt protecting the children. Either way, Bethany Anne has noticed something from both of them."

"So, what do we need to do?" Jean asked. "Set them up on a date?"

"No, we just need to get them to work together, I think. The problem is Jennifer has requested basically any position that keeps her away from Stephen."

"Why?" Jean asked while Cheryl Lynn nodded and pointed to Jean.

"We think because she believes she doesn't have a chance," Patricia said. "Other than that, I couldn't tell you."

"Well, that's an easy hook-up to figure out strategically, but tactically it will be a little more challenging," Jean said.

"Yes." Patricia said. "Okay, now we need to figure out someone for Scott."

"Scott?" Cheryl Lynn replied quickly. "I thought we would go for Eric next?"

"Why?" Patricia acted confused. "Does it matter which one is first? I figure that Scott's still hurting."

"Hurting from what?" Cheryl Lynn asked. "Was he hurt on the guys' night out?"

"Well, nothing he didn't heal from, none of the guys had to go into the Pod-doc the next morning. So, no naked shows there." Jean said raising her eyebrows up and down and smiling.

Cheryl Lynn looked at Jean. "You are unbelievable," she told her. "If I had a tenth of the amount of moxie you do, I'm sure my life would be radically different today."

"No time like the present to practice moxie, Cheryl Lynn," Jean told her. "Hell, start with Scott."

"What? No!" Cheryl Lynn was aghast. "What would I tell him?"

Jean started, "That you admire his massive arms and want to find out if it is true about big muscles and bigger…"

"Stop!" Cheryl Lynn said. "I don't even want to know the rest of that." She turned to Patricia. "What's behind door number two?"

"Well, first question. Are you interested in Scott? Like, really interested?" Patricia asked.

Cheryl Lynn put her hands in front of her on the table and played with them a moment before answering, "Yes."

"Okay," Patricia said, "Now that you've had the moxie to admit that, let's start talking about possibilities."

"You mean other than," Jean began to say when both women turned to her and said in loud voices, "YES!"

Jean rolled her eyes. "Just asking him over for dinner?"

"Wait, why would I do that?" Cheryl Lynn asked.

"Well, duh, you are the PR lady. Who's the most famous one in TQB?"

"Bethany Anne?" Cheryl Lynn said. "Oh, you want me to do a series on the guys next. With John, Eric, Darryl, and Scott showcased?"

"That is ingenious," Patricia said.

Jean shrugged her shoulders. "Hell, I wish I'd thought of it, so I could agree."

"You didn't consider that?" Cheryl Lynn asked her.

"No, I just figured we'd do another short feature on Bethany Anne, but you'd need to get some inside views. Now that I see what you're saying, I'm completely on board with a 'Bitch's View.'" Jean said.

"Why would we call it that?" Patricia said.

"Actually, it might not be a bad idea," Cheryl Lynn said. "The guys might not care, and we could title the show something like 'Guarding the Crown—A Bitch's View' or something like that."

"Isn't that getting a little close to calling her the Queen? I thought we didn't want to promote that piece in all of this?" Patricia said.

"We don't," Jean took up the argument. "But she is the head of TQB Enterprises, and there have already been people who claim she is both richer than royalty and stronger than half the rulers of countries in the world, so why not?"

"That could be interesting," Patricia agreed. "I'm not sure how Bethany Anne will react to it."

"Which part, the crown or the bitches?" Cheryl Lynn asked. "Because the crown part is probably fine, and she likes to dig the guys about the bitches part, and they like to own it like rock stars."

"Oh, hell yeah!" Jean exclaimed, leaning back in her chair, her arms in the air before slamming forward, her eyes on fire. "Can you imagine the fun we could have with tight black 'Bitches' t-shirts on those guys for a calendar? Do it for money so they can give it away?"

"I'm in for two," Patricia said, fanning herself. "I'm giving them away to friends, you understand."

Cheryl Lynn smiled at her. "I can't believe I'm saying this," she turned to them. "But that is such a kickass idea! A Bitch's calendar with studly men that I have to help photograph." She seemed to be lost in thought.

"I'm there for John's pictures, just saying." Jean put her finger on the table emphatically. "No other hussies should be allowed in."

"Oh, no you don't!" Cheryl Lynn said gleefully. "I've just thought of another idea to go along with it. Tickets!"

"Oh, that would make the day," Patricia said. "How would we sell them?"

Cheryl Lynn considered the question. "How about if we do several shoots in different locations around the world. Start in Australia, Pod them to the next place and finish in… well, wherever the hell the last country is for the day? That way, we get about an hour in each venue and sell tickets to multiple locations?"

"How do we plan that?" Patricia asked.

"Flash mob?" Jean suggested.

"Do what?" Patricia asked.

"That has possibilities," Cheryl Lynn said. "If we can figure out a way to make it happen safely, we could get a lot of good press this way."

"What's a flash mob?" Patricia asked.

"It's something that's happened because of the internet and cell phones. Usually, it's either planned, or a celebrity goes on the internet and says that they're visiting somewhere, and a lot of their fans decide to go see them. That's the flash part of the flash mob. So, the idea here is we say that we are going to be shooting in such and such a country, and then we livestream… the… hoooly crap," Cheryl Lynn stopped. "This could be huge."

"John goes first," Jean said. "That way the fewest people are around."

"The fewest women, you mean?" Patricia asked.

"Of course, we can let the LGBT group vie for Akio," Jean smiled. "See, I share!"

"Scott goes second, then," Cheryl Lynn said. "Hey, priorities."

"Don't you think they're are going to get suspicious?" Patricia asked them.

"Who CARES?" they both shot back, looked at each other, and laughed.

"You go first," Jean told Cheryl Lynn.

"Okay, they might get suspicious. So, how about a Spanish country and we put Eric at the end for that reason. Then, we have a predominately African-American country, and that's Darryl," she started. "Sorry, nothing else."

"We'll punt, as the guys say, until we get to that part," Jean said.

"Okay, that's three down and a few more to go. Good meeting ladies."

"We should have a secret team name," Jean said.

"Hmm," Patricia said. "If we can come up with one, it might become notorious throughout the ages. Women for centuries in the future pissed off because we took them off the market."

"Hell, who's asking for them to be off the market forever?" Jean said. "I might get tired of all that hunky man-flesh and want a soft artist type, who's into his feelings and… and…and…"

Jean looked down at the table and sighed. "Who the hell am I kidding? I want that man!"

CHAPTER TWENTY-ONE

MID-ATLANTIC

Captain Zhang walked through his Han class submarine, numbered 405. The damned ship was noisy, with the somewhat recent radiation shielding modifications helping to reduce the noise a little, and, supposedly, their health and wellbeing.

He had been told to change patrol location and they were arriving at their new destination in the next forty-eight hours. He had studied what he could of his two targets.

Both were modified Superyachts with tactical offensive and defensive weaponry. It was suspected they had a way to hole a surface ship under its waterline. There was no mention of what they could do to a submarine running deeply and firing torpedoes at depths of hundreds of feet.

His orders were explicit. Arrive in the area, approach cautiously, and acquire the ability to hit both boats within sixty seconds of a fire command.

If he had a supercavitating torpedo on board, he could do that safely from some distance, but he didn't.

He would pass underneath his own group, who would resume their previous range when his boat was in position. Then, it was going to be a game of seeing who would flinch first.

———

"Captain?" sonar called out. "We have a new visitor coming in from the Chinese deployment, depth approximately five zero zero, sir."

Captain Branon of the American fleet looked over. "Confirmed?"

"Aye sir, confirmed."

Captain Branon turned. "Communications, please pass on this information to those who are on our list, I'm sure they will want to know."

———

MANUFACTURING FACILITY 01, ASTEROID FIELDS

Bobcat walked through the mid-sized luxury liner presently in use as a hotel to his meeting with Omar Kolan, the hotel manager. While the ship had a captain, there wasn't much need for one. Its job was to sit still relative to everything else, hold position in space, and provide quarters to the workers.

For at least a couple of years, most likely.

Less if they could swing it, but that was a future problem. Today's problems didn't need to borrow trouble from the future.

He found Omar at the main desk, smiling at a lady with whom he was speaking as Bobcat approached. Omar finished with the woman who walked away after a quick glance at Bobcat.

Bobcat jerked his head in the direction of the departing woman. "Everything okay?"

Omar made a distasteful face. "One of the workers was not being respectful of her private space. Fortunately, some of Annane's men happened to walk by and she knew one of them. So, it was a comment more than a complaint at the moment."

"Damn, this shit always seems to happen," Bobcat muttered. "Do you want help with that?"

Omar shook his head. "No, I have a weekly fifteen-minute call scheduled with Bethany Anne in two hours, I'll bring it up then. I imagine she will have a unique perspective on the situation."

"Yeah, like showing them what happens to you if you do something to a woman. There won't be a free ride home for that shit." Bobcat said. "What are you doing about it in the meantime?"

"We have separate quarters for the women, with female Guardians. If any of the idiots happen to harass those women, it doesn't go very far."

"I can only imagine what happens if the lady growls at you and her eyes flash yellow," Bobcat replied, smiling. "So, got fifteen minutes for me?"

"Sure, give me a couple of minutes to call my second over to cover the desk. There is a meeting room through the doors over there to your right. It will seat four unless more are coming?" Omar said.

Bobcat shook his head as he started towards the door

Omar pointed to. "No. Just you and me for now."

A couple of minutes later, Omar joined Bobcat in the nicely appointed little room. It had a small round table with a red top, a gold carpet and gray chairs. Bobcat was sitting when Omar joined him.

"Pleasure to see you again, Mr. Bobcat," Omar said.

"It's just Bobcat, Omar," he replied. "Mr. Bobcat might be my father, but his name was George."

"Okay, Bobcat," Omar said as he sat down. "How can I help you?"

"I need to know how full we are on this vessel?" While Bobcat could get the stats from Samantha, he wanted the man's opinion, his gut response.

"We have filled twenty-five percent of the berths on this ship. I would not want to increase it past maybe half at this time. The ship, while modified for space, is not as designed as a hotel, and we don't have everything working as efficiently as we might wish."

"How long do you think it would take to make this ship more efficient?" Bobcat asked. "It can hold over two thousand if we double-berth people. Right now we're giving them one per berth, right?"

"Yes, we are," he agreed. "But we're working out all sorts of kinks with eating, water reclamation, and air in some parts of the ship. These could be serious problems if we're taxing the environmental systems before we get the kinks worked out."

"Okay, I needed to know. Bethany Anne might have to bring a shitload of Russians up here, and I've been asked to figure out where we can house them. The short answer is we can only hold a few hundred who are required for the manufacturing and mining operations at this time. Plus, you need additional engineering support to figure out the problems we're having that you guys can't nail down." Bobcat rubbed his chin, "So, I need to talk to Frank to find out if he has any suggestions for manpower."

"Wouldn't he tell you to speak to your country's NASA?" Omar asked.

"Ha!" Bobcat barked. "One, it isn't my NASA, and they really aren't that pleased with us at the moment." Bobcat chuckled. "Although hiring from them is funny as hell, we probably don't want to implement that option if we can help it. No, I'll ask Frank to help find you some people and get them working with Jeo. Furthermore, those over on the new ship can spend some cycles with you here. Maybe they have some technology that you can also use."

Bobcat considered what he had learned. "Omar, do me a favor. I want you to pretend you had an unlimited budget. What would you build for the solar system's most fantastic space hotel?"

"For how many?" Omar asked.

"Well, the biggest cruise liners right now can almost hold seven thousand people, fully berthed. Nimitz-class aircraft carriers carry five thousand. I'm guessing, twenty thousand?"

"Twenty thousand?"

"Or, I don't know, fifty?" Bobcat said, ignoring Omar's look of incredulity. "Well, maybe you should be thinking about a space station, not a hotel, okay?" Bobcat stood up from the chair. "Damn, I feel better with you thinking about this problem, Omar."

Bobcat left the stupefied man staring at the wall as he patted him on his shoulder, closing the door behind him as he walked away.

WASHINGTON D.C., USA

The President entered his small meeting room to speak to General George Thourbourah. He closed the door behind him, leaving his security outside and noticed a small container of fruit-flavored Tums.

Extra Strength.

He sat his notepad and pen down, popped the top and poured three into his hand. "I see we upped the quantity for the meeting. This an indication of how bad you think this is going to go?"

"Well, sort of," George said. "I know you're going to want to discuss reaching out to TQB, and I'm not sure how to answer that right now."

"So, you have nothing new?"

"Well, our Navy has spotted a Chinese submarine coming into the area around the TQB ships." George started.

"That's going to go well," the President said sarcastically.

"See, now you agree that they're just a powder keg waiting to go off," George pointed out.

"No, what I think is that the Chinese are doing what they do to us, but they're doing it to a group that doesn't operate like a country. The TQB ships are in international waters and have their ships registered with a foreign country. What are the Chinese going to do when something happens to their submarine? Blame TQB?"

"Probably," George replied. "They know who they're going up against. The Chinese are pushing their military might around. I've talked with Navy, the guess is that the submarine is going to get close enough to fire a torpedo and then force

TQB to accept their Navy's approach again."

"I don't think that's going to work," the President advised his liaison. "There are no negotiations to leverage. The Chinese don't have their entire Navy in this, and I doubt that TQB is showing all of their cards. I don't understand why TQB just doesn't get up and leave, it isn't like they're required to sit in any place, are they?"

"No. Although they are regularly supplied. They receive a cargo container at least once every twenty-four hours." George told him.

"How goes the stock market war?" the President asked.

George turned to another page in his report. "The stock market itself has been up and down, mostly down, so that's hiding some of the activity. However, we believe that over eighty-four companies are in the middle of this battle at the moment. This is the fourth wave we've detected on the NYSE and NASDAQ. Three in Europe and two in Asia."

"So, who are they fighting?" the President asked. "Because while I understand TQB is obviously huge and a powerhouse, if this is about their fourth huge stock market battle for hundreds of companies we know about, and probably a few hundred more we don't, who the hell are they fighting?" The President started to warm up to the subject. "Let's face it, between the two sides in this fight, I only see one side that is being out in the open. This other group is hidden, has used some sort of nuclear bomb on our soil—I'm going to get back to that in a moment—and is continuing to attack. So, I'm not too happy with not knowing more about this second group. Where are my reports on them? Why isn't intelligence figuring out who they are?"

George pursed his lips. "I'm not sure I have an answer for you. Intelligence doesn't have any significant connection between the companies at this time. Or at least, nothing above a twenty-seven percent chance of likelihood. You might as well just make up a reason for their connection as anything else that's plausible." George answered.

"I'll call them the damned Illuminati if this keeps up," the President snapped.

George smiled as he reached for the Tums. "Well, I did say plausible, Mr. President."

"Yeah, so you did," the President agreed. "So, I understand that we have actual reductions in the radioactivity out there in Colorado?"

"Yes. There's an anti-radiation powder invented by Tomihisa Ohta for the Fukushima disaster. It consists of a mixture of minerals including zeolite, said to capture radiation in water and absorb the isotopes of cesium, iodine, and strontium. Plus, another material just coming out of the labs. EPA worked with TQB on location to build special containers to spray the area, and together they seem to be cleaning it up rather quickly."

"You don't seem happy about this, George," the President said.

"Oh, I'm happy enough to say that the radiation, which wasn't a lot, is being cleaned up," the general said. "I just believe it's a false front."

"Ok, let's talk about that piece. I'm going to invite the TQB executive for a discussion," he told George.

"Is this on the schedule, or hidden?" George asked.

"Hidden, this time. I don't need the press to get wind of this at all," the President answered.

"How are you planning to get her in without everyone seeing this happening?" George asked.

"It will be after hours, brought in through one of the

tunnels to the DUCC," the President said.

"I see. Will you need me there?" George asked him.

"No, this is going to be a private conversation. What is said isn't going to be recorded. It will be an exploratory discussion to see if we can have open communications."

"Why aren't you setting this up with your people talking to her people and so on?" George questioned.

"Well, two reasons," he replied. "The first is the 'and so on' part you just mentioned. We need to be able to talk, and I'm not willing to have too many people beating their breasts for political points on this. I've had lower-level functionaries call, and they speak with equal parties. It became apparent that if I want to talk to the top, then it will be me doing the talking."

"Not very understanding of power, is she?" George said.

"Well, let's not forget we also have a significant naval presence watching their ships. If I'm not mistaken, our intelligence services are also trying to crack their computers, and I'm surprised I haven't heard about any covert operations yet."

"Well, they're on the drawing board," George said. "But we aren't going to attack anywhere on our soil, and the FBI and other government agencies can't seem to keep their paperwork straight to save their lives."

"And you wonder why they don't want to speak with us?" the President asked him, annoyance in his voice. "I want a list of every action against this company. This is damned ridiculous!" Making a few notes on his pad, the President continued, "Instead of trying to work with them, it's like we're purposefully trying to make their lives as difficult as we possibly can. Every person I speak with in Washington hates them. Most civilians love them. What is the damned problem? So, get me my list." The President grabbed the Tums bottle for another couple of tablets, and lifted it up to get George's attention. "Good idea, by the way."

George carefully schooled his face, "Yes, sir and thank you, sir."

———

"Yes?" A deep voice answered the phone.

"JG it's me, GT," a voice said. "The man wants to meet the woman, but without anyone involved."

"Okay. Any way to intercept?"

"Before the meeting? Possibly. But it means I'm out, and would need to disappear. Not exactly how I want to leave after thirty-five years."

"No, you're too high value where you are. Let me see what other assets can be used to accomplish this. Will the woman have to come in a certain way?"

"Absolutely. There's an office building near the primary location. The usual entrance is protected in that building. So, they drive in, get approved and escorted in through the tunnel from that side. No one sees, no one cares."

"So, the best time to acquire the suspect is going to be either pre or post-meeting. I'd prefer pre-meeting, myself. Although, maybe after the meeting would be better. That way, the man is ignorant until some agreed-upon situation doesn't develop. Will she have protection?"

"Not inside the tunnels, that won't be permitted. I imagine she will be covered by her guards until then."

"Can we fake the location request?" the deep voice asked.

"Hmm, that isn't a bad idea. There's a backup building that can be used. It isn't in service at the moment due to maintenance modifications planned for the next six weeks. But a mistake on the address, if caught, could be explained away."

"Is it possible to place our men in that location?"

"Yes. So, have her men in the car, allow her in, grab her, and take her out another way?" George asked.

"Yes."

"That's possible. But you're going to need to get some men with the correct uniforms. I can't supply those."

"That can be handled, but I need you to be there in the receiving location, to make sure I get my package or that the package is destroyed, GT."

"I understand. I almost think that's the better choice. I don't think playing with a live package is smart, JG."

"Sometimes, GT, you need to get a little payback before the bill is paid in full."

George hung up his phone when the line went dead.

CHAPTER TWENTY-TWO

MANUFACTURING FACILITY 01, ASTEROID FIELDS

really don't give a shit." Bobcat looked at the fourteen people tasked with building the ship at the table. He continued, "It's immaterial that we're building the first spaceship in space. That it's an alien design not made with gravitics in mind for thrust, that blah blah blah.

"I care that we get it done, that we get it fixed and that it's safe." Bobcat put up a hand to hold off commentary. "Safe doesn't mean taking for-fucking-ever either." He put his hand down. "So, get some bricks and pound some nuts if we need to. If you have ovaries, do the equivalent, I just don't know what that is," he said. "Nothing really worth doing takes less than a hundred and fifty percent or more of your effort. Pull out the impossible and beat reality with it. But get it done."

Bobcat looked over the assembled faces. "I'm getting reports back from Earth. There's a lot of shit going on, and my gut says we need this badass ship there, not here. We need a ship that can go down to the ground if possible, or close. That can handle missile shots and can fire back if need be." Bobcat smiled wickedly. "But if a twelve-hundred-foot spaceship suddenly turned up over my head, I'd need clean shorts before I launched shit at it. Well, I could probably just fling what was in my shorts. So, kick the tires and light the fires folks, this bitch needs to get done, dismissed."

Everyone smiled and grabbed their stuff, talking as they left. Jeo and Marcus stayed behind.

When everyone had left, and the door finally closed, Bobcat called out, "Samantha."

"Yes, Bobcat?" Samantha came back, her face showing on the wall.

"What's the real timeframe for finishing this ship? At least to the level that everything is working well enough?"

"Twenty-two days," she told him. Bobcat noticed Jeo look down at his screen and his eyes open wider.

"How many times have you been told, Jeo," Bobcat said as Jeo looked at him. "That I have all access? You don't think padding schedules hasn't been done for centuries? The technology is different, not the practice. You younglings, always thinking you're pulling something over on us." He smiled at the sheepish Jeo.

"Well, then what about your seventy-two hours?" Jeo asked.

"Wanted to see if you would give me the minimum, or shove everything you could into the seventy-two hours. Good to see you passed the pop quiz, my man."

"What were the odds?" Jeo asked to Marcus' snort.

"William and I both wanted to believe you would push it all in and not take the easy way out, so we actually didn't bet on the outcome. No one took odds," Bobcat said.

Jeo turned to Marcus. "That's kind of a compliment, right?"

"Absolutely. This is the first time I've ever heard them not agree to some sort of odds. They must think it would jinx it to bet against you," Marcus said.

Jeo looked down at the table, put his finger to the screen to move a few things and looked over at Bobcat. "I see some changes that might help. I'm going to go talk to a few people." He looked up at the wall. "Samantha, I need to get Tom and Trina together in meeting room B-1-12. Please see when they're available." He stood up and said to Bobcat, "We won't fail you."

"Dude, we all won't fail Bethany Anne," Bobcat replied.

Jeo smiled and left the room.

Bobcat turned to Marcus. "Okay, talk to me about the engines and the math, and use words I can understand."

"Well, let me go get my 'Hop on Pop' math book," Marcus started before Bobcat laughed and put up a hand.

"Okay, I deserved that. How about I ask you to give me the information in chunks I can process, and leave off the high-level stuff you know I won't be able to handle?" Bobcat asked him.

"Okay, not a problem. Effectively, we're now up to ninety-two percent efficiency. The math is making TOM's head hurt."

"So, he's bitching about it?" Bobcat asked.

"No, he's super excited about it. Apparently, nothing like this has ever been tried by his people, at least before he left. So, if nothing else he will either have figured out something they never tried, or he will have accomplished something as a single Kurtherian that will certainly not have been done by any other single Kurtherian when he gets to meet them again."

"What about us humans helping?" Bobcat asked.

"Well, when it comes to math, we might as well be doing their version of 'Hop on Pop' arithmetic monkeys, so we don't have much credibility," Marcus said.

"Even with our computers?" Bobcat asked.

"They don't count anything but what's in your mind. So, for them, our computers are considered calculators only and crutches as well," Marcus responded.

"What about ADAM?" Bobcat wondered.

"Hah!" Marcus barked. "Personally, I think they would have a group aneurysm if they found out about ADAM." Marcus thought for a moment. "So if they didn't know about ADAM in Bethany Anne's head, and she pulled some stunts with his help on them? They would probably worship her as the second coming of their version of a math deity."

"Oh, that would play so well to Bethany Anne. I wonder how fast she'd be pulling ADAM out and shoving him into something so they could all bow down to him in his new android body?" Bobcat said.

Marcus shrugged. "Don't know. But, getting back to the subject at hand, we're running into another major integration problem with the shields, and some of it has to do with the armament. If we push the guns out of the shield, then we can attain almost eighty-two percent efficiency after trying to equalize the protection conflicts. If we don't have the weapons, we have almost a hundred percent."

"So, anytime we push through the field, we're fucked, right?" Bobcat asked, "I mean, eighty-two percent is incredible, but I'm a bastard, and I want it all. In fact, I want a hundred and ten percent."

"Wait!" Marcus stopped, then looked around quickly, like he needed a drug in the worst way.

"Samantha, put the wall in whiteboard mode," Bobcat

said then turned to Marcus. "Marcus, use your finger!"

Marcus shoved the chair back and walked quickly around the table to the wall and started using his finger to write mathematical notations. Samantha drew them in black until Marcus said, "Orange," at which point she switched the next set of annotations to orange. A moment later, he wanted blue.

Bobcat watched for a minute, then shrugged to himself and pulled out his phone, checked the time on Earth, and dialed William to communicate through the Etheric.

"What's up?" William asked.

"Marcus the Amazing has resurfaced," Bobcat said.

"Oh? What's he doing without his whiteboards?"

"Drawing with his finger on the wall."

"No shit? He's using that functionality you wanted a couple of months back?"

"Yup, you owe me twenty." Bobcat agreed.

"Wait a minute," William protested, "That was only good for two months." There was a pause. "Which is today, you lucky bastard, what time?"

Bobcat replied, "I've checked, it's only four AM in Europe, so, I've got a few hours to go."

"Son of a bitch, that's cutting it close," William said. "Wait, weren't we in Colorado two months ago?"

"No."

"Damn, I tried. Okay, so what's he working on?" William asked.

"Something I said about wanting a hundred and ten percent of what I could get and being greedy," Bobcat told him.

"Oh, shit!" William responded.

"What do you mean, oh shit?" Bobcat asked. "That didn't sound like a good oh shit, William. Don't tell me I went one step forward, but two steps back with you."

"Maybe, sorry, got to go and check on something, bye," William disconnected.

Bobcat pulled his phone down to see the disconnection time. "Fuck."

———

"That should do it!" Marcus quit doodling on the walls. It had taken him forty-five minutes, one long wall and half a short one. Bobcat looked down at the scratches on his pad to note he had used seven colors, as well.

"What is it?" Bobcat asked, startling Marcus, who had forgotten he was in the room.

Marcus waved at the marks on the walls. "Your hundred and ten percent. The gravitic drives are not stuck with limitations like normal engines. They can be tweaked up and down considerably. We keep them to the same settings because that's what we're used to doing. It keeps our math, which is already difficult, from becoming more complicated. But in this case, it's caused our problems, too. When I start adjusting potentials and allow them to supersede the max we artificially created, they can compensate for the flux. It doesn't fix all of the problems perfectly, but I bet in practice we can hit ninety-seven percent effective while we push the guns through the field and attain a hundred percent within seconds after it is done."

Bobcat smiled at the rocket scientist. "Nice. Now, when can I get a hundred and ten percent?"

Marcus looked around in frustration for the non-existent pen to throw at his friend.

"What's up William?" Bobcat asked over his phone. He was scootering down one of the corridors when he drove around a corner and just about ran into two guys carrying a large box between them. "COMING THROUGH!" he yelled. He ducked, the box was lifted, and he drove under. It just scraped the top of his head. He yelled over his shoulder, "My bad!"

He continued down the hall until forced to slow in order to enter the large Pod hanger, which was empty at the moment. He parked the scooter. "Okay, sorry. What's up?"

"You want the good news or the bad?"

"Mix them like peanut butter and chocolate," Bobcat retorted. "Make something good out of this."

"Ahhh," William responded. "Okay. I'll try. So, the first problem is that we've figured out how to create a second field outside of the first. It isn't very powerful, but it *is* possible to accomplish. So, it will give us a new type of defensive shielding."

"So, how do we defeat it?" Bobcat answered, realizing why William had to leave so suddenly the last time.

"Well, the best we can do at the moment is layer the attack. The pucktards can't penetrate to the main shield in this formation without the first minor shield out of the way. So, we have to adjust our offensive strategy again," William said.

Bobcat said, "And, the other shoe drops. Okay, better to know about it now, and see how we can use it and why we might want to use it. There have to be reasons to do a double shield." Bobcat considered for a moment. "This isn't stopping us. Move forward and make sure we understand what we can. We need some sort of R&D location for the mad men and women to play with this gravitic stuff away from here.

I'm worried you're going to cross the streams and that would be bad, buddy."

"Ghostbusters style?" William asked.

"Yeah," Bobcat answered.

"Ummm," William responded. "Yeah, doing that too close is a bad idea. Okay, I'll move that problem to the right person. How are we with the ship?"

Bobcat looked around the empty Pod hanger. "Well, it's sparkly. Clean and mostly put together here in the hanger, but that bugs me. We are short people. Either we need to get some people moved over, or we need to move the ship closer to Earth, which is going to cause a problem. I hate having a massive, empty ship."

"Well, it isn't like Samantha can't do most of it for a short time, it is pretty automated," William said.

"That's just not right. Don't worry about it, I'm getting with Bethany Anne in a few hours to discuss personnel, and she is presently talking over things with Boris in Russia. She needed to help them out, and I understand we're going to have some more people join us. Damn, I never thought I would say I can't wait for Russians to join us." Bobcat chuckled and then sighed. "Dude, sometimes it amazes me what we can do as a race when we stop trying to fuck each other over."

"You and me both, boss. You and me both," William agreed.

CHAPTER TWENTY-THREE

QBS POLARUS, MID-ATLANTIC

Call coming in from Ad Aeternitatem, Captain Wagner," called Comms.

"Put it over here," Captain Thomas said as he heard the call beep.

"Captain Thomas, this is Captain Wagner," his speaker squawked.

"Hey Max, what's going on?" he asked.

"Hey, we were talking about the Chinese sub that's heading our way. Do you guys have a decision on how we handle this yet? Or have you talked with Bethany Anne?"

"Not yet, they just cleared their own ships, so I figure we have a little while. Other than sinking it, which I don't want to do as a first option, I'm open to considering other things than destruction," Captain Thomas said.

"Yeah, it might go there if we take too long, and they get too close. Even with a puck shield below the water we don't have a hundred percent protection if they get close enough. Well, not without sticking something almost right in front of them. If they happen to have a cavitational torpedo, we might be a little screwed."

"Agreed, we would have to go shields up and keep them up. I don't like that idea either," Captain Thomas mused. "Seems to show a little too much weakness. I really am not happy with the Chinese at the moment."

"Well, we had an idea over here. Do you think the teams could place enough gravitic engines on their sub to move it?"

"Like, force it to go somewhere else?" Captain Thomas asked.

"Well, that's one idea. But my XO suggested it would be funny as hell if we could pull them out like a fish," Wagner said.

Captain Thomas started laughing. "What? Tail up out of the water?" He thought about it. "We'd have to go slow when turning it down, but why the hell not? I'll get Bethany Anne's thoughts, but I'm pretty sure this would be a better solution, or at least a less destructive solution, than she might have on her own."

"Agreed," Wagner responded.

———

"So, that's the idea," Captain Thomas reported through the speaker as Bethany Anne viewed South America below her.

"Do we have enough power to do that?" Bethany Anne asked. "And how is it going to work?"

"We need to tweak at least fifteen of the ten-pound pucks and six of the five-pounders. I have people working on that right now. The setting changes are being done based on advice from TOM and ADAM. We'll drop them over the side and let them sink down. When they get close to the bottom, they'll engage and move next to the ship. We use the ten-pounders for the body, and the fivers for the conning tower. We're going to put the puck shield in place and have our defenses ready to engage if they fire anything. When we activate, it will mess up their communications, so no options to get commands from their leadership."

"Make sure everyone is safe. But I want you to request one American and one Russian ship, smaller ones, to get closer if they want to see you guys fish, okay?"

Bethany Anne heard her captain chuckle. "That would be a pleasure, ma'am."

"Okay, take video, will you? I'm going to be out a little while longer," she told him.

"Will do ma'am," Captain Thomas cut the connection.

TOM, take us down a little closer. I want a good seat to watch this when it happens. We can take some eye in the sky video. Damn, I wish I had popcorn!

———

"Sir?" comms specialist Jerrons said. "We have an invitation for one of our ships to come in closer. The QBS Polarus is saying that they are going to go fishing and that you really will want to see this."

Commander Fred Branon walked over to review the message. "Huh, looks like Bart is up to something." He turned. "Jerry! Get me a ride to the Independence, I'm going in closer."

———

The captain of the Russian Corvette Vyshniy Volochek reviewed the message from the QBS Polarus. While he wasn't happy with the apparent ease they had delivering the message, he was intrigued.

"Captain, the Americans are cutting out one of their own corvettes, the USS Independence and are heading towards the QBS ships," the comms specialist said.

"Very well. It looks like the QBS ships are going to do something and want us to see it. XO, make sure we are not between the QBS ships and the Chinese. I don't trust the Chinese not to try and get us involved in something. Put us outside the ring of the American corvette and off ten degrees further from the Chinese."

———

"Sir, we have changes in the ships above. We have one Russian and one American moving towards the QBS ships."

Captain Zhang pursed his lips. "Size?"

"Both seem to be corvettes, sir," sonar answered.

"What are they playing at?" Zhang wondered.

"Sir?" comms asked.

"Nothing." Zhang walked to his chair and sat down. "Sonar, what is in front of us?"

"Nothing that we can find sir," he replied.

"So, what are you doing?" Zhang said. "And what am I going to do to outthink you?"

———

"Puck defense is under water, sir," Jean Dukes commed.

"Very good, thank you," Captain Thomas replied and clicked off his speaker.

"Sir, we have confirmation the Fishing Pole pucks are on their way," another specialist told him. He nodded. "Good to hear. Let me know when Fishing Pole is surrounding our fish."

"Aye aye, sir," the specialist replied.

―――――

"Sir, the Russian Corvette Vyshniy Volochek is heading in our direction," the captain of the Independence informed the commander of the American group. Fred nodded his head. "Thanks, Ben, I bet they were invited to see this as well."

Fred looked around. "Hey, any way we can get some popcorn going? I think this is going to be something to see."

―――――

"Sir, the Americans are offering a spot near them, and they say they are popping the popcorn if we need some," specialist Gregor told his captain.

Captain Eugene Kuznetsov turned to his comms officer. "Popcorn?" Gregor nodded. "That is interesting. They are expecting a show, not something that will get them involved." He considered how this could go bad, smiled and said, "Make a notation and send the information back to headquarters. Tell the Independence we will provide the drinks."

―――――

"Five minutes to Fishing Pole activation, five minutes to Fishing Pole activation," the call went out to both TQB ships. Those crewmembers that could, left their stations and started crowding up on the decks. Many of them had their phones and video cameras out. Some took pictures of the Russian corvette as it got close to the American Independence. Both of the corvettes looked cool as hell with their angles and special hull designs.

Both deadly.

Both waiting to see what the QBS ships were about to pull off. A thousand meters above them, a small black Pod was watching the show as well.

───────

Inside the Chinese SSN 405, sudden, loud 'clangs' could be heard over the already noisy mechanicals operating the ship.

CLANG, CLANG, CLANG, CLANG, CLANG. The noises kept going on and on. The men could follow the clangs as they traveled down the ship, and then smaller ones around the tower.

"What is going on?" Zhang demanded.

"Sir, no idea!" sonar answered. "We have nothing on screen, sir."

Zhang grimaced. He had no orders yet to attack, and those commands would not arrive until they were in position. "Comms, contact," he started as comms called out at the same time.

"Captain, we have lost all communications," comms said. "VLF and ELF are offline."

"Bring us up to one hundred chi and stabilize," Captain Zhang ordered.

"One hundred chi and hold, aye sir!"

The submarine proceeded to move up to a one hundred chi depth. As the ship started to stabilize, groaning could be heard.

Then all hell broke loose.

———

"Commander, loud clangs heard underwater," Captain Ben Rose turned towards his commander. "I think the movie just started."

Fred turned to him. "Where's that popcorn? I'm going outside."

Fred was handed a bag of microwave popcorn, which smelled delicious. He stepped off the bridge and walked around to the front of the ship. He could see the Captain of the Vyshniy Volochek and raised his popcorn bag to him. He could see the man salute him back with a bottle. Fred turned back and dropped some of the buttered popcorn in his mouth. He looked around. "Is somebody recording this?" He heard back three confirmations. "Okay, just wondering." He turned back to the sea.

Fred was halfway through the bag when large amounts of roiling water caught his attention about a quarter mile away.

Twenty seconds later, the popcorn bag completely forgotten in his hands, Commander Fred Branon watched as the submarine was lifted out of the ocean.

By its tail.

Into the air.

Over two miles away, too far for Fred to hear, there were hundreds of people cheering and clapping on the decks of the QBS Polarus and QBS Ad Aeternitatem.

A thousand meters above them, a contralto voice, said into the silence of her Pod, "You don't fucking push my people. If you do, you won't like the results, I swear it."

>>**Bethany Anne, I have a request routed through Cheryl Lynn that the President wants to speak to you.**<<

President of what?

>>*The United States, she said*<<

Oh. Bethany Anne was sitting in her Pod, taking an hour for herself. ***Put him on the speakers.***

"This is Bethany Anne, Mr. President," she said.

"Hello, Ms. Anne," the President said.

Bethany Anne chuckled. "Sorry sir, that's my name, I don't have a last name. Just Bethany Anne."

"Sorry, I was a little confused about the name situation," he said. "I wanted to reach out to you regarding many of the changes going on with your technology and see if you would be willing to meet and discuss a few things that are occurring. I'm sorry, but this would be outside of normal channels."

"Yes, I'm open to a discussion. Where are you thinking? You may not be aware, but it's a problem every time I show up in America. Mysterious requests to arrest me happen all the time," she said.

"I happen to have a report coming to me, letting me know all of the different annoyances that have been aimed in your company's direction. I apologize, but your technology and method of handling challenges are throwing a lot of people into a level of discomfort they are ill-equipped to handle."

"No need to apologize to me. I'm sure, as an American, you understand the concept of talking softly and carrying a big stick, yes?" Bethany Anne asked, taking a trick of Ecaterina's to try and hide her American roots.

"Yes, I am," he said then paused a moment. "Just curious,

where are you right now? There is an office pool wondering where on Earth you are as we are speaking."

Bethany Anne looked out the window down at the globe below. "Above Africa, sir." Bethany Anne heard a lot of 'I'm out,' 'not my guess' and something else mumbled.

The President came back. "Nope, no one is a winner."

"Did anyone say how high?" Bethany Anne asked, amused that there would be betting in the President's Office.

"How high?" he asked.

"Yes, I'm about two hundred miles above Africa, so if you wait a few minutes, I'll be above South America."

She heard a loud, "That's me!" and laughter in the background.

"So, you're really up in space? This connection is astounding," he said.

"Yes, actually in space. I apologize, but I've got another situation I need to address. I know you have people to deal with your schedule, and my preference would be to keep this quiet, as I am neutral and prefer to also be seen as neutral. So whomever you have designated, please have them work with Cheryl Lynn and I will work my schedule as best I can to fit yours."

"Thank you, Bethany Anne. I look forward to meeting you," the President said.

"My pleasure, and I do as well," she replied before the connection was closed.

What situation do we need to address? TOM asked her.

My emotions, TOM, my emotions.

CHAPTER
TWENTY-FOUR

WASHINGTON D.C. USA

The black SUV was waiting for them as their Pods dropped down to the darkened parking lot at half-past one in the morning.

Three Pods landed, five people got out. The SUV driver stepped out and walked over to the men.

"John, Eric," he said as he clasped hands with the first two he came to. "Someone want to tell me why I got dropped from flying, and now I'm driving?" Captain Paul Jameson asked.

"You'll have to speak to BA about that," John said, with a thumb to one of the Pods. "She's in the middle one, waiting for you." John smiled at the pilot to reassure him before he and Eric followed Darryl, Scott, and Akio to check out the SUV Paul had driven from Florida.

Paul walked to the Pod, the doors opened, and Bethany Anne was sitting inside wearing a black executive suit with a maroon shirt underneath. "Hello Paul, long time no see!" She smiled at him as she sat up and stepped out of her Pod. She grabbed his offered hand and shook it before giving him a hug. "What? You think I'm not willing to hug one of my people that's been with me forever?"

She stepped back to look him up and down. "I see you're keeping in shape."

"Habit, I'm waiting to get into the next big thing," he said.

She cocked her head and asked, "What would that be?"

"Well, I requested twice to get into the Black Eagles, ma'am. Both times, I was told opportunity comes to those who wait."

"So it does, Paul Jameson, so it does," she agreed. "You know why you were told twice?"

Paul exhaled. "I'm hoping because I needed to get something through my thick skull?"

"No, it was because I had to be sure that your initial antagonism towards those above you had burned off. Furthermore, *you* needed to know it had burned off. How did you feel each time it happened?" she asked him.

"A little dejected, but I went back to work," he considered it further for a few moments. "I didn't feel neglected. Like I wasn't being listened to. Merely that things were going on that had a focus, and while I needed to wait, it wasn't to just cool my heels." He eyed her hopefully. "I take it that I'm getting my request to move up to the Black Eagles?"

She smiled. "Better."

Paul's head jerked back just a bit and to the side. "Better? Is there a new type of fighter?"

"Oh, you could say that, Paul. You see, there's an entirely new ship up there," Bethany Anne pointed to the sky. "One that isn't going to be, commanded like one down here. It's my ship, Paul. I'm going to need someone to fly her, and I don't want someone thinking in two dimensions."

"How big?" Paul asked.

"Fucking huge." Bethany Anne deadpanned. "But I'm told it can stop on a dime and give you nine cents change if that helps?"

"Well, it gets my attention, that's for sure," he said, his eyes narrowing as he tried to figure out what ship would be 'fucking huge.'

"I'll make you a deal, Paul. If you fly this ship for one month, and then want to go to a Black Eagle squad as either a fighter jockey or the unit commander, just tell me, and we'll make it happen. But, unless you want it, you have flown your last jet aircraft." She looked at Paul, who was trying to understand.

"No more jets?" he asked.

"Only if you want to, they're a little slow, but I can understand the desire to fly the old stuff," she said and winked at him. "So, if you accept my offer to see what's behind door number two, then this Pod behind me is going to take you back to your plane to get your clothes and everything you need. Then you are going on a fourteen-hour trip to where your new ship is waiting for you. I'm told they desperately require your help to dial stuff in. You'll be one of three, directly under me. You are the pilot. I'm going to need guns, but I'm pretty sure I know who that will be. I am also going to need an XO, and I'm pretty sure I know who will sign up for that."

"Jean Dukes for guns?" Paul asked, smiling.

"Yes." Bethany Anne agreed with a chuckle. "The one and only."

"Hell yeah, I can't pass up a chance to see where this is going to go," he held out his hand. "Ma'am, Lt. Commander

Paul Jameson, reporting for duty."

Bethany Anne grasped his hand firmly. "I accept. Now get in this Pod and get yourself out to the Asteroid Belt."

Paul dropped her hand and stepped around her to get in the Pod. As he sat in the chair and started strapping in, he looked back up and asked, "Asteroid Belt?"

Bethany Anne turned around. "Yes, make sure you take some reading material. I'm told the trip can get a little boring after the first hour or two of looking at the stars." She closed the doors and hit the front twice. The Pod slowly moved up, paused, and then quickly disappeared.

Bethany Anne turned around. "One down."

She walked towards the SUV and slid into the back seat as Scott held the door open for her. She noticed Darryl in the seat in the very back. "Short straw?" she asked him.

"That damned Akio is lucky as shit, that's all I'm saying," Darryl grunted as he tried to find a comfortable position in the smaller back seat.

Akio was already in the seat next to Bethany Anne as she slid in the middle, "Akio?" He smiled and shrugged. "I do what they ask, they say pull a straw, so I choose a straw."

Bethany Anne looked dubiously towards her Elite Queen's Own. While she thought he was probably doing something fishy, she couldn't figure it out quickly, so she dropped it.

By the time the SUV left the parking lot, the Pods had left. Fifteen minutes later, the vehicle arrived at the address provided them. A single guard stepped out of the shadows to wave them in. The guys saw the man step back into the shadows once they passed through.

"My Queen, these are not the right guards," Akio said. "These are here to kidnap you and take you to another, someone who wants you either dead or alive."

"Motherfucking President can…" John began when Akio cut him off.

"It isn't the President doing this," he said. "This is some group that I can't figure out reading thoughts from this distance."

Bethany Anne heard Darryl behind her. "Lucky little mind-reading shit!" Perhaps Darryl had figured out how Akio had been so fortunate.

"How do you want to play this, Bethany Anne?" John asked.

"I want to trip this trap and figure out how to go find this mysterious guy. Give me a second." Bethany Anne opened her consciousness to hear the vibrations, the energies, the thoughts around her. She shut down those of her men and started jumping from one mind to the next, seeking something… seeking…

"Got him," she said, her eyes still closed. "They're expecting to shoot you guys and gas me. In other words, gas everything and then, when I'm out of the way, fill you guys with lead."

"Damned rude," Scott mumbled. "I've had enough lead in me recently, I'd rather not go through that again if I can help it." He turned to Bethany Anne but was shocked to see her eyes shining red, fangs out, countenance determined.

"Ah, John?" Scott murmured, reaching toward him in the front seat.

"Huh?" John said as he turned left down a ramp to continue towards the bottom. They had been told they needed to descend three levels where they would meet the security.

"Ah, John?" Scott said again more forcefully, tapping him on the shoulder.

John turned quickly to look at Scott. "What?" It was then

he noticed Bethany Anne's face. "Oh."

John turned back towards the front. "Okay guys. New plan. The plan is to stay the fuck in the SUV so these poor sons of bitches can suffer whatever the hell they deserve for wanting to kill us."

John finished driving down the additional level and pulled towards the men standing guard next to a door. He kept his lights on, keeping the waiting men a little blinded as the vehicle slowly came to a stop. Fifteen feet away from the SUV, the two uniformed men had their thumbs in their belts, their faces angled slightly away from the vehicle.

Bethany Anne's head turned to her left. "Three." Then glancing towards her right, "four." She finished, looking ahead, "Two."

Akio faced the front seat after noticing her face. He had not ever seen Bethany Anne so deadly calm. Eric caught Akio's eyes and shook his head. "Stay in the car," Eric mouthed to Akio, who nodded his understanding.

That was when Bethany Anne disappeared, and the shrieking began. Seconds later, one of the men in their head-lights stared at them from lifeless eyes, his neck broken. The other grabbed his throat, as Bethany Anne opened the door with his hand on the security glass. Seconds later she disappeared inside.

John exited the vehicle, saying, "Well, let's see if any of these poor fuckers need anything."

Scott got out and called from his side, "Three here, beyond the need of any support."

"Same here," Akio said from the left.

"Can somebody let me the fuck out?" Darryl called. "This backseat is for pigeons!"

Eric laughed as he went around Scott's door and grabbed

a hidden handle in the seat, "It's here genius," he told Darryl as the whole seat moved forward and Darryl was able to squeeze out.

"I'll ride on the damn roof next time," Darryl growled as he pulled his Sig Sauer P227 Tactical and started towards the door.

John had already gone through the door after he heard a couple of pistol shots inside.

The men caught up to him as he was studying another soldier, this time with a bite in his neck when they heard a scream.

Akio and Scott stayed behind while the other two followed John down the hallway, their pistols drawn.

They caught up to Bethany Anne, holding a man in a general's uniform high against a wall screeching at her. "What are you?"

"Your worst fucking nightmare, George!" she replied in a menacing voice. "Someone who sees your inner thoughts, your inner sins, and your inner knowledge and rips it out as I please." She grew a nail a few inches long on her left hand. "Now, where do I start cutting, George?" She took the sharp nail and trailed the tip down his uniform coat, cutting slices into the fabric. "Who is JG, George?"

George shook his head violently.

"Joshua Guildenstern?" George's eyes opened wide.

"What are you doing? Stop it!" He tried to fight but was easily pinned to the wall by John holding an arm and a leg on his left side, Eric on his right. Bethany Anne let go, turned around to straighten her jacket before once again turning back to the frightened man. "Once again, who is Joshua, George?"

>> **I have four Guildensterns within an hour of here.**

Two are happily married, one is a lawyer, one is an industrialist. <<

Tell me about the industrialist.

ADAM described Joshua's large holdings, his family history, what could be accounted for, and his present location.

"So, Joshua lives out in Virginia?" Bethany Anne asked George aloud. "Yes, I can read your mind, you useless morally bankrupt chucklefuck." She tapped her finger against her lip. "You're going to text him and let him know that there was a problem, but the package is tied up tight. You have to wait until an unexpected event, make something up, happens before leaving. We will get to Joshua tonight, trust me."

"Bethany Anne?" John said.

"Yes?"

"What do you want to do with all of the evidence?" John looked around as he spoke with her. "Lots of blood." He paused a moment. "Lots."

Bethany Anne turned to George and spoke, silk over steel, "So, how were you guys going to clean it up?"

"Cleanup crew, in two hours," he rasped.

"So, if there are no bodies, but blood everywhere, what will they do?" she asked him.

"Clean it up, but report it," he replied.

"How long before that happens?"

"I'd need to see the mess," he said. Bethany Anne nodded to the guys who dropped him to the floor.

John grabbed him by the collar and started walking him out of the room while Eric told Bethany Anne, "You aren't going to be able to go see the President like that," he told her, pointing to her outfit. She looked down in disgust at all of the blood she had splattered over herself.

"Son of a bitch," she said. "Cheryl Lynn is going to kill me."

"Well, I'd offer to wet a tissue to get the two blood splatters around your mouth, but I think that would be about as useful as pissing on a fire," he told her.

Bethany Anne rolled her eyes as she turned towards the door. "Wow, Eric. Way to tell a girl she looks bad," she muttered as she followed Darryl out of the room.

Eric walked behind her. "Hey, BA, I'm just keeping it real." He waved his arms wide in explanation, talking to her back as he walked out of the room, carefully stepping over the blood splatters in the middle of the floor.

———

General George Thourbourah stood next to the column by the SUV, staring blankly into the distance, his mind screaming but his body not responding.

He was in purgatory as six people spoke around him.

"So, we have ten minutes to figure this out," Bethany Anne said. "Or I need to cancel the President's meeting."

"I say we make this jerk-off help us," John said, flicking a thumb in the direction of the general. "It was his dumbass plan to kill us all in the first place.

"Yeah, but we need corroboration, and unfortunately, I killed them all." Bethany Anne said. "Perhaps not a moment of clear thinking."

John snorted. "No, probably not. But don't jump all over yourself. You found an outlet that could be justified and it was easy enough for you to go out and do it. Now, we just need to figure out the solution that doesn't make us all seem like bloodthirsty killers."

Everyone but the general stood a moment to look at the dead bodies, the blood splatters and then returned to looking at Bethany Anne.

"Okay, I get it," she groused and fought the urge to flip them off. "Next time, I'll knock more heads into unconsciousness instead of knocking them all the way off."

"Secret Service is not going to accept the President coming here," Darryl said as he looked around at the blood everywhere. "This is one photo away from a scandal."

"Okay, I've got an idea, but it sucks beyond sucking, boss," Scott said.

"Let's hear it." She turned towards him.

"He," Scott started, pointing at the stunned general. "Has to be the hero of the night."

Akio turned to look at Scott. "I don't follow this," he said.

Scott started selling his idea. "Bethany Anne was attacked, she was in the middle, the General comes here, saves the night and then... and then..." Scott sputtered, "Well, then the story falls down," he sighed.

"Likely when I kick his ass again," Bethany Anne said as she looked at the mess. "Gott Verdammt! Why didn't I just leave some alive?" She looked around for something to kick, but everything was concrete.

"What about Virginia?" John asked.

"Joshua?" Bethany Anne said. "Frank has found out a shitload about that dried-out animal fondler. I'm for getting to him tomorrow or the next night. Tonight, I need to meet with the President."

She turned around. "Okay guys, this jerkoff is going to go back to his life, thinking that many of us got killed, but you guys took me away. Someone shoot his ass where he won't bleed out..."

"Wait!" she screamed when four guns all cocked quickly, aiming at the general.

"Dammit, one bullet, not one bullet from each of you!"

she laughed. "Although, that was almost funny as hell. Draw straws to see who gets to do it. I'm going to jump to Florida and take a vampire-fast shower and will be right back. Stage this place to look like there was a lot of fighting and drag some bodies around. I'll take two of you back who get dirty. Three of you stay clean." She looked around, "Ok, snap snap guys!" She took a step and disappeared.

Darryl muttered, "Akio isn't drawing first!"

––––––

Thirteen minutes later, Darryl was driving with Akio riding shotgun. Scott was in the back seat beside Bethany Anne. John had too much blood on him from following her, and Eric won the draw but got blood on himself when he shot the general.

The new location, compliments of the general, was another building, but as soon as they entered, they could see lots of people. They made it to the bottom when Akio said, "Yes, all good. No deviousness in any of them."

"Okay, see you guys in a few minutes," she said as Akio stepped out of the SUV and opened her door. Nodding to him in thanks, she walked up to the guard in front of a nondescript gray door. "I believe I'm expected?"

The man nodded with a smile. "Yes ma'am, you are. Please have your men stay with us, there will be two guys inside to pat you down and make sure you're clean, ma'am."

Bethany Anne allowed herself to be searched and waited as they performed a metal search to make sure she had no weapons. She was escorted down a corridor that was at least two hundred yards long. She ended up in a small room, before a door on the opposite wall was opened. The nicely appointed meeting room that she was ushered into had a long dark wooden table, leather chairs around it and a wall of screens to her left. Ahead of her, the President was seated, looking at the newspaper.

He looked up and smiled. "Hello, Bethany Anne, thank you for meeting me here this evening."

"Trust me, Mr. President, I've already been blessed. Getting to speak to you is the icing on the cake," she told him and turned on her best smile.

CHAPTER TWENTY-FIVE

WASHINGTON D.C. USA

So, I'm to understand your meeting went well, Mr. President?" George asked.

"What?" the President replied, as he sat down and opened the Tums bottle in front of him, "With who?"

"Why, with the TQB Chairwoman, Bethany Anne."

He frowned. "No, I was stood up, George. Damned rude, if you ask me," the President said. "While she eventually sent an apology to explain she got violently sick, it seems pretty suspect to me. Sometimes foreigners have the worst manners."

"I see. Well, I'm sorry to hear that, sir." George said as he moved his papers around.

The President waved a hand. "We can try another time, but not before I cancel on her once. I try not to be petty, but this President doesn't appreciate rudeness."

"Of course not, sir," George agreed. "So, we're following

up on the Chinese submarine incident. Another time that TQB has inflamed the passions of a powerful nation against them."

The President frowned. "More rhetoric, George? I'm not happy with being stood up, but let's not jump to conclusions. Why was there a Chinese submarine so close to their ships anyway?"

George kept the wince out of his eyes. His conversation with JG had been difficult, but the massive amount of dead bodies and blood everywhere, plus his own gunshot wound that he had carefully hidden from everyone so far told the man they had tried. His memory was a little vague, but they had gotten three of the guards in some way. He didn't believe it was her usual detail, so, unfortunately, they didn't know who would be missing and presumed dead.

"Well, Navy's guess is that the Chinese were going to put the squeeze on them," George said.

"Exactly. So they grabbed the submarine and pulled it out like a fish." The President shrugged. "I've seen the video, I love it."

"Yes, I understand it's prime viewing across the fleet," George agreed. "But the Chinese are seriously pissed at the moment."

"This time it's not our problem," the President said. "Make sure our hands are clean in this episode, I don't want any splatter on us."

"No, I think it's fair to say that TQB is taking full responsibility for ruining one of their submarines," George replied.

"Something about them having to scram the nuclear reactor right?"

"Yes, it didn't work too well angled up like it was. So, TQB's two ships floated away with the Chinese ship in tow until they had a place to put it down and let the seamen out. Some things came off the Chinese sub, and the TQB ships left the area."

"Where are they now?" the President asked.

"West of South America, in the Pacific."

"Which way are they heading?"

"They're heading towards China, sir."

The President stopped for a moment and shook his head in frustration. "Dammit." He reached for the Tums bottle one more time.

———

CHINA

Stephanie Lee looked around the room. It was clean.

This is the control room, the male voice told her.

"How long have you been here?" Stephanie Lee asked.

Eight centuries, the female voice said.

"Why are you here?" Stephanie Lee continued.

To raise up those on Earth who deserve to move forward in an enlightened and empowered way. To prepare for the tests and trials, the female voice spoke in her mind.

To defeat the weak and worthless, the male voice added.

That, too, the female voice confirmed.

"You two need names," Stephanie Lee said.

Then I shall be Yin, the female voice said.

I shall be Yang, the male finished.

"That works very well, I like them." Stephanie Lee sat in the central chair. While she wasn't a huge woman, the chair was built for someone smaller.

"Where are you?" she asked.

We are touching you from both here and elsewhere. We cannot fully engage here in your dimension without a body, and we had not yet found an adequate host to share our intelligence and wisdom until you arrived, Yang said.

"I see," she said. "And my father?"

Has spoken with us since he became the Clan leader before you were born. We have been making plans for the future, with contingencies for contingencies. Unfortunately, we did not see the rise of other Kurtherians on this planet. That was a mistake, Yin said.

Stephanie Lee stood up. "Where is this Transference Pod?" She started walking out of the control room. If she didn't do something soon, she would talk herself out of her future. Just like her father had, apparently.

She wouldn't allow that. She would be as she had originally planned.

Having power and authority.

Turn left here, Yin spoke to her as she stepped into a hallway. *Put your hand on the black square on the right, now stretch your hand wide.* A door opened before her. It was a simple room, with a rectangular box in the middle. Everything was made from metal, gray. There was no rust on anything.

Step to the Transference Pod and place your hand on the right, yes on the smaller square.

The Pod opened for her, the white inside clashing with the darkness of everything else.

When you lay in here, you will come back as the ultimate, Yang said. *You will be the Leopard Empress.*

She looked around and found a place to take off her robe before getting inside the pod, pushing another square inside. The Pod closed with an audible click.

RELEASE THE DOGS OF WAR

A minute later, another human entered the room. Stephanie Lee's father bent down to gently pick up the sacrificial robe she had been wearing.

He had a tear in his eye. Eight years ago, he thought that the best chance, the one his clan had been genetically marrying and having babies to accomplish, had left the mountain and would not be back. The best opportunity in fifteen generations had sprinted away, and he hadn't commanded her to be brought back.

Because, he thought, it had been a mere childish spat.

He turned and walked out of the room. The transference would take days.

Inside the Pod, Stephanie Lee's face was composed, peaceful, while her mind screamed silently in pain.

―――――

PLA GENERAL STAFF HEADQUARTERS, BEIJING

The four men stepped into the darkened and quiet room and nodded to each other. No names were to be used, but any agreement reached would be put into effect.

After the appropriate respect had been shown to each of them, the political representative spoke. "Welcome to our new naval representative." Heads nodded in greeting. "It seems that the last plan failed to accomplish our goals."

"We tried to express the futility to the last representative," Intelligence told Navy, "But pride interfered."

The political representative agreed and continued, "Where are these ships now? I understand they left our submarine on an island?"

"Yes, Ascension Island, near Georgetown," the naval representative answered.

"They have moved to the Pacific Ocean," Intelligence replied.

"Where are they going, or are they sitting still in the water as they were before?" Political continued.

"They are moving towards us," Intelligence said.

"Do they expect to do something else? They would what, attack our nation?" Navy asked.

"Unlikely," Intelligence said.

"Still, this has caused us to lose much face," the political representative said. "Therefore, the three of you need to review options. If they want to make us a fool, then we will return the gesture.

If they want to take it further?" he paused. "Then we push back until they break. We do not back down. Not even Russia or the United States does that to us."

His lips pressed together. "I have a meeting with our business side. We will bring economic attacks against them as well. They thought it funny to pull our submarine out of the water like a fish? We shall see who is gasping for air in the end."

He nodded to the other three men and then pushed back his chair and turned, opening and closing the door quietly behind him.

The three men looked at each other before the naval representative put his hands, clasped, on the table. "Suggestions, gentleman?"

———

RELEASE THE DOGS OF WAR

You see, I'm not really here right now, a female voice said.

Joshua's eyes opened quickly. He looked around his bedroom, trying to see in the dark. His huge bed, a four-poster with wooden columns surrounding him, was dark gray in the minimal light coming through his shades in the early morning.

He had heard a whisper in his mind, a dream he supposed. But it had sounded so real, so tangible.

So close.

The conversation with the general had not gone well. George's memory of the ambush was fuzzy. But he had confirmed that the President had not met with her later that night so that much was true.

Still, the feeling that he was missing something important was unsettling him, and now it was affecting his mind while he slept.

In the morning, he would pack and head out. He would need to lock down the computer equipment downstairs after pulling the solid-state hard drives to take with him. That information was his past and his future, his security.

It was everything that made him what he was, and the foundation for so many others at the same time.

He considered what he needed to do and turned to look at his alarm clock, the faint blue numbers glowing twenty-three minutes past three in the morning.

He was restless. Joshua pushed the covers off and sat up in bed. His feet blindly searched around for his slippers before finding them and sliding them on. He hated the cold stone floors but at the same time, couldn't stand carpet all over the house.

Reaching over and touching the base of his lamp, he turned it on to the lowest setting. His body shook involuntarily, and he looked over his shoulder. The feeling of being watched didn't go away.

He felt like a child, but he still got down on his knees on the floor to look under the bed, making sure that no one was there.

No one was.

He put his head on the cool floor and could feel the sweat beading on his forehead. The stress was getting to him. He thought about how close George was to him and decided that George would have to be cut out. He hated losing such a valuable asset, but George knew who he was and had been involved in the attempted attack.

They would be coming for George. He lifted his head and made a mental note to start the process to remove George from the equation.

He got up and went into his bathroom. It had a walk-in shower, Jacuzzi tub and bath. There was a lap bath to the side as well so he could swim against the water jet streams for fitness.

He really did hate the cold.

If there weren't so many damned important people in this area of the country, he would move somewhere a bit more predisposed towards decent weather. He brushed his teeth to get the nasty film off and put his toothbrush back.

Grabbing his silk robe, he tied it around his waist. He had two and a half hours before his house lady would come to start his breakfast and take care of his room.

He walked down the hall, descended the wooden steps, and turned at the end beside the stairway. A door at the back opened to provide access to space under the stairway, and he stepped in. He reached up and pulled on a string to click on the light. Stepping over a box of Christmas decorations that the people had left behind when pulling everything down last season, he pushed on a small section of the wooden wall. It clicked, and a portion of the wall opened and allowed him to step inside.

He walked down the small, carpeted hallway to his computer room. Calmly, with the ease of repetition, he put his palm on the plate and spoke for the recognition software. He waited for the locks to cycle before pulling on the door and entering the climate-controlled room.

The computers weren't anything special, just old. Old enough that there weren't any embedded security problems from foreign manufacturers. Joshua had seven more of these machines, set to the side. All ready to be pulled out of their packaging and put in place when this one failed.

He walked up to the keyboard and monitor, then typed in his password to open the command set and put in the commands to lock down the hard drives. Once complete, it was a matter of a few seconds to issue the shutdown command.

It took an agonizingly long minute and thirty seconds to completely shut down before he could push the lock button, and then pull out the unique hard drive setup. Joshua turned around and went back through the doors, closing them carefully before he turned to go back up the stairs.

He walked into his room and put the hard drive on his bed before going into his closet and grabbing his travel bag. He would call his pilot at 5 AM, notifying him that he would want to leave as soon as a flight plan was filed to the Caribbean. Then he would figure out the next best location.

Church.

What the hell? Joshua stuck his head out of his closet to

look around. Why would he think of church right now? He hadn't thought about a church in over thirty years. Ducking back into his closet to grab two pairs of shoes, he quickly walked out and tossed them on the bed before going into his bathroom for his grooming kit.

Coming back out of the bathroom, he added the kit to the items on the bed and went to his dresser for underclothes and jeans. He grabbed some t-shirts and threw them on the pile too.

Five minutes, two dress shirts, and some cash from his safe later, he was stuffing everything in his bag. He had written a quick note to tell his housekeeper he would be gone at least two weeks.

When he left the house, he had not noticed that the number two on the note to his housekeeper had an additional zero added to it. Apparently, he was now going to be gone for twenty weeks.

Joshua got into his car and texted his pilot that he wanted to leave as soon as possible. He had a message back within seconds that he was up at the airport already servicing the plane for periodic maintenance review if he wanted to leave now?

"Fucking great!" Joshua muttered to himself. "Finally something going right in my life."

He pointed his Jaguar down the street and floored the gas pedal. His neighbors could bitch, but he wouldn't be around to hear it for at least a couple of weeks. It took him forty-seven minutes in the early morning traffic to make it to his private hanger. The door was open, and his jet was lit up. He parked the Jag in the back of the hanger and grabbed his stuff before leaving the keys on the office desk for his service guy to go get it cleaned and to run it at least once a week while he was gone.

He walked over to the jet, jumping up the few steps to get on and turned right to head to his seat. Dropping his bag on the left seat and he seated himself on the right. He wiped his face with both hands, never noticing that the plane was beginning to taxi already. Closing his eyes as the plane waited in line, the engines powered up and the tension in his neck relaxed. Soon, they were airborne.

Time to wake up, Joshua Guildenstern.

Joshua's eyes flew open to see a woman sitting across from him.

"What the hell?" He turned to look around, but found himself in the airplane as expected. His bag was missing from the seat beside him. "You can't be here, it's impossible!"

"Oh, but I'm here," she said.

A man came from the front of the airplane and Joshua looked up to call his pilot, but found himself looking at a man he didn't recognize. "Who the hell are you?"

The man smiled malevolently at him. "I'm the Queen's Ranger, Barnabas."

"Who?" Joshua practically squeaked. "Ranger?" He started to stand up when the woman lashed out with a kick and shattered his kneecap. Joshua screamed in pain and dropped back into his seat, trying to cradle his knee.

"The defendant wasn't told he could stand up," she admonished him. "In fact, the defendant is only here for the punishment phase, the trial has already happened."

Joshua bit down on his pain. "You can't be here!" He looked around, "You weren't here before we took off!"

She turned in her chair. "Did you hear that, Barnabas? Apparently, your ability to play with memories is impossible."

"What?" Joshua tried to make sense out of what they were saying.

She turned back to Joshua. "Your useless organization was created in seventeen seventy-six. Barnabas was born hundreds of years before that." She looked over to the strange man as she spoke. Joshua tried to look at both of them, but a sudden stab of pain got his attention. It was then he noticed she had a well-dressed shoe pushing on his kneecap. He tried to slap it away, but it was gone, and all he accomplished was twisting his own leg.

He wanted to cry, but grown men didn't cry.

"Pay attention." He looked up to see she held his treasured hard drive. "We appreciate you grabbing this. ADAM, our pilot at the moment, will enjoy reviewing the information and finally pulling apart everything your perverted group has tried to create." She tossed the drive to the other man, who caught it easily. Joshua was watching the catch when she snapped fingers in front of his face, startling him to turn towards her.

"You have no idea how badly I want to cause you untold pain, pain that wracks you for years. Something, by the way, I could easily accomplish," she said. Joshua's eyes widened as she put a hand up in front of her face and the two of them watched as one of her fingers grew a black nail three inches long. "Pain of just a few cuts, with rubbing alcohol, I don't even need to use nanites to waste your body."

Both of them were mesmerized by the ebony gleam of her nail in the light of the cabin before it slowly receded, leaving a typical finger, and she looked at his face again. "But, alas, I'm not allowed to fall into the cycle of retribution that my feelings call for, so I cannot, must not, do that which I crave."

Joshua's face was covered in sweat now, beads of liquid starting to slip down his cheeks.

"So, I'm here to let the Ranger do what he chooses to do.

I'm here to tell you that you stole my love from me, you guilty fucking savage. May you rot in HELL!" She hissed at him, her eyes flaring red at the end. She stood up quickly, turned away, and walked towards the front of the plane.

Joshua turned to the man and tried to smile, but the Ranger's face was a mask. And that mask was the essence of promised pain, pain that was coming, coming for him.

"Hello Joshua, my name is Barnabas," he started. "While it is true that Bethany Anne is limited in what she can do..." eyes turned red and fangs grew out of his mouth, as he finished,

"I am not..."

———

An hour later, as Joshua's Learjet flew towards the islands, two figures disappeared off of the plane to appear in a closet on a small island just east of Miami, in Key Biscayne.

The man needed to take a shower, to remove massive quantities of blood.

The woman would seek the screams she had heard on the plane in the lonely nights, when her empty arms and heart ached with loss, to feel the satisfaction of justice in her memories.

Now, she still had one to find. If it meant she tore up a country to locate the bitch?

Then so be it.

THE ETHERIC

Johann couldn't see in the grayness of everything. He was just about out of supplies and wasn't sure what to do now.

He didn't know the amount of time he had been in this one location, this one place. Occasionally, a box with supplies would appear, always in the same place every time, keeping him chained to the only lifeline of food that he could discern.

This place was a void, it existed without a sun and moon, without stars or clouds, trees or the wind, just mist.

Just, nothing.

He tried yelling but heard no return sounds from the grayness. It consumed his voice and gave him silence in return. He never felt anything looking at him. It was all quiet, all loneliness, all himself.

He was trying to read the words on the box of crackers he had eaten, carefully parsing them out one at a time when he caught something in his peripheral vision.

He turned to look in that direction and thought he might have seen a light.

There it was again! He strained to see what it might be and looked at his meager food stash. Should he leave this area? Could he find this place again in all of the grayness?

He looked up hurriedly to see the one light had become two, both red. Both coming at him.

He started sweating in the cool air when he realized they weren't lights, they were eyes.

Bethany Anne's eyes.

Johann started grabbing what food he could, stuffing his pockets and then grabbed the fork and knife, his only weapons and turned away from the direction of the red eyes and ran.

She had been in his dreams, promising him pain. More pain than he could possibly imagine when she came for him. He had awoken thirteen times, every time sweating and afraid.

She was here.

He could hear her voice in his head, drilling through his ability to think, to plan. He could only run in his terror.

I've come, Johann.

Johann did his best to jog, but every time he turned around, her eyes were the same distance away, flaring red in the gray mist.

I'VE COME! she screamed into his psyche.

Johann bolted upright, his heart beating wildly, his clothes soaked in sweat as he looked around in desperation trying to slow his breathing. The remains of his food were stacked in a pile near him.

"God!" he cried out weeping, wiping his red eyes. "What

is the bitch doing to me?" he spoke to the nothingness.

Like always, it never replied.

Johann used his dirty shirt to wipe off his face as he crawled to the food stash and opened the cracker box. He pulled out six crackers and started eating the first, a tiny nibble at a time. He reached over to pick up the piece of cardboard he was using to keep track of how many times he slept. He used his fingers to tear another small rip. He grabbed another cracker and started counting the little rips.

His face turned ashen in the gray light.

There were thirteen.

———

MICHAEL'S NOTES

Release the Dogs of War - The Kurtherian Gambit 10:
June 26, 2016
One month after the previous book's release.

Hello again!

It's the end of June, 2016 and this is the TENTH book you are reading…Well, if you didn't read the short stories (which you totally should, because they are kickass!) Either way THANK YOU.

It is due to your continued reading, enjoying and feedback that these stories still make it out each month. That it's WORTH doing each month. Because, without your reading, what's the point? Without your support, where would the extra energy come from to keep this crazy schedule going?

My challenges this month were different than previously. I was having a serious problem with trying to pull together the threads, the arcs if you will, for this book. I have a great friend by the name of Kat Lind who happens to be an industrial psychologist among many other degrees, and she helped talk me through some of my issues.

Thankfully.

I am a visual person, I like to think in images (as I'm learning) and I didn't have an image for this book. Oh, I could do a bunch of explosions (kind of got that out of my system in Bitch's Night Out—sorry). But, I wanted to lead the direction towards so much more while still destroying a few people along the way. Just, not individually every time. Plus, the desire to introduce the next big thing… MORE KURTHERIANS… Mwuhahahahahahaha…

<*cough* *cough* *ach*, Ugh, furball>

Sorry, I got ahead of myself there.

Bethany Anne, how I wanted to just let her rip and tear and destroy and kill and so on and so on. The problem with that, is she is constrained by her role and the expectations that others have on her as much as she is constrained by her personal desires. Well, the logical personal desires, not so much the emotional ones. Plus, who wants to read a book of just killing and more killing? (Yes, my hand is up, but I don't count.)

There is a LOT going on. We have the Queen's Rangers now and I can say that I didn't plan that at all. When I was typing the "What am I going to do with you, Barnabas?" from Bethany Anne, I was really talking out loud to myself, *what the hell am I going to do with you?* So, that was a new thing and I loved how it is working out with Tabitha.

That brings up a good point. You know that story that we are going to read in about 4 or 5 weeks? Next month or so? SUED FOR PEACE. Yeah, neither of us know what's in that book yet. No kidding, no lying—just truth. No *fucking* clue. Well, except Stephanie Lee, Kurtherians, China, politics and a 'Fucking HUGE' spaceship.

Speaking of big-ass spaceship. Sorry on the cover!

I seriously thought we were going to have that scene in this book, but it ended up with a submarine pulled out of the water like a fish. They just couldn't get the ship done in time. Which, I completely realize sounds weird.

My bad.

Then, the episodes with the women talking. Hell, that was so much fun! I did have some concerns when I wrote that, so I asked some fantastic women to look it over to make sure I didn't go too far. These are older ladies, grandmothers full of decorum in fact.

They told me I didn't go far enough. *<blushing problems>*

Wow, I have some more learning to do, apparently.

I look forward to kicking a piece of China's ass. A lot of those assholes are doing EVERYTHING I point to in my books. They are stealing company secrets and using them. They are placing hidden spy software in the hardware we buy from their companies and while I admire it from a survival of the fittest mentality, it pisses me off because it is just wrong. Like, ethically wrong. Their leaders are morally bankrupt. Not exactly the type of people you want to face the future of our world alongside. Not that we have a choice. Oh well, maybe another future is coming for us, not the dystopian one I can imagine. Remember, China's leaders are thinking and implementing plans for fifty to a hundred years in the future. Their descendants finishing stuff they start now. Damned impressive.

Our leaders can't think beyond the next election.

Oh, speaking of imagine.

Imagine that something goes wrong with all of the computers, a cyber-war is unleashed, in fact. Civilization implodes because our interconnectedness across countries, reliance on technology and inability to procure fuel, food and parts incites such a civil disturbance that we damn near kill ourselves across the globe.

Those spy satellites up above us? Useless. Most power systems have melted due to the cyber-warfare.

Now, imagine a person finds himself brought back to reality, having fought for a hundred years to break free from another dimension, one he used, but didn't have near the affinity to use like one he loved.

The *one* he needed to find because she had left the Earth a hundred years or so before. Before this time had happened. She had made sure the Earth was safe, and was still protecting it, even if she was unaware of the present issues.

She's out there, among the stars.

Now imagine this man had to force the world to his will to drive it back from the edge of the catastrophic results of their stupidity. Whether they wanted to make his future happen or not.

The Dark Messiah - The Second Dark Ages will be arriving this winter. He has a promise to fulfill and he will help, or destroy, any who dare come between him and *fulfilling his promise to her.*

Because, whether it happens that day, or a hundred years in the future or more, Michael *will* fulfill his promise.

A promise even Death has learned to respect.

———

Now, for something completely different. I decided I wanted to see about giving a few Kindle Fires ($50) away to some readers who are presently serving in the military. I thought, how cool would that be to give away four of those? I get to support both readers AND some members in the military which I love. I have a lot of military fans, and quite a few who are helping me put these books together with their insights and corrections and stuff.

Then, I found out (thanks!) a Kindle Fire sucks for reading on base out in the sun, it's heavy, it has poor battery life etc. etc. So, I asked about the next higher one. Then, I asked which Kindle would be best to give away to active military or vets who are interacting with me on Facebook and received their input.

The answer, it seems, is the $210 Kindle Paperwhite 300PPI with Wi-Fi and 3G.

That was a little bit of a surprise. A tad more than I was budgeting and frankly made me swallow once or twice. That was until I said 'fuck it!' and decided I was going to do it.

And I did. The first Paperwhite to give away is right here

with me as I'm typing this. But, here's the problem, how do we figure out who wins the first one?

I figure a raffle is the best solution.

Next, I'm trying to figure out how to give more of these away? I can afford four Fires a month right now, but I'm not so sure about four or five Paperwhites each month.

So, guess what I did? I brainstormed until I think I came up with a way to make it all happen, if I can get enough support from readers (not only just Kurtherian Fans, but a lot of readers) we can make something REALLY COOL happen.

Here is the plan. You will have to let me know if you want to get involved, the plan sucks, or whatever. Either way, I'm giving away two Paperwhites, minimum.

This idea is to see if we can come together as readers where I support you, we support the military and I get to highlight other Indie Authors like I've been doing before.

Finally (and really, really important) - Keep it self supporting (as in, it helps pay for the Kindles and the infrastructure.) I think I have an idea and this is what I'm thinking:

1) Readers sign up for an email newsletter that promotes books. Each book highlighted is from an Indie Author with prices from ARC (Please read for free, and give a review if you would - so helping complete newbie authors) to $0.00 (free) and KU and full price across multiple genres. Think of it more as a weekly catalog perhaps? Maybe once a week or every two weeks, depends on how much freaking work it takes for me to do it.

2) In the email, I will link to my website which will display all of the offers, but most of them will have Amazon Affiliate links (I can't put affiliate links in the email, against Amazons TOS (terms of service) and they would ban me.) Not that it matters for ARCs or

$0.00 or KU books, because affiliate links don't procure any money for those links. What it might do, however, is provide an income IF you see an interesting book, and then go on to buy something else while you are there. There is no cost to you, the reader, to do this. Amazon will eventually pay me a small percentage.

3) Using the affiliate income, I can pay towards the Kindle(s) and the Kindle shipping costs (which can be expensive around the world), the email list costs and other subscriptions to make this work and (God Please) allow me to hire someone to do the newsletters. I really, really don't like putting newsletters together. I can, and I will, but I don't find it fun.

4) Finally, Kindle Paperwhites! The good stuff, not the Fires, are selected by raffle to give away and provided to the military personnel compliments of the email reader selected for that giveaway. Right now, this is only US military as I haven't the foggiest notion how to do this for those in countries we connect with. I'm WILLING to do it, but don't know HOW to do it. I think it would be cool to be able to also support those in other countries militaries.

Readers win by finding good books by Indie Authors and supporting giving Kindles at the same time. Obviously, Indie Authors win by getting in front of readers. Some book lovers in the Military win because …KINDLE! I will win because I have figured out a self-supporting method to help everyone I want to help and (maybe, hopefully?) it will grow if the Affiliate Income pays to help it grow.

The worst thing that will happen is I buy and give away two Kindle Paperwhites (which I'm going to do, whether this works or not), so no harm there.

If you are willing to jump on the PaperWhites for Military Members Book Newsletter - Just click here:

http://kurtherianbooks.com/readers-supporting-military-book-newsletter/

You can sign up for the email newsletter (seperate from your Kurtherian Gambit email) AND PLEASE Nominate someone (drop your contact info and I'll get in touch with you to get their info) - links on the page and a FAQ as well at the link above.

PLEASE click on the link above and consider joining that email list. The email that comes will link to a page on my website highlighting authors, ARCS (free read for review if you are willing) and other stuff. I explain more (including it is NOT a NON-PROFIT and why) on the page above.

If you help me get that list to 10,000 names, I'll write a special short story and release it for free. Just share that link above and encourage anyone you know that loves to read, supports the Military (U.S. for now) and Indie Authors. The emails will be simple and will point to a website to get more info (Amazon TOS).

I'm in contact with a military support group (http://operationsupplydrop.org) to help make MORE happen if we have the Kindles for them, so what the hell?

LET'S DO THIS!

So far, the Readers helping Military Readers email list (with minimal sharing in 48 hours) is at 82 so far. My Kurtherian Gambit email list is at 715 - but that took 10 books and 8 months. I'm hoping we can hit 2,000 signed up in just 2 months. That would be freaking cool as hell. I'm going to spend money to make this list happen, but I could use any help you can offer, as well.

You don't need to ask me, just share and we can get sign-ups as quick as Bobcat goes through beers.

Now, what's coming up?

I'm going to have a few short stories in anthologies out (I think) July and August. The first is a short that speaks to Michael's changing over a thousand years ago and the second is a Ranger Tabitha short called Tabitha's Vacation. It is set up to be a hundred and fifty years in the future.

There is a story by Paul C. Middleton called The Boris Chronicles - Evacuation coming out next week where I am a co-author (minor) on the book. It is happening between books 9 and 11. You get hints to this stuff in this book when Bobcat talks about needing space for Russians. Paul is at the editing stage right now... Well, he is in Australia, so he is actually probably sleeping right now.

I'm going to drop a thousand word snippet TOTALLY UNEDITED!!! At the end of this Author Notes to give you a taste of what I'm doing with Tabitha... She has attitude and it shows.

A lot.

Thank you all for reading these author notes, for joining me on this crazy adventure called The Kurtherian Gambit, for supporting the awesome things going on with the email list and supporting people who are using their lives allowing someone like me to make stories that we enjoy.

Michael Anderle
June 28th, 2016 - Just hours from Publishing.

UNEDITED
- SNIPPET 01 -
TABITHA'S VACATION

One Problem, One Ranger.

I walked into Rossini's Bar on Planet Bectal with what my boss calls a physical ailment of a short temper with a bad case of I-don't-give-a-shit. I was grumping to him for the third monthly meeting in a row about nothing to do when he came to check on me in my area of the sector and as my doctor, he prescribed a two-month vacation for my medicine.

My boss knows me too damned well.

He isn't going to lose my services for the three months. It's three because I need two weeks travel both ways, and he knows I know he is still getting work out of me. So, he can kiss my ass on the actual travel time. I booked that on the nicest, most expensive luxury liner on this side of the Galaxy for my vacation, everything else was going to be work. Perhaps fun work, but work nonetheless.

Here on Bectal's world, I would just be doing my job. Poking the alien equivalent of ant-hills, looking under disgusting rocks and kicking over dilapidated buildings to see what maggots from the local equivalent of the criminal world scurried away. Hopefully faster than I could figure out what the hell they've done wrong and if necessary, shoot them.

My usual area of responsibility was two solar systems back and one up and damned if it wasn't getting too boring. It had taken me thirty years, but I'd finally gotten most organizations to understand The Queen Bitch's Rule for her Rangers which is 'One Problem-One Ranger.' The corollary to it, from my boss, is Rangers have no limits for our backup, it just can't be another Ranger.

One time, on the Sver'an planet, I got into a shouting match with the equivalent of the local Warlord. I hadn't wanted to lay waste to half a city just to pull out his good-for-absolutely-nothing second cousin from his whatever-the-hell the third parent was called in their family group.

So, in front of him and his men, I told him I would call for a battalion of the Queen Bitch's Guardians if he didn't produce the miscreant.

That rat-faced POS just stared at me and called my bluff. He didn't know us Rangers very well. So, I did.

Call that is.

Because as a Ranger, we have a direct link to the Queen Bitch herself, Bethany Anne. The conversation back then went something like this:

"Tet-gurky, you will produce your psychotic murdering little prick from god-knows-what-you-call-the-baby-momma or I'll call in a battalion of the Queen's Guardians to pull his useless ass out of this city."

I was rather angry at this time. It was my third time to this hell-hole of a planet, and the inhabitants were having problems with the Queen's version of justice. Which is to say, 'be nice to each other, or else.' Some alien species had a real problem with the nice part. Oh, it isn't that they don't understand the concept, it is pretty universal, it's that they have lived so long with the concept of those who have strength rule, that when someone comes along with more strength, they have to test it.

A lot.

All the damn time, it was starting to piss me off. Sure, the first time people test Bethany Anne's rules I get it. By the second time, I'm wondering if this area just didn't get the memo (and I call to make sure the PR department sent the damn memo). By the third time, it's just a case of who is backing down first, them or me.

It's sure as hell not going to be me.

So, it was my third time to speak to Tet-gurky when I figured he had to have read the memo, and they had done the research, and the rumors about Bethany Anne's Guardians had to have made their way around the planet from the fighting two solar years back.

But, the little prick answered me, "Do it, Ranger Tabitha." He spread his furry little arms around his Warren with the other fifteen leaders of his clan, "I don't think we are so significant to the Queen Bitch that she would waste such valuable resources as a battalion of her finest soldiers to locate one little problem child."

"He's not a child, Tet-gurky, he has created his own little psychopaths with baby momma's," I answered.

"You say, psychopath, we say the strongest is always right. He was the strongest." Tet-gurky's sibilant laughter spread to the fifteen little rat-faced throats around him, and it pissed me off.

It wasn't my job to kill them all, no matter how upset I was at being laughed at. My job was bringing the little bastard to justice for killing someone on the world under my jurisdiction. So, fuck'em.

Bethany Anne?

Hello, Tabitha!

Do you have a second to chat? I asked. While she is a friend, she is still the Queen and even after a hundred and fifty years, I treat her as my liege first, my friend second.

Yes, I'm en route to check on a diplomatic mission. We are in the middle of a transition, recalculating the heading. I fucking hate this shit. Some of the ships with us are so damned slow.

Well, if you didn't ride in the fastest chariot of the group, perhaps you wouldn't be so impatient.

Yeah, well, some things don't change with age. But, enough about me, what's up with you? You rarely call just to say 'hi.'

Sorry about that. Bethany Anne was right. I did rarely call just to chat. *I've got a problem here on Sver'an where I need to pull out a POS. I either need to get help from the local Warlord, who is related to the little creep, or drop a lot of shock and awe to either make them produce the freak. Or actually, tear apart this city to get to him. So, I told him to produce, or I'd request help.*

He called your bluff, did he? Bethany Anne replied to me, humor in her voice.

Yes! Little turd-magnet says he doesn't think his little cousin-or-other is important enough for you to support me.

Did you change your body to produce red hair? She asked me.

No, why? I responded, confused.

Because your language when you change your body to produce the red-hair drops back to when we first met.

Oh, hadn't noticed.

Either way, tell him that the I will speak to him within two galactic-standard hours, or he can keep his cousin. If I'm waiting more than five minutes when I get there, I'll find his cousin, and he and his men are forfeit. Please keep the area calm until then.

Wait, what? I just need a battalion. I'm not asking you to show up.

I understand but think about your reputation. When you threaten a Queen's Battalion on this no-where little planet, and the Queen Bitch shows up?

Yeah, but which rep? The one with the criminals, or the one in the Rangers? My group is going to laugh their asses off. I complained.

Well, the rep with the Rangers is your own to deal with. Besides, Barnabas is going to think this is funny as hell.

Yeah, well he would, I grumped.

Alright, Pilot says the new course is locked on and I've told the group I'll catch back up to them on the third jump. Besides, you can tell the other Rangers I was bored.

You are bored.

See! When you tell the truth, the truth will set you free.

With that, she closed off our connection.

———

...TO BE CONTINUED...

MICHAEL'S NOTES

Part Two

Still here?

Wow!

I was literally exporting for the final update before dropping this on Amazon and thought about one other item.

Death.

As in, Michael's death.

The BIG M…

Oh, holy crackers did the reviews come FAST and FURIOUS (hard focus on 'furious') right away. When I just checked, **It's Hell To Choose** has 98 Reviews compared to **We Will Build's** 97. The ONLY book in the series with more reviews is **Death Becomes Her** with 149 (Almost 150 WOOHOO! (Then, like 200 is a goal ;-))

So, in 1 month, it jumped to the *second highest reviewed book*. Death, apparently, brings out some opinions, really f'ing fast.

Really fast.

Really…painfully…fast.

By now, you know that Michael is coming back in his own series in the Winter as he focuses on pulling the Earth out of the Second Dark Ages so he can get to the stars, and fulfill his promise.

So, please. Don't hate on me.

Just saying, I was crying too.

Later ;-)

Michael

SERIES TITLES INCLUDE:

KURTHERIAN GAMBIT SERIES TITLES INCLUDE:

First Arc

Death Becomes Her (01) - Queen Bitch (02) -
Love Lost (03) - Bite This (04)
Never Forsaken (05) - Under My Heel (06)
Kneel Or Die (07)

Second Arc

We Will Build (08) - It's Hell To Choose (09) -
Release The Dogs of War (10)
Sued For Peace (11) - We Have Contact (12) -
My Ride is a Bitch (13)
Don't Cross This Line (14)

Third Arc (Due 2017)

Never Submit (15) - Never Surrender (16) -
Forever Defend (17)
Might Makes Right (18) - Ahead Full (19) -
Capture Death (20)
Life Goes On (21)

New Series

THE SECOND DARK AGES

The Dark Messiah (01)
The Darkest Night (02)

THE BORIS CHRONICLES
* With Paul C. Middleton *

Evacuation
Retaliation
Revelation
Restitution *2017*

RECLAIMING HONOR
* With JUSTIN SLOAN *

Justice Is Calling (01)
Claimed By Honor (02)
Judgement Has Fallen (03)
Angel of Reckoning (04)
Born Into Flames (05)
Defending The Lost (06)

THE ETHERIC ACADEMY
* With TS PAUL *

ALPHA CLASS (01)
ALPHA CLASS - Engineering (02)
ALPHA CLASS (03) *Coming Soon*

TERRY HENRY "TH" WALTON CHRONICLES
* With CRAIG MARTELLE *

TRIALS AND TRIBULATIONS
* With Natalie Grey *

THE ASCENSION MYTH
* With ELL LEIGH CLARKE *

THE AGE OF MAGIC
THE RISE OF MAGIC
* With CM RAYMOND/LE BARBANT *

Restriction (01)
Reawakening (02)
Rebellion (03)
Revolution (04)

THE HIDDEN MAGIC CHRONICLES
* With JUSTIN SLOAN *

Shades of Light (01)
Shades of Dark (02)

STORMS OF MAGIC
* With PT HYLTON *

Storms Raiders (01)
Storm Callers (02)

TALES OF THE FEISTY DRUID
* With CANDY CRUM *

The Arcadian Druid (01)

THE CHRONICLES OF ORICERAN
THE LEIRA CHRONICLES
* With MARTHA CARR *

Quest for Magic (0)
Waking Magic (1)

SHORT STORIES

Frank Kurns Stories of the Unknownworld 01 (7.5)
You Don't Mess with John's Cousin

Frank Kurns Stories of the Unknownworld 02 (9.5)
Bitch's Night Out

Frank Kurns Stories of the Unknownworld 02 (13.25)
With Natalie Grey
Bellatrix

AUDIOBOOKS
Available at Audible.com and iTunes

THE KURTHERIAN GAMBIT

Death Becomes Her - *Available Now*
Queen Bitch – *Available Now*
Love Lost – *Available Now*
Bite This - *Available Now*
Never Forsaken - *Available Now*
Under My Heel - *Available Now*
Kneel or Die - *Available Now*

RECLAIMING HONOR SERIES

Justice Is Calling
Claimed By Honor
Judgment Has Fallen
Angel of Reckoning

WANT MORE?

Join the email list here:

http://kurtherianbooks.com/email-list/

AND NOW

http://kurtherianbooks.com/readers-supporting-military-book-newsletter/

Join the Facebook group here:

https://www.facebook.com/TheKurtherianGambitBooks/

The email list will be sporadic with more 'major' updates, the Facebook group will be for updates and the 'behind the curtains' information on writing the next stories. Basically conversing!

Since I can't confirm that something I put up on Facebook will absolutely be updated for you, I need the email list to update all fans for any major release or updates that you might want to read on the website.

I hope you enjoy the book!

Michael Anderle - June 28, 2016.

Printed in the USA
CPSIA information can be obtained
at www.ICGtesting.com
LVHW091234110524
779935LV00002B/178

9 781981 790050